# Surrender
# to the Unknown

Rebecca Mattson

D1715145

# DEDICATION

In memory of my dad, Lavern Hammer, the Scandinavian who reminded our entire family every St. Patrick's Day on his birthday that everyone is Irish at least one day of the year!

# ACKNOWLEDGMENTS

**First, I want to thank my sister Gloria**—this story's adventure began when you said, "I have an idea for a story". Thank you for the creative idea that sparked my imagination and set me on my journey to publish my first romance.

**To my dear Aunt Candice**—your encouragement and mentorship mean the world to me.

**To my daughter, Rachel**—you held my hand through my final revisions and editing process, encouraging me the entire time. As an avid reader, you became the reader's perspective I needed. Our love for good literature will always bind us together, and I look forward to continuing our collaboration on my next book.

**To The High Kings**—Darren Holden, Brian Dunphy, Finbarr Clancy, and Paul O'Brien, whose music and kind-hearted spirits have touched my heart and soul to the core.

To learn more about The High Kings, visit their website: https://www.thehighkings

*May the sound of happy music*
*And the lilt of Irish laughter*
*Fill your heart with gladness*
*That stays forever after.*

# Chapter 1

The sun peeked out from behind the clouds as Caitlin Sullivan pulled up in front of her childhood home. When she stepped out into the open, a cool March breeze took hold of her long auburn hair and blew it in every direction. She brushed it back before hurrying carefully down the icy sidewalk and up the two steps to the front door. Memories and the wind were messing with her today.

Caitlin had started the morning off in a reflective mood, thinking through the choices she had made over the last decade. She loved high school and her college experience, excelling at her studies, and genuinely fulfilling her father's nickname for her as a child: "little smarty-pants". But, when she graduated, she made the mistake of putting on a pair of rose-colored glasses, believing her degree would help her land the perfect job.

She smiles at this memory now—in the same way you remember your first crush—so wide-eyed, so innocent. Caitlin loved history but loving history and teaching history are not the same. After five long years of writing lesson plans and dealing with behavior issues, she realized she didn't have the fortitude to inspire a bunch of teenagers along the same lines. Her first attempt at a career seemed a failure.

So, she found herself back at the drawing board, pen in hand, and supportive parents on either side. She applied to graduate school at Boston College and received a Master of Arts degree in Archival Management and Public History. Through the process, she fell in love with the idea of being a historian—a "history detective"! At least that's how she described it to her friends. Caitlin finally felt ready to "obtain the key facts she would need to assist her in unlocking the mysteries of the past." Just the kind of nerdy adventure she longed. Soon after, an internship at a local museum led her to her first job in public history. At that moment, she felt prepared to move forward in her personal life.

Despite the Irish blood running through her veins, when it came to romance Caitlin severely lacked "the luck of the Irish". Maybe she needed a little Celtic love potion. Like most people, she'd gone through the occasional ups and downs as she played the dating game, but recently her love life had paralleled a tragic ride on a roller coaster that had flown straight off the track. Her way of handling the devastating crash was to run back home—far away from the man who had broken her heart. Home provided the constant source of consolation she needed. Thanks to several months of sipping caramel macchiatos with her sister, along with their in-depth conversations, her heart had begun to heal.

Today was a brand-new day, and she looked forward to a little distraction. For the last two years, Caitlin's father had struggled over the death of her mother, Kathleen. She could see him losing interest in the things her parents used to do together: taking long walks, riding bikes, attending the theatre, or seeing a movie. They had even gone golfing and fishing together. Now he spent most of his time surfing TV channels without really watching anything. Even his weekly bowling nights with the guys from work had become almost nonexistent. Earlier in the week, Caitlin and her sister Abbey had finally talked their dad into letting them sort through their mom's personal belongings. Today was the day it would happen! They had put off this vital task for far too long, and a cloud of dread hung oppressively over the entire house.

As Caitlin stood at the front entrance of her childhood home, she reflected on the last visit she had made earlier in the week. While at work, her father had severely pulled some muscles in his back. Over the next two days, his pain level had continued to increase, making it difficult for him to move. When he finally declared defeat, Caitlin and her sister convinced him to visit a doctor. After a thorough examination, the orthopedic surgeon recommended surgery to repair the muscle. He informed them complete healing would take six to ten weeks with rest and proper physical therapy. Knowing their father and his Irish stubbornness, Caitlin and Abbey predicted it would probably take the full ten weeks. They had put their heads together to develop a plan on how to support him in his recovery.

"The biggest challenge to Dad's healing process is making sure he follows the doctor's orders," Abbey stated the last four words with emphasis, as though she were issuing a groundbreaking statement.

"We can't be with him 24/7 to make sure he follows them," Caitlin accosted Abbey, throwing in one of those classic sibling eye-rolls that always seemed to accompany their disagreements.

Abbey would not back down, so Caitlin solemnly conceded. "You're right; he'll need more assistance during the start of his recovery. My hours at the Museum tie me up during the weekdays. I can sometimes help during the evenings and possibly on the weekend. What about you?"

Abbey thought carefully, running several options through her mind. Then a light went on inside her head, making her look like a deer caught in the headlights. "I've got it! I have the perfect solution." She paused again, wheels spinning.

"Well, I'm waiting," Caitlin moaned, standing with her arms, crossed in front of her.

Abbey walked around with perpetual ideas and scenarios running through her head, a regular think tank if you asked Caitlin. If someone had a problem, they need only refer to her younger sister for the solution.

"What do you think about me moving out of my apartment and back home with dad until my wedding?" she posed.

Caitlin couldn't contain the laughter escaping her mouth, "You've got to be kidding! Isn't that a little extreme?"

"Not really, it would have several benefits. First, I'll be getting married in June, and I won't need my apartment any longer. Moving out now would save me three months of rent and utility bills—a total win-win. There's a waiting list of people wanting to rent at my building, so I don't think I'll be charged any fees for breaking my lease," became her final point.

"Abbey, I can't disagree with your reasoning, but what about work? You can't be here all the time." They both had busy work schedules and a family wedding to finish planning. Caitlin realized she would have to try to look at things from her sister's perspective this time. The Sullivan sisters' lifetime challenge when it came to tackling a sticky situation: one saw the glass half full and the other half empty.

"Caitlin, my shifts vary as a nurse. When you or I cannot be around to help Dad, we could hire someone to assist us. I have such an easy commute from here to work; it wouldn't be a burden."

Caitlin couldn't help but laugh at Abbey's willingness to help. She was a modern-day Florence Nightingale. She would make sure the proper measures were carried out to successfully help their dad fully recover while ensuring everyone else around did the same, even if it meant shortchanging herself on sleep.

So, that settled things. Caitlin promised to pitch in and help when she could. They also hired a middle-aged woman named Susan Brown, a part-time in-home caregiver. She would provide the additional assistance their dad would need when they couldn't be around during his initial recovery. When they first met Susan, they were pleased to see she could magically bring a smile to his face, something they had seen less often since their mother's death.

Coming back to the present moment, Caitlin remembered where she was standing. The solid oak door before her and her heart in her throat. It was going to be a challenging day for her emotionally.

Before Caitlin could knock, Abbey threw open the front door. "Greetings, Sis! It's about time you got here. Are you ready to get to work?"

Caitlin gave her sister a quick hug, sneaking a peek at the disarray of the house. "Let me hang up my coat first, and then I'll meet you in the bedroom." She hoped they would make quick progress on the task at hand. She didn't want to spend too much time thinking about their mother today. Caitlin still struggled from grief over losing her, but she had never confessed this to Abbey. Part of the guilt she carried stemmed from her living such a distance away at the time of her mother's illness.

She knew she had to stop dwelling on the past. Caitlin didn't want her younger sister to see her break down today. Abbey was her rock, but Caitlin didn't know if her support would be enough to pull her out of the depths of despair. On top of everything else going on, Caitlin was still struggling over the breakup of a serious two-year relationship. Strong emotional currents flooding her life were fighting against her ability to climb to safety. Recently she only seemed good at silently drowning in her sorrows.

"Where should we start?" Abbey cheerfully asked the minute Caitlin entered the bedroom. It, too, was a mess. Their dad had piled numerous items of their mother's in the bedroom out of sight to remove all memories of Kathleen from his current living space. Aside from one large photo of their whole family in the living room, any visitor would be clueless about their mother's former existence. A significant number of items had been heaped haphazardly on both the queen-sized sleigh bed and the mahogany dresser.

"I think we should box up Mom's clothes first," Caitlin suggested as she opened the bedroom closet and began to browse through its occupants. "Dad said if we came across anything of sentimental value, we could keep it."

"Good to know," her sister responded as she began folding some of the clothes she'd pulled out of the nearby dresser.

Caitlin, quickly lost in thought, handled clothing items as if each piece of fabric was a precious artifact. Each one filling her head with a multitude of memories.

"Do you think her burgundy cardigan is still in there?" Abbey asked as she began to walk dreamily toward her sister. "It was my favorite, and I often borrowed it from her whenever I felt chilled."

Caitlin rifled through her mother's sweaters, and sure enough, there it hung on a sturdy hanger. She pulled it gingerly off its wooden support, laying it gently in her sister's arms. Abbey lifted it to her face and breathed in deeply, her memories bringing a smile to her face.

Caitlin tried to clear her mind. Unlike her sister, she did not want to revisit the past. Caitlin and her dad were a lot alike. Shake it off, she told herself.

"What else do you think we might find?" asked Abbey, who seemed to be enjoying the walk down memory lane. She always had a way of seeing the light at the end of the tunnel, whereas Caitlin often seemed blinded by the confused emotions clouding her mind.

"Seriously, Caitlin, snap out of it," she scolded herself. Hoping Abbey hadn't heard her, she quickly turned away, spotting an item of clothing that immediately and inordinately lifted her spirits, "I don't remember Mom saving this."

She tugged on the scarf draped around the collar of her mother's old winter coat. "Look, she saved the scarf I made for her in 8th grade. You remember when I first learned to knit?" She smiled at the memory. "Not the best craftsmanship, but she kept it all these years." In a sudden swell of emotions, her heart quickly caught up with her mind, and she choked back a cry. It was hard.

After a moment of reflection, Abbey broke the silence. "I'm glad moving home has convinced Dad to let us sort through Mom's things. It will help him move forward. He's had such a hard time letting go."

"I know it's been difficult for all of us. Mom's death happened so suddenly."

"So sudden... It's hard to believe she's already been gone two years, but we were so fortunate to be able to keep her at home those last few months. Can you imagine how different a hospital stay would have felt?" Abbey surveyed the room, considering all that remained. "The hospice care nurses made this room her haven in the end. Just look around. All her favorite artwork, photos, books, music, and souvenirs are in here. It's so heartwarming."

"And Dad appreciated being able to keep Mom at home. He was never more than a few steps away from her during those last two months," Caitlin reflected.

It had been a long road getting to this moment in time. Cancer doesn't just claim one victim; it claims a whole family. Even with Abbey's positive outlook on life, it had made a mark on her. She had devoted quite a bit of her time to their father the first year after their mother's passing, which delayed her from moving forward with her wedding plans.

Suddenly, angry over the memory of the pain and suffering their mother went through, Abbey sighed. "Cancer is such an ugly beast! It doesn't seem to care who it makes suffer."

"Yeah. Mom fought such a hard battle and still lost it in the end. Dad is a prime example of a living casualty of war." A chapel-like silence entered the room for a brief moment until a robin, perched on the tree outside, decided to make her presence known.

In typical Abbey fashion, she quickly redirected her attention and started barking orders again, proof "Head of Nursing" would surely be her title down the road at the hospital. She had a way of taking control of a situation and getting the job done.

"Dad said we could donate Mom's clothes to charity, but we need to put her other things in storage."

"Uh-huh," Caitlin muttered very quietly. Abbey didn't notice her response until she glanced over to where her sister was sitting on the bed, head hanging down and hands clasped in her lap, twiddling her thumbs anxiously.

"Caitlin, are you all right?"

"I'm fine, but I can see why Dad avoided this task. There are so many memories in this room," she sighed.

"Good memories," reminded Abbey, placing a comforting hand on her sister's shoulder.

Caitlin nodded, but her chest remained heavy as she continued to help box up the rest of the room. They separated the clothes from other items like photo albums, a few mementos, and some framed family photos. Caitlin questioned Abbey about where their dad wanted more personal items stored. She revealed the attic was the desired location for the time being until he felt well enough to look through them. From that point on, they put things in gear and finished motoring through the boxing and labeling of everything else, stopping only now and then to discuss an item one of them questioned as a donation or keepsake.

They had completed their task in just under two hours and decided to immediately haul the donations outside and put them in Caitlin's car. They moved as quickly as possible since the wind had picked up, and light flurries were falling. Without their coats on, speed was of the essence to prevent any chill from setting in. It took them three trips back and forth to the car before returning to the bedroom.

Abbey had an idea, "Caitlin, what if we take the remaining boxes up to the attic right now, so they're out of the way? It will make the job of moving the rest of my belongings back in this weekend so much easier. Then, we can hang out with Dad for the rest of the day."

"He'd like that," she agreed.

It had been ages since either sister had climbed the creaky staircase to the attic. As they trudged up the stairs, Caitlin asked, "When was the last time you were up here?"

"I haven't been in the attic since we were kids. I don't remember anything too exciting or worthwhile stored up here other than a few boxes of Christmas decorations." Abbey took several steps into the attic to reach for the light switch. In the process, she ran into something.

"Ouch!" she cried, dropping the box she'd been carrying.

Caitlin emptied her arms and rushed to her sister's side. "Are you all right, Abbey?"

"Yes, I just bumped my leg." Abbey rubbed her knee as she leveled her eyes with the top of a trunk she'd never seen before.

"Hey, an old steamer trunk," Caitlin observed.

Curious, Abbey began to unlatch it to reveal a variety of items. They knelt beside each other and started to rummage through its contents, much like they used to search through their toy box as kids. A few items they discovered were some old, yellowed documents, an antique-looking checker set, a Bible written in what looked like the Gaelic language, and a man's weathered blue-gray Irish flat cap nestled on top of some old photos.

Caitlin began to caress the documents as if they were prized possessions. She lovingly glanced from one to the other until something caught her eye. "Look, Abbey, these are immigration papers from Ellis Island." *Wow*, she thought, *what history*! "They show Grandpa's family arrived on June 20, 1927. And look, here's great-grandad's certificate of citizenship, it's dated April 5, 1930. How amazing!" She hesitated before relinquishing the items to her sister.

Caitlin began to imagine the doors this information could open, revealing additional facts about their family history. She had always longed to know more about her ancestors. Caitlin valued the close ties her family shared while at the same time hoping to learn more about past generations, knowledge surely worth treasuring. She knew it seemed a bit nerdy, but there were mysteries to be solved regarding their ancestors that had been left behind in Ireland—and she was equipped to solve them.

All wrapped up in the excitement of her sister's find, Abbey reached in and extracted an old photograph. "Look! A wedding picture."

"Whose?"

"It looks rather old." Abbey turned it over to discover someone's neat handwriting. "Wait, someone wrote names on the back for identification. William Aeden O'Sullivan and Johanna Caitlin McGillycuddy. August 11, 1883."

Caitlin took the photo for a closer look. "It's an image of our great-great-grandparents. What an interesting maiden name."

"I see where you got your name, Caitlin." Abbey reached in to pick up another photograph. She could tell it wasn't as old as the first. "Here's another of three boys. Does anyone in this image look familiar to you?"

"No, it's a little blurred."

"Wait, there's something written on the back of this image as well. It's harder to read than the first, but I think one of the names is William, too."

"Let me see." Caitlin carefully took the photo from her sister and started to study the image. "It could be the right time-frame for one of these boys to be our Great-Grandpa William." She held it closer to one of the lights in the attic to get a clearer view. The boys' ages gave away their identity, and the youngest resembled snapshots she had seen of her dad as a little boy.

"Well, have you figured it out? Who are they?"

"Yeah. Grandpa told me about his uncles. If I remember correctly, this is Ryan, the oldest of the O'Sullivan boys," she pointed to the far-left side of the picture before moving her finger to the next oldest. "This must be Brenden, and the youngest boy has to be Great-Grandpa William. It must have been taken shortly before Ryan died."

"Did Grandpa ever tell you Ryan's cause of death?"

Caitlin answered immediately, "Influenza. His family lived in Dublin at the time, having moved there from Killarney. In the city tenements where they resided, many suffered from the filthy conditions and the crowdedness. It's probably safe to say they also had poor health care."

"Things haven't changed much from the past; the flu is still a common contagious disease and one of the top ten leading causes of death in the U.S."

Caitlin couldn't resist smiling at the nurse-like comment spilling out of Abbey's mouth. "Is that the reason you always nag Dad about getting the flu shot every fall?" chuckled Caitlin. She realized this was a yearly battle between the two, and when she looked up at Abbey casting daggers at her, she realized her comment was unappreciated.

While Abbey had been listening to her sister, she had continued to rifle through a few more items before pulling out another piece of yellowed parchment. "Look what I found—a marriage certificate." She skimmed over its contents. The edges were worn, and she found it a challenge to read the elegant fading script. "It seems our great-grandparents, William Michael O'Sullivan and Lauryn Sinead Kelly, were married at St. Andrew's Catholic Church on June 3, 1916." She paused, looking directly at Caitlin. "Do you remember any of the stories Grandpa Pat used to tell about his father's family?"

Caitlin began to paint a picture of how the family continued to live in Dublin after Ryan's death and until Brenden and William were old enough to support themselves. "Once his dad and uncle had jobs and a place to live, Grandpa said his grandparents returned to Killarney. They still had relatives living in the area and could live a less hectic life there than in the big city."

"Did Grandpa say if his family ever visited with them before they left for America?"

"He told me the only time his dad ever saw his parents again was at his wedding. Grandpa said he never got to meet his grandparents because they weren't in the best of health."

"How sad. Caitlin, do you know what happened to Brenden? I don't remember Grandpa talking about his uncle."

In a rather dramatic voice, Caitlin began to repeat the tale their grandfather had told. "A battle of wills began right then and there. One brother tried to convince the other to travel with him to America while his counterpart presented his best case for staying. In the end, Brenden warned William he needn't bother to contact him after he left the country because he wouldn't be answering back. William wanted a better life for his family, so the threat fell on deaf ears. Despite the angry words shared by a fear-filled brother, our great-grandfather took the risk of traveling by boat with his family to a foreign land to start a new life. Henceforth, cutting himself completely off from the rest of his family."

What a heartbreaking story thought Abbey. "I can't imagine letting anything like distance get in the way of our relationship, Caitlin. We are bonded for life."

Touched by her sister's words, Caitlin reached over and hugged Abbey. Both sisters agreed they couldn't fathom anything ever separating them for long, let alone the rest of their lives. They found it hard to relate to such a situation.

"It's sad to think that after Grandpa arrived in America, he never saw nor heard from his relatives in Ireland ever again," Caitlin reflected.

Abbey resumed her search through the trunk, "Look, Caitlin, this looks like an old birth certificate. Is that Grandpa's name?"

"Let me see," she requested, gingerly taking hold of the faded document. "Patrick William O'Sullivan. Yes, it's Grandpa's! Birthdate March 17, 1920."

"How difficult do you think it would be to trace our family tree? I'd love to know what became of Brenden and his side of the family." The more excited Abbey became, the higher her voice rose as she squeaked out her final thought. "Maybe we could even find some of our relatives currently living in Ireland!"

Caitlin smiled. "That could be fun. It should be fairly easy in today's age of technology." Finally, remembering the task they had come up to the attic to accomplish, she suggested, "Let's find a place to put these boxes first, then we can discuss this further with Dad."

So, here is where Caitlin's adventure started to unfold, a newly sparked interest in tracing the O'Sullivan family's Irish roots.

The following week, the two sisters began to brainstorm a list of steps they would need to take to solve a family mystery three generations old. Could they find living relatives in Ireland and reunite their families? Maybe a project like this would distract their father during his recovery. Only time would tell.

# Chapter 2

As a public historian, Caitlin had been involved in many intriguing investigations over the past few years. She had learned how to follow clues and draw conclusions using artifacts found in the most unassuming places. Many of her acquaintances did not understand why she loved history so much—why she was always digging through collections of old documents and books found in the archives of local libraries and museums. But, honestly, it was the thrill of the chase, the joy of solving a mystery. She found great satisfaction in putting the pieces of the puzzle together to create a clearer picture of a specific event or person from the past.

In her current position at the Minnesota Historic Center, Caitlin noticed people seemed to take her work more seriously than when she taught history in a public high school. To her, history wasn't just about dates and facts. It was a meeting with the joy, suffering, and lessons of those who had come before you—connecting the present with the past. It reminded her of how far humanity had come on a road well-traveled.

Over the past two weeks, Caitlin had begun to piece together their family tree by using information from the documents she and Abbey had found in their grandfather's trunk. She got frustrated quickly—names and dates only told part of the story. Time seemed to be melting away, and she felt no closer to revealing the key facts about her paternal ancestors that would help her find any of their descendants now living in Ireland. She believed she was grasping at straws, but excitement raced through her veins at the thought of taking her fine-tuned research skills and using them to finally solve their family mystery. If given a time machine, Caitlin would have immediately jumped on board and risked life and limb to shake some sense into William and Brenden O'Sullivan before they closed the door on their sibling relationship. After the sting of love lost, she couldn't fathom choosing to abandon one's family in hopes of a better life. Her family served as her support system. There had to be more behind the story.

Seeing no other alternative, Caitlin decided to pin her father up against the wall on Sunday afternoon. She hoped he could shed some light on the topic. It didn't take long for her to realize he'd been stubbornly sitting on a hidden treasure trove of information. When she started to question him about his own family, the silence became so thick you could cut it with a knife. Without warning, he suddenly leaped across the room, pausing when he found himself standing in front of the wooden TV cabinet her mother had painted white years ago. It had seen better days, and the door creaked as he yanked it open, hard enough to send an old photo album tumbling out. *How long has it been stashed there?* Caitlin speculated.

"What have you got there, Dad?"

"Just some old pictures of your grandpa's I've had sitting around since his funeral," Caitlin remembered her dad hauling some of his things back to the house. *So that must be how the trunk found its way into the attic*, she realized.

Her father decidedly heaped not one but three photo albums on the coffee table. Caitlin noticed one stood out as much older than the other two. She knelt and carefully opened the old family album, invoking many emotions as she slowly flipped through the old black pages with four gummed photo holders at the edges. With careful observation, Caitlin realized she had stumbled upon images of her father as a young child living in Boston with his parents and two younger siblings. A few months ago, she would have agreed these were just old family photos, but today these images were of greater importance. With each crooked smile and weathered edge, they could begin to help tell the stories she had yet to hear.

"Dad, can you pull out some of your favorite photos of your

father and grandfather? They might help stir up a few memories from your childhood?" He shuffled through a few pages. Earlier, when she had asked her dad to help her with this new project, he had adamantly declared he'd be of no help due to his poor recollection of his childhood memories. She waited to hear him repeat himself, but instead, he began to hem and haw momentarily before dislodging an image from the album and beginning to share.

Half an hour and four photos later, her dad began to look a little haggard. He leaned back against the sofa and exhaled, his worn and weathered hands rifling through his silver-streaked head of hair. A habit she had been noticing more and more lately. "Ah, Caitie, your Aunt Mary has a better memory for details. You should see if she can help fill in some of the holes in my stories. We used to sit around and listen to our Grandpa weave tales one after another of early life in Ireland. I just never paid much attention in my youth. I don't recall half of what I heard."

Caitlin laughed, "What a good suggestion, Dad. I'll give Aunt Mary a call and tell her what we've been doing. Maybe she can add some details to your stories as well as share a few of her own."

"Great! Now, I think this old man needs to get to bed."

Caitlin's father placed a quick kiss on her cheek before he hiked up the stairs. Her train of thought immediately shifted as she contemplated the next step to take in her research. Maybe searching through available Irish Catholic Church records would help her find a few more birth, marriage, and death records than what she already had on hand. It was essential to pay close attention to names, dates, and locations, weeding out any misleading information along the way. Sometimes you might find a similar name from the same community, comparable (at least in her mind) to a criminal case creating false evidence. These pieces of evidence tended to "mislead or misdirect" investigations, whether criminal or historical. But the skills she had learned throughout her internship made her ready for this additional challenge.

Caitlin was determined to fulfill her grandfather's dream of finding the missing pieces to the puzzle and uniting his family once again after all this time. A task worth taking on. Caitlin believed it would fill a void in their lives and better yet finally change her luck?

On the following afternoon, Caitlin worked up the courage to call the National Library in Dublin to ask a few questions about her search. On the other side of the Atlantic, in the Genealogy Services Department, an energetic woman close to Caitlin's age answered the phone. Meghan, a research assistant at the Library, loved her job immensely. Today her enthusiasm showed through her cheerful voice.

"National Library Genealogy Department, Meghan speaking. How may I help you?"

"Hi, my name is Caitlin Sullivan. I have a few questions about some family research I'm doing."

"That's what I'm here for Caitlin, what's your first question?" Caitlin took the first step outside of her comfort zone and handed the torch to someone else who could bear light on the subject. Meghan listened carefully to the questions directed toward her, responding with confidence. She jotted down a few notes as they continued their conversation, sharing encouraging words along the way.

An hour later, when their conversation ended, Caitlin's nerves had calmed. Meghan had answered all her questions, for the time being, and she knew what steps to take next.

"Thanks for your time, Meghan."

"Not a problem. Now remember what I said, you should think about hopping on a plane and crossing the pond for a personal visit to the National Library."

Caitlin made light of the thought, as pleasant as the idea sounded. She had neither the time nor the money for such a venture.

When her family gathered for supper later in the week on St. Patrick's Day, Caitlin spilled all her information on the table, causing a domino effect of questions and emotions. It was just par for the course whenever Caitlin started a new pet project.

"Caitlin, why don't you take some time off from work to travel to Boston for a short visit with Aunt Mary?" suggested Abby, passing a plate of corned beef across the table.

"Yes! She'd love to see you, and I know she has a precarious pile of family documents she's gathered over the years," added her dad.

Abbey knew her sister. Once on the hunt, she wouldn't be able to rest until she'd tracked down some of Brenden's descendants. She continued with what Caitlin could swear was a little wink,

"Then you could follow Meghan's suggestion and continue on your journey to the National Library in Dublin."

"I'll think about it," Caitlin hesitated, mentally weighing the options as she scanned the faces seated around the table. Her sister had spoken her piece. But when Caitlin's gaze fell upon her father, she noticed the sparkle in his eyes and knew he had made the final decision for her. Somewhat slow to move on any significant decision, she knew deep down inside she was ready to take on this emotionally charged adventure. Caitlin would be fulfilling her grandfather's dream of returning to Ireland in search of his family. What did she have to lose?

Joy welled up from within her at the notion of connecting with long lost relatives. In a way, Caitlin had started to believe her past misfortunes had something to do with a kind of family curse. Maybe she would never find love and be able to move on until she had removed the wedge causing the division between the two brothers and their families.

Her father seemed to read her mind. "Caitie," he said so compassionately, a lump formed in her throat, "your grandfather always talked about finding his uncle's family someday, but he never got the chance. It would mean the world to me to connect with them and share our stories".

Caitlin's heart sank. Travel to Ireland seemed financially beyond her reach, mainly due to her recent job change, "But, I have neither the time nor the money to take a trip like this."

"Ah, Caitie dear, I've got some money saved away thinking your mom and I would get to do some traveling when I retired. Now it's just sitting around waiting for someone to use it."

"What!? Dad, that's too much…" Typical Dad, squirreling away funds for a rainy-day adventure. If only he could travel with her, but the doctor had very clearly advised him against traveling for several more weeks. "I'll pay you back when I get a chance, Dad," she vowed, not wanting to take advantage of him.

"Nonsense, my treat!" her father insisted. He was a generous man who always meant what he said.

"Ah!" Abbey squealed. "It's perfect! If you travel in April, we will still have time before you leave to look at wedding and bridesmaid dresses. And Susan and I have everything under control where Dad is concerned. What have you got to lose by taking a little time off to devote to this family cause?"

Abbey had a way of convincing a polar bear to vacation in the desert; there was no arguing with her. In the end, Caitlin couldn't resist the personal challenge she had set before her. "All right," Caitlin sighed. "You both have me convinced! I think I can manage to get a week off in late April, and then we'll have all of May to complete any final preparations for your wedding."

"Go for it, Caitie," her father agreed. "You would benefit from a little adventurous undertaking right now. I only wish I could go on it with you."

"Me, too, Dad. Just think of the possibilities down the road for a trip together—for the whole Sullivan clan!"

Abbey looked at her fiancé, who had been quietly listening to the conversation, "Tim, wouldn't Ireland be a lovely place for a honeymoon?"

One more unfinished wedding plan, he realized. "I've always wanted to kiss the Blarney Stone."

"Oh, you're full of blarney, Timothy Baxter," she chuckled. Caitlin couldn't help rolling her eyes. Tim and Abbey were so cute and corny it hurt sometimes.

As she drove home later in the evening, she realized she had a lot to do. And it all began with creating a compelling enough presentation to convince her boss for time off to gallivant to Ireland. She went to sleep, feeling exhausted.


Caitlin had cleared her travel plans within a week, and over the next two weeks, she collaborated virtually and through email with Meghan at the National Library. Each time a new question popped into Caitlin's head; they would connect. They had built such great camaraderie that they began to share more about their personal lives along the way. What Caitlin found most interesting were the stories Meghan told about her two brothers, who seemed to be opposites in personality.

"Now, Meghan, what do you like best about having brothers?" Caitlin asked in early April just before ending their work session, her departure to Ireland only a few weeks away. "I only have one sister and can only imagine how different it would be."

"Oh, I don't know. Is there anything good about having brothers?" she joked.

"Seriously, now, tell me."

"My brothers have a protective way about them. When I first dated my husband Brian, they would give him the hardest time. They even threatened to do him bodily harm if he did anything to upset me."

"You can't be serious," challenged Caitlin.

"I'm telling the truth; they've embarrassed me more than once. I wish I had a sister like you. It must be nice to have someone with whom to share your secrets. Only a foolish woman would reveal her innermost thoughts to a brother—the reason I never kept a diary in the house when I was growing up."

"It is. I'm awfully close to Abbey. Things will be slightly different, though, once she's married. She won't need me as much."

Meghan could hear the sorrow in Caitlin's voice. "Once you come to Ireland to visit, we can spend some time together just hanging out. Maybe you can be the sister I never had."

"I can't wait!"

Regardless of what the future would bring, Caitlin was thankful to have made an Irish friend in the process. If she was successful down the road in finding some of her relatives, they might both get to know each other's families as well. The thought warmed her heart.

# Chapter 3

The first leg of Caitlin's journey took her to Boston. She boarded the plane on an early Friday afternoon, strands of thin April light piercing the glass of her cabin window. She looked forward to spending the weekend with her beloved aunt, who had just recently moved into a new luxurious residence on Pier 4 in the Seaport District. Her aunt had described the nine-story building as luxury living with views on three sides—the Financial District, Harbor, and Airport.

Welcomed upon arrival by the efficient concierge service, Caitlin felt like royalty as a young gentleman in uniform escorted her up the elevator and to the doorstep of her aunt's boutique two-bedroom lodging. She was impressed by the service and fully prepared to kick back and enjoy a relaxing weekend. Within minutes of her arrival, her aunt's upscale home had started to feel more like a five-star resort or private country club. Luckily, she wouldn't be staying long, or she might never want to go home.

Over the past thirty-five years, her aunt had worked hard as a financial advisor, and with no husband or children in tow, she had managed her funds wisely. It enabled her to afford a relatively comfortable lifestyle at the tail end of her career.

"Oh, how I've missed you, my dear," her aunt sighed as she opened the impressive front door. Caitlin immediately melted into her aunt's embrace and lingered a while. The four months they'd been apart had seemed like ages.

Once free, Caitlin immediately noticed the floor-to-ceiling windows shedding light into the beautiful home with crystal clear water views. "Aunt Mary!" She gasped. "I can't get over how beautiful this location is. I want to see every nook and cranny of your lovely new home."

"It's not as large as my former townhouse on Beacon Hill, but the location is worth the downsizing," she admitted.

"With all the amenities available to you at this location, you'll manage," Caitlin pointed out with conviction. "I went on-line to the website and was blown away."

"I love the picturesque waterfront view the most. Everything I want is at my fingertips. I have access to exclusive retail boutiques, upscale dining, and an array of fitness and wellness options."

"It sounds wonderful."

"There's even enough room for you if you ever wanted to move back. Of course, until you've found someone you'd rather live with," Aunt Mary hinted.

"Like a husband?"

"Possibly."

"You've always been more than generous, but nothing you say or do will convince me to move back to this area as much as I loved living here in the past." A disappointed look appeared on her aunt's face.

Well, it didn't hurt to suggest it, Aunt Mary reasoned. She missed having Caitlin nearby. She loved her as if she were her very own daughter. "Caitlin, my dear, let me show you around. I've only been living here for a few months, but already I feel like I'm in Heaven. I could not have found a better location to which live. But first, you must tell me everything you've been up to since you moved back home."

So off they went, walking and talking throughout the condo about every topic imaginable. Nearing the end of Caitlin's brief tour, the conversation had shifted to her father's health.

"How is your father doing?" Aunt Mary asked, with a look Caitlin immediately recognized as sympathy. "I feel awful about his injury. Even though I've talked to him several times on the phone, he's managed to avoid giving me too much detail."

"Oh, you know my dad. He doesn't like to talk about himself, especially when it comes to his health. He's making steady progress, though. We should know in about two weeks when he'll be able to go back to work."

"Maybe he should just retire," she suggested.

"With Mom gone, he needs to keep busy. I don't think he's quite ready to put his feet up for the long term." Caitlin described her father's specific injury, surgery, and physical therapy regimen as they stood in the living room. Caitlin stopped to admire the exquisite hardwood flooring and top of the line finishes.

"How do you and your sister handle everything while trying to work full-time?" her aunt pondered as they began to move again.

"We have help from Susan. She's the part-time health assistant who comes in when we need her. She's part of the reason my dad is making such a steady recovery," Caitlin's oral dissertation ended in the kitchen, where she discovered a state-of-the-art wine refrigerator and exquisite marble countertops. Each detail she set her eyes on seemed grander than the one before.

Aunt Mary removed a bottle of wine from its resting place, "You must be hungry. I've prepared something for us to enjoy while you tell me more about your new job."

She began to pour them each a glass of Pinot Grigio, serving appetizers consisting of Sesame-Soy grilled chicken with avocado on cucumber slices and fresh mozzarella and basil on Caprese Toast. They were followed by a light meal of roasted vegetables and baked fish with a light cream sauce, allowing their conversation to flow into details about Abbey's upcoming wedding on the first Saturday in June.

"I have a lot planned for us to do tomorrow, Caitlin," Aunt Mary said excitedly, the last dish put away on the drying rack. "I suggest we get a good night's sleep and get an early start in the morning."

Caitlin, feeling exhausted from her travels, didn't argue. "We do need to schedule part of the day for you to fill me in on what you know about our family history."

"We'll have plenty of time for everything tomorrow, don't worry. Now get to bed."

"I've always known you to be a wise woman, so I'll follow your advice." Caitlin picked up her suitcase and headed to the spare bedroom. She was looking forward to seeing more of this newly upscaled neighborhood in which her aunt had moved. The minute her head hit the pillow; she fell sound asleep in the luxurious queen-sized bed with its exquisite night view of the harbor.


Later the next day, in between a trip to check out one of the boutique fitness studios in the area and fine dining at the Seaport, Caitlin got to listen to her aunt share a few stories about her grandfather's life in Ireland. Mary also surprised her niece with a shopping trip to pick out a special outfit for an evening out in Ireland.

"Aunt Mary, you don't need to buy me anything."

"No, but you know how I love to spoil you and your sister now and then. Everyone needs a nice evening dress." Caitlin's aunt always had the knack of getting her way, and she wasn't about to complain. She'd learned a long time ago that accepting generosity can be an expression of love.

Walking along the storefronts, Caitlin reminisced about the Sunday afternoons she'd spent with her aunt when she had lived in Boston. Her aunt had a way of making her feel appreciated, especially since her mother's death. Besides her sister, Aunt Mary had become her closest confidant, and Caitlin could trust her deepest feelings and concerns without worrying her aunt would reveal them to anyone else.

They shared many common interests, and when Caitlin had lived in Boston, they would often go to the theatre, concerts, and historic locations together. Caitlin even humored her aunt now and then and attended a Red Sox game with her, even though Caitlin favored the Twins.

Just as they approached the boutique Aunt Mary wanted to enter, the fragrant smells from the restaurant next door reminded Caitlin of all the delicious meals her aunt had prepared for her over the many Sundays they'd spent together. Besides being a good listener, what her aunt had most in common with her mother was the ability to cook exquisite meals. Something Caitlin had never learned from either of them.

"Come on, Caitlin. It's the shop I told you about."

Caitlin emerged from her memories; her vision embraced by the gorgeous, patterned dress in the window. "Oh, how fun! Let's go in. I'm right behind you."

They browsed meticulously through the racks of dresses together, pulling a few for Caitlin to try on. Then the task of modeling each one for her aunt began.

Just before trying on the last dress, her aunt hesitated briefly before broaching a touchy subject. She cared about her niece and had been upset by her hasty exit from Boston right before Christmas. "Now, I hate to bring up this subject, but I think you should try to connect with Jeremy while you're still in town. I know you had a bad break-up, but..."

"But nothing," Caitlin retorted. "He was seeing someone else behind my back!" Surprised by her own emotional outburst, Caitlin took a deep breath before continuing in a calmer voice, "I spent two years working on a relationship I believed would lead to marriage. There's nothing further I have to say to him."

"But Caitlin," her aunt began to explain, "I told you he broke things off with the other woman over a month ago. He's called me several times to ask about you."

"Really? Come on, Aunt Mary, only a guilty coward would try to get back into my good graces by taking advantage of my relationship with you. If Jeremy calls again, feel free to tell him I'm doing fine!"

Not used to being reprimanded by a niece who generally accepted her suggestions, Aunt Mary took a deep breath. "Well, I guess you know best, Caitlin. I just thought you should know he seemed so embarrassed by his lack of judgment and sincere about his love for you."

"I respect your point of view, Aunt Mary, but if he cheated on me once, who's to say he wouldn't do it again?"

"I suppose it's possible."

Caitlin placed a hand on her aunt's shoulder and, in a serious voice, said, "Everything will be fine. As you can see, I've moved on! I'm ready for a new adventure. Now, let me try on this last dress."

At the end of their shopping excursion along the waterfront, Caitlin walked away with a long-sleeved A-line dress in a beautiful chartreuse color—the cotton blends of the material soft to the touch—a casual yet elegant look on Caitlin. Her outfit was complete after purchasing a pair of black leggings to go with the knee-length dress. Evenings in Ireland could get a little chilly, and the outfit seemed perfect for a spring night out on the town. Her aunt talked her into adding a matching purse and an attractive pair of black dress boots because… "One needs an adventurous outfit for an adventure abroad!" In the end, Caitlin could not resist a pair of dangly gold earrings and a matching necklace that looked nice with the rounded neckline of the dress, topping off the already perfect ensemble.

Aunt Mary couldn't get over how lovely her niece looked—her new outfit accentuating her beautiful auburn hair and curiously intelligent green eyes. The question was, would Caitlin have the occasion to wear it? The dress had been purposefully designed for a special outing to catch the eye of an equally handsome man. Would her niece have this opportunity in Ireland? She sure hoped so if she was determined to leave Jeremy in the dust.

As they strolled back to her residence, Aunt Mary couldn't help herself. She made a final plea to Caitlin. "Now, don't forget me while you're on your trip. When you wear this outfit, I hope you'll feel obligated to call me immediately to update me on your trip and the lucky Irish lad you've cast a magic spell on."

Caitlin couldn't help giggling. "You are a hoot, Aunt Mary! I promise I'll keep you updated while I'm gone, but don't hold your breath on the other wish. I've decided I'm just unlucky in love. Besides, my main focus on this trip is family research and finding some of our relatives, not searching for the new love of my life."

"I can't tell you how much your traveling to Ireland means to your father, your Uncle Will, and me. I'll say some prayers for you while you're gone. Reconnecting with family believed lost forever would be a blessing."

Sunday afternoon arrived too soon for them both. Caitlin hugged her aunt tightly, tears beginning to pool in her eyes. Just one more reason to take this vacation of a lifetime, she reflected, to visit the home of my ancestors. "Thanks again for being willing to drop me off at the airport when I could just as easily have taken a cab. I'll take any extra time with you I can get these days."

"It's just not the same here without you, Caitlin. I've missed our time together. You're like a daughter to me. Well, at least we had a great time catching up."

"As far as your missing me, in just two months, we'll all be together to celebrate Abbey and Tim's wedding. I'll share all of the details from my adventure with you then." She paused momentarily before diverting back to the task at hand, "Will you be ready to leave in about fifteen minutes?"

"Yes, I'll be ready, silly girl. Now go and get your things so you can be off on your little escapade. I know you won't be sorry about your decision to take this trip," her aunt said before hurrying off to get her car keys.

Caitlin could feel the butterflies in the pit of her stomach. In just a few short hours, she would be jetting off across the Atlantic amidst a bunch of strangers with dreams and goals of their own. Caitlin couldn't help but consider what their stories would be. Or, what motivated them to travel in the same direction she was going? She smiled as she buckled up in her aunt's passenger seat and reflected on all she longed to uncover. Only time would reveal the extent of her success.

Not far away, at an outdoor cafe along the St. Charles River, a dark-haired gentleman sat finishing dinner at his hotel. Several women candidly glanced his way and smiled, hoping to catch the attention of his steel-blue eyes. He was a handsome man, lost in thought. He'd just spent the last few days at the New England Cluster Dog Show. While he had enjoyed his time there, he'd missed his loyal canine, Duncan.

Irish Red and White Setters were Donovan O'Malley's area of expertise. He raised and bred this beautiful yet vulnerable breed in Ireland, and some of the pups Duncan had sired were now showing well in America. At one point in time, the breed had been nearly extinct in Europe and was still considered vulnerable in the UK. He had proudly taken on the task of continuing to secure a future for this line of beautiful, family-friendly dogs. People loved them. They were loyal and adorable.

Donovan felt a little homesick even though Boston had proved to be a beautiful and intriguing city. He looked forward to collecting Duncan and whisking him back to their peaceful home in the countryside. His parents had been lovingly watching over his companion while he'd been away.

Donovan found it hard to believe his parents had already been living in Dublin for five years. They'd moved into the city from their family farm to be closer to his younger sister and her family. His nephew Liam had just turned one when his brother Sheamus proposed an idea to them. Their partnership with his brother initially seemed a wild idea, but the pub and inn they purchased together proved a profitable business venture. The previous family had already run the establishment successfully for almost four generations when the youngest members decided to sell it.

His parents wanted a change of pace but being close to their grandson happened to be the icing on the cake. So, without much fanfare, they agreed to go into business together. Donovan's parents suggested he move into their current family home to oversee the management of their family business. The timing of their move had worked well for Donovan. He had just finished establishing a veterinary clinic down the road from their family's farm in County Kildare. A year after the move, his sister gave birth to her second child, Grace.

Frequently his parents watched not only their grandchildren but his dog. His niece and nephew had always wanted a dog of their own, but his sister and brother-in-law currently felt their lives were too hectic to add one to the mix. Occasionally, he'd leave Duncan with his parents to serve as a surrogate pet. Over the past few years, he had benefited from a little dog therapy and canine friendship. He hoped his sister and brother-in-law would realize someday what a difference a dog would make in their own lives. Until then, he didn't mind sharing Duncan.

After signing his meal receipt, Donovan glanced up, his attention drawn to a family with two active young children seated at a nearby table. Seeing them joking and fooling around reminded him of something his mother would often say, "Donovan, your father and I are still praying you and your brother will settle down and give us a few more grandchildren."

A flood of oppressive memories surrounded him. He recalled having such plans just three years earlier. He had gotten engaged, but two months before the wedding, his world had come crashing down. Marie, the love of his life, had died in a car accident. He'd been trying to fill the empty cracks in his broken heart ever since. Donovan began to pour himself into his work to forget his loss, but he hadn't been able to move past the memories of the way her love for life seemed to fill his entire being. Since her death, looking at other women was like entering a thick fog. They might be within arm's reach, but he just didn't see them. They didn't pique his interest enough to take a chance on love again.

Emotionally exhausted by the thoughts running through his head, he envisioned relaxing in the Sky Club at the airport and then reclining in his first-class seat on the flight back to Dublin. Things had been calm on the home front while he'd been away, so he had nothing to distract him from getting some rest after a few busy days in Boston.

Logan Airport seemed lively as Caitlin observed the entry at her drop off point. Aunt Mary bid her a fond farewell, and off she went into the thrumming bustle of the airport. Caitlin tried to convince herself flying business class would help her forget her fear of flying, but she could feel her heart rate increase when she walked further into the airport. Caitlin had to be honest with herself. She tended to feel most comfortable when both of her feet were solidly planted on *terra firma*. She didn't fly often—it had been almost two years since she'd last stepped on a plane, and now she'd be flying across the ocean for the first time in her life.

As she waited to check her bags, Caitlin's brain went on a massive overload. Questions regarding her motivation for taking this trip had wormed their way to the surface: Would her detective work pay off? Would she be able to successfully follow the clues she had gathered to track down family members living in Ireland? And where exactly would they lead her? There were so many unknowns. What if these relatives didn't even want anything to do with her family?

Caitlin found herself so distracted by her nervousness she unexpectedly walked directly into a rather tall man attempting to make his way through the airport.

"Pardon me," he apologized with a smileless glance in her direction, leaving her staring as he confidently pivoted around her before sauntering toward the Delta Terminal. She couldn't help but notice he seemed to stand out in a crowd but not because of his height. There was just something about him—she realized she felt somewhat unnerved by the fact the man had hardly given her the time of day. She was stressed further by having to wait nearly half an hour to get through the security line. It prevented her from calming down after her run-in with the nonchalant stranger.

On the other hand, Donovan, a seasoned traveler, leisurely strolled through the TSA precheck with hardly a care in the world. Well, except for one piece of advice for the woman who had bumped into him. *People should give themselves more time when traveling, so they don't need to rush and mow people down in the process.*

An hour later, Caitlin felt thrilled to be finally boarding the plane. Upon entering, she found her seat just one row behind First Class. A young woman, already seated to the right of her unfortunate middle seat, shuffled through a magazine while trying to tune out the other passengers entering the plane. She looked harmless enough.

To Caitlin's chagrin, her section's front row lacked under-seat storage, forcing her to rethink where she would place her items. In the process of hoisting her carry-on-bag into the overhead storage bin, someone bumped into her from behind, causing her to drop it. Several things spilled forth onto the floor.

"I'm so sorry, my dear," apologized an elderly woman with the sweetest Irish brogue. "I'm not steady on my feet these days. This is my seat," she explained, pointing to the aisle seat next to Caitlin's.

"Here, let me help you," volunteered a deep voice spread as smoothly as butter on a warm piece of toast.

"Thank you." Without looking up, Caitlin could feel the heat of the man's presence when he knelt to assist her in retrieving the items she'd dropped. A fresh citrus scent drifted in her direction as his hand briefly touched hers, sending heat racing up her arm causing her cheeks to flush. She hoped he wouldn't notice when he stood back up, bag in hand.

At first, she didn't recognize him. The smile on his face had changed his entire outward appearance. Her cheeks turned a deeper shade of red when she glanced over at him and realized it was the man she had run into earlier.

"Oh, my! Thanks again for your help," Caitlin stammered, mesmerized by his charisma and the Irish lilt in his voice. She lowered her head, and frantically prayed this handsome dark-haired gentleman would not recognize her.

"My pleasure," he crooned as he quickly stored her bag in the overhead bin before allowing her to squeeze past him to her seat.

Caitlin noticed the attractive, long-haired blonde had lost interest in her Vogue magazine, now seemingly captivated by the live model who had stepped off the page and out into plain view. He had begun to assist the older woman with her seatbelt. A charmed storybook hero, indeed.

Other passengers trying to get to their seats were becoming impatient due to the traffic jam. The "Good Samaritan" announced calmly, "I'll be out of your way in just a moment as soon as I finish helping this lovely woman." Listening to the lilt and lift of the words that flowed from his mouth was like being rocked gently in a boat at sea. Comforting and safe. The man's voice and charming smile pacified the restless line of passengers waiting to get situated in their seats as if he'd hypnotized them.

"Now, who may I thank for the assistance, young fella?" asked the older woman.

"Donovan O'Malley at your service," he said so only she could hear him, "And what might your name be, my dear?"

The woman giggled. "I'm Noreen Murphy," she said with a twinkle in her eye.

"Well, Noreen, I hope you have a very relaxing flight."

Caitlin observed his retreat, wondering what in this man's past had given him such self-confidence. The rest of the passengers began to flow steadily past them until all were seated.

Shortly after they secured the cabin door, the plane's engines hummed as they backed away from the jet bridge. Donovan took that moment to look over his right shoulder. He spied Noreen relaxing with her eyes shut, a smile painted on her face. The attractive redhead—who had almost run him over earlier—sat nervously, rubbing her hands together. What an intriguing start to his journey home.

For fear of focusing only on the massive plane about to lift into the air, Caitlin began to strike up a conversation with her elderly seatmate. "Hi, I'm Caitlin."

"I'm Noreen Murphy. I'm so sorry about all the commotion I caused earlier," she said sweetly.

"Oh, it's no problem. We're all settled now, and I'm looking forward to a quiet and restful flight."

"Me, too." After a few more minutes of quiet conversation, they both reclined their seats and closed their eyes, hopeful they would both get some much-needed rest before landing.

Five hours later, a sudden movement from Noreen awakened Caitlin. She'd been dreaming restlessly about leaving her father behind when Noreen grabbed Caitlin's arm with her right hand. Jolting awake, Caitlin noticed Noreen's left hand fly directly to her chest. She immediately pressed the call light for help from a flight attendant, fearing the worst for her seatmate.

"Are you all right, Noreen?" Caitlin asked, trying to remain calm.

"I'm having some trouble breathing, and my chest feels rather tight," she gasped.

"It's OK, Noreen, I'm here." Caitlin said a silent prayer as the closest attendant came rushing over from First Class. Shortly afterward, an announcement came over the intercom in the form of a call for medical help.

A woman came forward from a few rows back while Donovan joined them. "I'm a nurse," the woman stated. "How can I help?"

Caitlin couldn't hear what Donovan said to the nurse and flight attendant, but she could hear them moving emergency equipment toward them. The nurse asked Noreen a few questions, then took her blood pressure, conferring with Donovan throughout the process. He helped place an oxygen mask on her face before they carefully transferred her to his First-Class seat.

Within fifteen minutes, things had quieted down, and Donovan had taken Noreen's seat. "Will she be all right?" Caitlin asked.

"She's stable for the time being you don't need to worry. When we arrive in Dublin, they'll have EMTs waiting to take her to the nearest hospital."

"So, are you a doctor?" asked Caitlin.

"Yes, but my patients are generally animals. I'm a veterinarian. Now I advise you to try to relax a bit before we land."

Comforted by Noreen's stable condition, Caitlin drifted back to sleep, not realizing her head had taken residence on Donovan's shoulder. He just smiled and closed his eyes, hoping to get a few winks of sleep as well before they landed. Not exactly the relaxing flight he'd hoped for, but his seatmate was charming company, nonetheless.

# Chapter 4

A muffled noise projected from the airplane speakers caused Caitlin to wake from a deep sleep. Without moving her head, she slowly opened her eyes, feeling the gradual descent of the plane. Her entire body tensed when Caitlin realized her head had been resting on the shoulder of the "Good Samaritan". She quickly shifted to sit up as straight as a pillar before shyly glancing to her left. Out of her peripherals, she could see a broad grin stretching across Donovan's face.

"Good morning," she mumbled, raising her eyes to meet his as she tried to gain her composure. "Did anything else happen while I was sleeping?"

"No, it's been very peaceful. Nothing further to report on Mrs. Murphy at this time."

Silence. Their train of thought on the same wavelength, each wondering the other's name. Would they be fools if they got off the plane, not knowing this one fact about each other? Donovan beat her to the punch, drawing a long breath. "So, as I recall, we were never properly introduced. I don't know your name."

"Caitlin," she shared hesitantly, too nervous to think of giving this chivalrous man more than her first name.

"Donovan ..." An announcement emanating from the speakers interrupting their exchange.

"Good morning everyone, we are fifteen minutes from landing at Dublin International. Please make sure your tray tables are up, and your seats are in their forward positions. The captain asks all passengers to remain seated once the aircraft has landed until emergency personnel can remove a passenger from the plane. Thank you for your patience regarding this matter."

Caitlin sat back with eyes shuttered and sighed. "Are you all right?" Donovan asked.

Slowly, looking straight ahead, she replied, "I'm fine. I'm just relieved we'll be landing soon. I get a little nervous when I fly." Caitlin couldn't believe she had just revealed her fear to this virtual stranger.

"Ah, I'm sure you're not the first person to feel this way. Just breathe easy, and we'll soon be on the ground." Suddenly the plane hit a pocket of turbulent air, causing the seats to shake from side to side. Frightened by the sudden movement, Caitlin impulsively grabbed Donovan's hand, and without embarrassment, held on tight.

He gently squeezed it in response, "Relax. We're almost there. Now close your eyes and breathe deeply." The jarring of the plane seemed to last forever from Caitlin's point of view, and she continued to hold fast to Donovan's hand, only letting go when the plane began to taxi toward the gate.

One of the flight attendants strolled toward them, eyeing Donovan with a smile. "Sir, Mrs. Murphy said she'd feel more comfortable if you'd ride with her in the ambulance to the hospital. The attending nurse needs to catch a connecting flight. If it's all right with you, we can have your luggage delivered to the hospital if you give me your baggage claim ticket."

"No problem," he promptly responded. "I can spare the time." He stood to remove his wallet from his pants pocket, swiftly extricating both the ticket and his business card. Caitlin sat, mouth awkwardly and unintentionally hanging wide open. She was amazed at how quickly Donovan had volunteered to accompany a virtual stranger to the hospital. She stared, admiring his tall, muscular build and rather handsome, almost regal-looking face. A real-life Prince Charming if her childhood memory served her well. Obviously, she had read one too many fairy tales in her youth.

Yes, Donovan was easy on the eyes, but he'd proven to be a compassionate man, more importantly. Caitlin quickly lost in her thoughts—which was standard for her— found herself seriously contemplating what it would be like to start a new relationship with a man like Donovan. He seemed to be the kind of partner she'd prefer. But the sudden jerk of the parking plane brought Caitlin back to reality. *Snap out of it.* She scolded herself. *No sense in pining after a man you barely know who lives an ocean away from you.*

The plane slowed to a complete stop, and soon two paramedics eased a gurney onto the aircraft, carefully lifting Noreen onto it. Caitlin stood up and moved toward Donovan before he could leave. She placed a hand on his arm, not knowing what she intended to say, but once again — mercifully—he beat her to the punch. He turned toward her, and in a smooth Irish lilt, his croon sang a lullaby, "Caitlin, it's been a pleasure meeting you. I hope you enjoy your stay in Ireland."

Caitlin nodded and, without thinking, hugged him awkwardly. "Thank you. It's been great meeting you as well. Let Noreen know I'll be praying for her."

Taken a bit by surprise, Donovan stiffened up. Deep down, he appreciated Caitlin's honest emotions, but he wasn't used to this type of affection from strangers. Stepping back slowly, Donovan made a promise to pass along Caitlin's message. Then he turned away, a slight smile lingering on his face. As Donovan exited the plane into the Dublin Airport's sterile air, he realized Caitlin's beauty and kindness had already enraptured him. But he admitted to himself it would be best if he never saw this woman again. Donovan wasn't willing to allow himself to get involved in a relationship while he still carried around the pain of losing the love of his life. He didn't want to feel that way again, and Caitlin seemed to be the kind of woman a man could easily fall for.

When Caitlin reached the baggage carousel, she replayed the events of the flight repeatedly in her mind. A feeling of melancholy settled in the pit of her stomach. She would probably never see either Noreen or Donovan again. She surmised Donovan's unavoidable charm had cast a spell on her.

Once she had successfully collected her bags and somewhat successfully collected her head, she calmly waited for a taxi to take her on the short trip into Dublin and to O'Malley's Pub and Inn on Pearse Street. Anxiety began to build as reality hit the fan. She'd be staying for the next few days in Dublin! After three generations, a descendant of William Aeden O'Sullivan had set foot on Irish soil once again, in the city of her grandfather's birthplace. Engulfed in emotion, she took several deep breaths as she stepped into the taxi, and it began to carry her closer to her destination.

The moment they arrived on Pearse Street, the sight alone of O'Malley's Pub made her heart stop. The pub was precisely how she imagined it—a golden accented doorway with green lettering so royal it was as though the very hue originated at this establishment. With ease, the taxi driver hopped out and plunked her luggage onto the sidewalk, leaving her stranded in front of the entrance to the Inn.

"I guess he's in a hurry," she said to herself, not even having a chance to thank him.

Caitlin slowly turned full circle, mouth still agape, to take in the surroundings. A dog appeared suddenly from around the corner of the building, dragging a young boy behind it. Such a beautiful dog—its medium-length, white fur with deep chestnut patches fluttering in the breeze. It appeared to be well-groomed, clearly demonstrating the great care the owner took of their pet.

Without warning, the boy lost his hold on the leash, and the robust, solid, and sinewy dog gracefully covered the ground between them before lifting its front legs and placing its large paws square on Caitlin's shoulders almost as if to embrace her. She braced herself but still ended up dropping her bags in the process. The dog seemed to grin at her, and she couldn't help staring into its beautiful brown eyes and laugh.

"Duncan, down, boy!" commanded a gray-haired gentleman in a firm voice standing behind the young boy.

"I'm so sorry, Miss, Duncan can get a little excited," the man apologized, picking up the leash the boy had dropped and pulling the dog back to his side. "Are you all right?"

Caitlin bent over and began to pet the enthusiastic bundle of joy, particularly his long silky triangular-shaped ears. Duncan wagged his tail exuberantly while turning up his face toward Caitlin. At that moment, her heart melted. It was love at first sight. She felt stunned. Each meeting along her journey thus far, even canine, had been serendipity. A wave of gratitude began to pour over her.

"Yes, I'm fine. It's okay. I love dogs as much as your dog seems to love people."

He let out a deep sigh of relief, then offered his hand to welcome her, saying, "Actually, I've never seen him greet a stranger like this before. I'm Sean. This is my grandson Liam."

She reached out and, with a firm handshake, spoke to him with self-confidence. "Glad to meet you, Sean. I'm Caitlin." She turned toward Liam and gently shook his hand, "And it's great to meet you, Liam. Is this your dog?"

"No, Duncan is my uncle's dog. Are you here to stay at the Inn?" Liam blurted out before his grandfather could say another word.

"Why, yes, I am," she confirmed. Liam grinned from ear to ear. Such a little charmer, she noted.

"Ahh, your last name wouldn't happen to be Sullivan, would it?" Sean asked.

"Yes."

"Meghan's friend and our guest from America! My wife Bridgett and I have been expecting you. Welcome to Dublin. It's lovely to finally meet you after hearing so much about you from our daughter." Gesturing to her bags, he offered, "Let me help you with your luggage. Follow me, and I'll take you to my wife so she can help you get settled in your room."

"Thank you. It's so generous of you and your wife to arrange for me to stay at your Inn."

Sean gave her a warm smile. "Liam, can you take Duncan upstairs while I help Miss Sullivan?"

"Please call me Caitlin," she encouraged. He nodded in return.

Liam smiled at Caitlin, then took off with the dog toward the entrance to the Inn. Intricate wood carvings decorated the frame of the doorway, painted a cherry red. The sign saying "O'Malley's Inn" in gold lettering was easily visible to passers-by. Liam looked back, and enthusiastically shouted to her, "See you later, Caitlin!"

"You too, Liam," she called after him, following Sean into the relatively small lobby. Passing through the quaint entryway, she noticed interior double doors connecting directly to O'Malley's Pub. Straight ahead, a friendly-looking middle-aged woman stood talking to Liam by the reception desk. She looked up and immediately noticed Caitlin. Smiling widely, she rushed over to them.

"Caitlin, welcome! I'm Bridgett O'Malley," she exclaimed, embracing her like a long lost relative. "Meghan has told us so much about you. I feel as if I already know you."

"I feel the same. I'm so excited to be here and grateful for your hospitality."

"Did you have a pleasant flight, dear?"

"Yes and no," Caitlin responded hesitantly and immediately began to explain about poor Mrs. Murphy and the excitement on the flight from Boston.

"Our oldest son actually traveled home on the same flight! He just called and said he'd be late picking Duncan up, but he didn't say why. I hope the woman will be all right."

"I hope so, too," Caitlin sighed, wishing she had a way of checking up on her. Not knowing if she was going to be all right made Caitlin ill at ease. She was the type of person who needed closure—no matter how small the issue—before she could move on in life.

"Well, didn't the gentleman who helped the woman tell you his name? Maybe he'd have some information to share."

"Why yes, but only his first name, Donovan."

"Donovan?" Bridgett couldn't believe it. "Our son's name is Donovan."

Sean looked at his wife. "It sounds like something he'd do."

"The Donovan I met said he was a veterinarian," Caitlin added.

"Then it must have been our son. The chances of there being more than one vet on your plane named Donovan is slim. When our son stops here to pick up Duncan, we can find out more about how Mrs.… oh dear, what was her name again?"

"Noreen Murphy," Caitlin offered.

"Ah, yes … how Mrs. Murphy is doing."

Caitlin couldn't believe this was happening. Just when she thought she'd washed her hands of Donovan, God had dropped him right back in her lap. The "Good Samaritan" and their son were one and the same, but no matter, she hadn't changed her mind about the subject. She would not get involved with the good doctor.

Bridgett moved behind the ornate reception desk and pulled out a room key. "Sean can check in with Donovan and see when he'll arrive at the Inn. In the meantime, let's bring your things up to your room so you can get settled. You must be hungry! Can I have some food sent up?"

"I'm fine for now. I think I'm going to lay down first and get some rest. I'm meeting Meghan at the library this afternoon."

Sean had been following the lively conversation carefully as he watched the animated expression evolve on Caitlin's face. Such a sweet lass, he thought, but he could tell she wasn't a seasoned traveler. "Relaxing a bit would be fine, but don't go falling asleep. You'll get terrible jet lag. When you do come down for lunch, I can let you know what I found out from Donovan. I'm sure everything will be fine. Now, go on with Bridgett, and she'll get you situated."

As Bridgett led Caitlin toward the stairwell, she began to share details of the quaint and historic Inn and Pub. Caitlin noticed the blue carpeting and white walls created a continuous color scheme stretching down the hallway and up the stairs. To the right of the stairwell, she found an alcove containing a wooden desk and a rack overflowing with travel brochures. Bridgett paused as Caitlin stopped to grab a few to browse through later.

"We've put a lot of work into updating the Victorian charm of this Inn, which was originally built in 1885. It has no elevator, so you'll need to follow me up these stairs to your room on the second floor."

Bridgett held the door open for Caitlin at the top of the first landing. She entered a hallway covered with intricate, floral-patterned wallpaper with dark oak trim around the doorways and as baseboards. The vision took Caitlin's breath away. Everything seemed so well preserved. It was like taking a step back in time. Classic rug runners lay protectively on the hardwood flooring adding additional charm to the hallway. Her room was the last one on the right.

Upon entering the room, her eyes took in the blue and gray-toned color scheme, which had a calming effect on her senses. Its two large windows let ample sunlight in through the sheer curtains, with pull shades available to cast out any unwanted light when necessary. She appreciated the warmth and coziness of the room. Spying an armchair positioned near one of the windows, Caitlin imagined herself perched there later in the evening just to watch the locals. A few other strategically placed pieces of furniture created the homiest setting. She realized she couldn't have found a nicer place to stay in Dublin. Despite the Old-World charm, Caitlin noticed her room had its own modern bathroom with elegant tiles and updated shower fixtures. She wouldn't be complaining about these lodgings any time too soon.

Caitlin looked out the nearest window to admire the view of the busy street below. "Meghan mentioned you live right here at the Inn."

"Yes, Sean and I live in a suite we remodeled when we moved here five years ago. It's on the third floor above the Breakfast Room in the neighboring building—right above the pub, if you find yourself over there and fancy a cup of tea. But be careful, my 80-year-old father-in-law Aengus lives with us, and he's known around town as a mischievous leprechaun," Bridgett explained.

Caitlin, drawn immediately to Bridgett's sense of humor, wanted to know more about the O'Malley family. "Meghan told me her home is on the outskirts of the city, but what about your sons? Do they live nearby as well?"

"Sheamus lives in a one-bedroom flat just a few blocks from here while Donovan lives a 45-minute drive west of Dublin on our family farm."

"It's nice that they live so close to you. Your Inn is such a lovely place. I'm glad I'll be able to stay here this week. It's such a short walking distance to so many places, including the National Library."

"That's why it works so well for Meghan. We keep an eye on our grandchildren when they're not in school, and both their parents are working."

"I met Liam earlier. He's adorable. I missed seeing Meghan's daughter, though."

"Meghan and the children are staying for supper tonight. Why don't you join us, too? Then you'll get to meet Grace and the rest of the O'Malley family before the end of the day."

"Thanks, it would be my pleasure."

"Now, why don't you get settled in and rest for a while, but make sure to come down early enough so I can take you over to the pub and introduce you to Sheamus. He'll make sure you get a good lunch before heading off to the library to meet with Meghan."

"Thank you, Bridgett. It sounds like a good plan."

"In the meantime, I'll call Donovan and see if I can convince him to join us for supper. It would be nice to visit with him and hear about his trip. He can also update you on Mrs. Murphy's condition at the same time."

"That would mean a lot to me. Thank you," said Caitlin appreciatively before Bridgett left, shutting the door quietly behind her.

"Great, just what I wanted to avoid, getting to know Donovan better!" she complained to herself, pacing back and forth on the plush carpet. She found an empty glass on the desk. Picking it up, she shuffled into the bathroom for some water. "I have no idea why I feel so strongly about avoiding a man who has every quality a lass would be looking for—in a husband," she fumed, glancing at herself in the mirror. *Really, Caitlin! Did you just say the word "husband" aloud?* She scolded herself.

# Chapter 5

Caitlin relaxed in O'Malley's Pub just before noon, enjoying a delicious Cobb Salad as she watched the foot traffic bustle past the large ornate window. Sitting in the very city of her grandfather's birth brought back memories of him. Her grandfather had longed to visit his homeland, but it felt surreal to be here without him. She said a short prayer, asking for divine intervention. She knew her grandfather would have given her his blessing. Now she was preparing to take the next step toward reconnecting with the O'Sullivan family after almost a century of separation, and she couldn't help feeling nervous.

After a short while, fully re-fueled, Caitlin headed off on the short ten-minute walk to the National Library. Today's weather seemed to be perfect for a stroll in the city. Since she had enough time to spare before her appointment, she stopped along the way to take a few photos, determined to document her adventures.

While Caitlin focused on the past, Donovan found himself knee-deep in the present, just a few miles away. After awkwardly accompanying Noreen to the hospital in the ambulance, he'd patiently awaited the doctor as he finished evaluating her. Although impatient to retrieve Duncan and head home, he decided to stick around so Mrs. Murphy didn't feel alone.

After what felt like ages staring at the muted waiting room television, a young nurse emerged from the emergency room and entered the waiting area. "Dr. O'Malley, they just transferred Mrs. Murphy to her room. The doctor believes he'll probably release her tomorrow, but just to be safe, he wants to keep her overnight for further observation. You've permission to see her, but don't be too long. She needs to get some rest. We expect her son here within the hour. Rest assured; we'll take good care of her until he arrives. Feel free to leave anytime you want."

"Thank you for being so kind and caring toward a frightened woman," Donovan said with a grateful smile. "Your staff has been wonderful, and I appreciate you letting me check in on her."

A little flustered by his effortless charm, the nurse responded, "Of course! She's anxious to see you. I think she called you her tall, dark, and handsome doctor."

Donovan chuckled as he walked down the hall and quietly entered Noreen's room. He didn't want to disturb her if she'd fallen asleep, but she lay staring at the door as if she'd been expecting him. "Donovan, you're still here."

Donovan looked at the pale face of the older woman framed by a white pillowcase. "Mrs. Murphy, I couldn't leave without checking on you first."

"Call me, Noreen," she interrupted.

"Noreen, one of the nurses told me you'd be on your way home to your husband tomorrow, and your son should be here soon."

"Yes, I'm in good hands, but before you go, lad, I want you to write down my phone number. If you're ever near Killarney, I'd like you to give me a call. I'd love to see your handsome face again so you can meet my husband." Donovan couldn't help but blush when hearing the praise, even from someone much older than himself. What a charmer!

He pulled out the bedside drawer, where he discovered a pen and a pad of paper. He began to write down the phone number she recited, then placed it in his wallet.

Now, who could resist such an offer, he wondered. "The next time I'm in the area, I promise I'll stop by to visit. Before I leave, will you promise to have your son contact me when he gets here? I'd like to be able to answer any questions he may have about our flight." He placed one of his business cards on her bedside table.

"Of course, Donovan."

Taking her hand in his, he patted it gently. "Now why don't you close your eyes and get some rest. Your son should be here within the hour. If you need anything, just buzz the nursing staff, and they'll rush in to help you." Lifting her hand to his lips, he placed a light kiss upon it. She smiled and whispered her thanks before closing her eyes, letting exhaustion take hold of her.

Donovan made his way into the hallway then proceeded to stroll toward the nurses' station, pausing briefly to glance out the window. He was glad he could be there for Noreen today, but it forced him to realize he still carried guilt over not being in the right place at the right time for the love of his life.

He realized, after all these years, he still blamed himself for his fiancée's death. If he'd been driving the evening of her accident—he believed he could have maintained control of the car when hitting black ice—avoiding the massive oak. He anguished over the memory of Marie being found half an hour after the accident, trapped behind the steering wheel of his car. Why couldn't God have sent someone to save her when he couldn't be there? Why couldn't the ambulance have gotten to the scene of the accident fast enough to prevent her death from internal bleeding? His heart began to ache from the memory of seeing the accident photos a few days after her funeral, and he hung his head in shame, his eyes blurred.

Everyone reminded him it wasn't his fault. Confused, Donovan wondered what had dredged up all these painful memories. He believed he'd gotten beyond the intense grieving and feelings of guilt. Then he realized Caitlin, the lovely lass from the plane, had stirred up emotions within him he had thought buried. He'd felt a tug on his heartstrings the moment they'd first met, and now he struggled to block the vision of her cascading auburn hair and long-lashed emerald green eyes before he went crazy with questions of "what if?" Thankfully, he realized the memory of Caitlin and his unwanted feelings would soon fade, and he'd never see her again. Thank God, because, based on what he knew of her, she was the kind of woman who could get under a man's skin. He already felt drawn to her and saw no benefit, at this point in his life, in getting to know her better.

Donovan stopped at the nurses' station to pick up his luggage the airport personnel had dropped off a few hours earlier. Finally, the time had come to retrieve his beloved Duncan and head home to get some rest, some much-needed rest. His mother always said routine was good medicine for the ailments of life. So far, it had helped to heal his wounded heart.

Donovan checked his phone on the taxi ride into town. He saw a missed call and a voice message from his dad. He realized a quick lunch with his parents was in order. Staying in Dublin another hour or two wouldn't make much of a difference. His staff knew his arrival back at the clinic would be delayed when he had called earlier from the hospital.

Upon arriving at the Inn, Sean greeted his son in the lobby with a firm embrace. "I tried to get a hold of you earlier, but now that you're here, your mom and I have a proposition for you."

"Didn't you see my text, Dad?"

"No, when did you send it?"

"Just a few minutes ago," Donovan tried to say in a calm voice. Sometimes his dad's inability to use technology baffled him. "Why don't you and Mom just join me for lunch, and you can tell me all about your proposition?"

"Sounds like a plan. Let's check in on your lovely mum first!"

Heading toward the registration desk they spotted Bridgett stepping out of the office. She immediately directed a radiant smile toward her son.

"Well, you sure look happy to see me."

"Of course, I never get to see enough of you." Bridgett hugged her son briefly then exclaimed, "Now listen to me, you're not going to believe who's staying here!"

Donovan chuckled, entertained by his mother's apparent delight. "Is it someone famous?

"No celebrity, but someone I think you might know."

"How intriguing, I can't stand the suspense," he said somewhat sarcastically.

She held his hands and looked intently into his eyes as though she expected a reaction, "Her name is Caitlin Sullivan. She said you met on the airplane coming home from Boston while helping a woman who had become ill on the plane."

Donovan's heart began to pulsate immediately. "Caitlin? She's staying here?" he stammered. *Just my luck*, he thought, *the one person I hoped to avoid.* He began to feel anxious, palm-sweat anxious, not his typical reaction to a woman. Deep down, she already had a tight hold on him.

"Yes," his mother confirmed with a smile, "and I think it would be nice if you stayed and had supper with us tonight before going home. We invited Caitlin to join us. She's currently at the Library with your sister, trying to track down some of her Irish relatives. Just imagine," she gasped, "she could be related to someone we know; her grandfather was born right here in Dublin!" Bridgett paused, as though she'd almost forgotten this final detail, "More importantly, she wants to hear how Mrs. Murphy is doing."

Donovan could understand how worried Caitlin might be about Noreen and felt somewhat obligated to share what he knew. He figured he could resist her charm long enough to give her an update. One meal in her company with his entire family there, what did he have to lose?

"All right, I guess I can put off my departure for a few more hours. Why don't you and Dad join me for a bite to eat in the pub, so we catch up?"

"I don't have time right now. Why don't you enjoy some lunch alone with your dad? I'll store your luggage behind the desk. By the time you've finished eating, I should be able to go upstairs with you for a short visit. Your grandad will be happy to see you as well as Liam and Grace—and of course—Duncan! He'll be happy you're home."

Donovan and Sean walked through the double doors connecting the Inn to O'Malley's Pub, ready for some father-son bonding time. He didn't get to see his parents as often since their move to the city. He had his hands full running his clinic and overseeing the management of their 240-acre family farm.

He and his parents jointly owned an Equestrian Center designed for all types and standards of horse riding. They scheduled organized rides every day for all levels of horse riders over the cross-country course or trekking. Finn, their manager, took care of the business's day-to-day running along with employing an extensive staff to care for the grounds, animals, and guests visiting the farm for recreation. Over the last few years, Donovan had added clay pigeon shooting, archery, and an air-rifle target shooting range to increase their visitors' options.

He had excellent horse handlers, but he cared for any animals with serious injuries or health conditions with help from his clinic staff. In addition, he checked in with Finn regularly.

Donovan spotted his younger brother as he entered the pub. A simple wave of the hand caught Sheamus' attention. He moved toward them. "It's been too long, Donovan," Sheamus said as he gave his older brother a big bear hug. "I thought you might have gotten lost in America. I know you have no sense of direction."

"I'm glad you think you're funny, Sheamus. America is not a place where I would intentionally get lost. Boston is a busy city with much to do, but I wouldn't want to be trapped in it for long, although I did enjoy seeing the dog show. Duncan has sired some fine pups, and I enjoyed visiting with some of their owners and seeing how much they've grown."

"Say, Thomas Callaghan and his band, The O'Tooles, are stopping by tonight to sing for a couple of hours," Sheamus mentioned. "You should come down to the pub after supper to hang out with them."

Donovan stopped to consider the idea. They were good friends with Thomas and his band and liked to sit around and jam together as often as possible. It had been several months since they'd last had a chance. "Tempting as it would be to hang out with them tonight, I really should be getting back home."

*Just like Donovan to put work before all else,* thought Sheamus, hence the lack of family time with him. "Come on, Donovan, stay in town a bit longer. What if I tell you Thomas mentioned The High Kings were back in Dublin after touring the countryside, and your good friend Brian Dunphy might be stopping by later tonight?"

That got Donovan's attention, another friend he hadn't seen in a while. He'd been a fan of The High Kings for nearly ten years now, becoming close friends with them just about a year ago.

His brother, becoming impatient as he waited for an answer, repeated himself. "Now, are you going to be sticking around long enough to join us? Thomas promised lively music and a rollicking good time."

Donovan paused before answering. Staying to sing tonight at the pub was another change in his plans, and he felt hesitant for some reason, "Well, I don't know…"

"Sure, you can," said his dad, who'd been listening intently to the discussion between his two sons. "Let me text your mum and tell her you're staying here tonight. She can get a room ready for you. Tomorrow you can commute to work from here. One more night away isn't going to make a difference when you've already been gone almost a week. Besides, Meghan and her kids are staying overnight. It's been a while since we've had the whole family together."

Sheamus grinned at Donovan. Their parents always did this. They seemed to love pulling on the strings of Donovan's life like he was their puppet, "It'll be a grand time tonight; it isn't often we have Brian in town. The High Kings are quite popular these days. I believe they're getting ready to return to America for another tour early this summer. Imagine that!" Sheamus pointed out.

Donovan finally admitted the truth to himself; time with family and friends was too important to pass up. "All right, I could use a little family togetherness, and I'd enjoy the opportunity to sing with friends."

Sean had already gotten a response from Bridgett. "You're all set for tonight. Your mum's having your things brought upstairs."

Donovan hesitated momentarily and then admitted to himself he hadn't spent much time with his parents lately. What kind of son was he? "Great, why don't we order our lunch, and then I'll call Finn to let him know I won't be home until tomorrow morning. I also need to check in with the clinic to make sure they don't need me this afternoon." If all went smoothly, he'd be able to relax and have a fun-filled evening with his entire family.

Caitlin would be pleasantly surprised when she joined his family for supper tonight. They were a friendly bunch and were sure to include her in all aspects of their family time together. Donovan only hoped she wouldn't be entirely overwhelmed by their exuberance on her first day in Ireland. *Am I a fool to even care?* He wondered.

# Chapter 6

As Caitlin approached the National Library's main desk, joy took hold of her when she caught sight of a raised hand greeting her from across the room. She immediately recognized Meghan from their Skype sessions over the past month. Meghan moved quickly from behind the desk to join her.

"Caitlin, it's so good to finally meet you face to face," she spoke cheerfully over a brief hug.

"I feel the same."

"Did you have a pleasant flight?"

Caitlin took a step back and immediately began to report her unusual experience. "It was relaxing until the elderly woman sitting next to me had a medical emergency."

"Oh no, how awful! Is she going to be all right?" Meghan asked with genuine concern ringing through her every word.

"I think so. A man I met on the plane rode in the ambulance to the hospital with her. Your parents think it was your brother who had arrived on the very same flight." Caitlin went on to explain what she knew about the man.

Meghan repeated what her mother had said earlier, "Well, it's too much of a coincidence for it to be anyone other than my brother. Was he about six feet tall, dark hair, and blue eyes with a neatly groomed beard?"

"Yes! Handsome as well as polite," she added.

"I don't know about handsome; I guess most women think so. Polite, definitely, and he is a fairly serious individual. I'd be surprised if it weren't my brother."

Meghan looked at the change in Caitlin's demeanor after discussing her older brother. She had seen that look before on the faces of countless women. Caitlin had already fallen for her brother's undeniable charm. He seemed to have some kind of magical powers when it came to the opposite sex, and they were often vying for his affections. Regardless of the degree of their interest, he never seemed to notice his innate ability to attract women. Both of her brothers had been born with good looks and charismatic personalities.

"Why don't I take you on a short tour of the Library before we get started with our research," she suggested, trying to get her mind refocused on the task at hand.

"I'd enjoy that, Meghan."

After a brief pause, she began, "The Library was opened in 1890 and designed in a classical style by Cork-born architect, Thomas Deanne. As you can see, it is rather spacious and has fine craftsmanship in masonry, marble, hardwoods, and glass." Meghan seemed to immediately go into the tour guide mode, a common hazard for Museum staff members of any sort.

Meghan walked Caitlin through the wood-paneled Genealogy Advisory Service area. As they entered the next room, Caitlin admired the mosaic floor with the emblem of an owl. The stained-glass windows in the front hall were spectacular and portrayed famous people in the worlds of literature and philosophy. As they moved toward the main Reading Room, Meghan pointed out the carved figures representing the continents of Europe, Asia, Africa, and America on the mezzanine landing of the main staircase. The room itself was horseshoe shaped and almost 50 feet high in the center. Light streamed in through the large central dome and side windows high in the walls.

Caitlin looked up to admire a plaster frieze of cherubs. "It's all so amazing!" came flying out of her mouth. Meghan agreed. The Library had always carried a special place in her heart, one of majesty and intrigue.

Caitlin was impressed by what she saw. "This is an incredible building. Not only do people have access to many diverse resources, but the beauty of the architectural structure and artworks within is awe-inspiring." Meghan could only smile at Caitlin's response because she felt the same way about the National Library.

Meghan continued the tour. One of the things she wanted to point out was the location of the varied resources available to visitors. "Here, you can see we have a copying service. It allows our visitors to have photocopies made of most items in our collections." She went on to explain the National Library was a closed stack reference library, meaning books and other items in their collections could not be browsed or borrowed. They limited retrieval to professional library staff only, like Meghan.

Caitlin immediately realized how carefully organized the Library was—it held the most comprehensive collection of Irish historical documentation in the world. Caitlin knew it was an invaluable representation of Ireland's history and heritage. What a treasure to any person of Irish descent, she thought. "I'd like to step into your shoes right now and trade jobs with you. Working here would be a dream job for me! Both of my parents come from Irish heritage, and I love Ireland's history and folklore."

"One thing I love most about working here is getting to meet people like you who are on a mission to delve into the past and build a bridge to the present," Meghan admitted. Working daily with people on the road to discovery brought joy into her life.

Caitlin looked at the expression on Meghan's face. She enjoyed her job, and Caitlin couldn't wait to have her own experience. Her grandfather had dreamed of his family back home in Ireland, and today, Caitlin found herself much closer to finding some of those relatives. In the future, she hoped she would get the chance to do something like this for people back home. "Truthfully, I'm here to learn as much as I can from you. At the museum where I currently work, my boss wants me to offer similar services when I return."

"Wonderful! Make sure you ask me any questions you think might help you," she encouraged, wanting her new friend to get the most out of the visit, which had taken her so far from home.

"Honestly, Meghan, I think your enthusiasm is a big part of the success of the services you offer here. You have great persuasive skills as well, hence the reason for my visit."

"Come on, enough of your inflating my ego. Let's head over to my office. I know we have a limited amount of time to accomplish what needs to get finished today. To save time, I've already gathered together some documents for you to review."

Once they'd arrived at Meghan's office, Caitlin took a seat in the enormous leather-backed chair, positioning herself confidently at the very edge. "When we were talking on the phone earlier, I told you my great-great-grandparents were living in Dublin along with both their sons, William and Brenden. In 1915 they returned to Killarney, where some of their family were still living. Their sons remained in Dublin until my great-grandfather immigrated to the United States with his wife and son."

"Yes, we decided the first question we want to answer is— did Brenden continue to live with his family in Dublin after William left?"

"Right, I tried to access the on-line census records, but I didn't have any luck."

Meghan pulled out a legal-size Manila folder with several documents in it. "The 1926 census report isn't scheduled to be released until 2027."

"Just my luck!" Caitlin could feel her streak of bad luck spread like wildfire. Maybe coming to Ireland had been a waste of time and money. Was she kidding herself after the past month of research? It had been almost a century since her family had stood on Irish soil. She found it difficult to believe she would ever be able to set eyes on any of Brenden's family, her Irish kin. She felt defeated before they'd even begun to look at the information Meghan had found. She sighed, "I'm sorry... I do not know what my problem is. I'm not one to give up at the drop of a hat, but I have a lot more invested in the process when it comes to finding my own family. What do we do next?"

Meghan could hear the stress in Caitlin's voice. She knew the key to success in researching family was not to give up before truly getting started. "We'll take the information you already know about Brenden, his wife Colleen, and their three children and branch out to other available resources. I was able to get copies of the birth certificate of all three children. Fiona was born in 1913, Anna in 1917, and their son Declan in 1920. Declan and your grandfather were born the same year." Caitlin rifled through the photocopies delighted to see the names and dates on these official copied documents.

"You mentioned Brenden and William's parents moved back to Killarney when they left Dublin. So, I used the Roman Catholic Parish registers we have on microfilm here at the Library to further trace several records."

"And—what did you discover?"

"I have a copy of your great-great-grandparents' marriage certificate from St. Mary's Cathedral in Killarney, as well as the baptismal records of all three sons," she continued. "I also found out Brenden and his wife may have returned to Killarney after your great grandfather left for America since their funerals were both held at St. Mary's along with your great-great-grandparents." Meghan pulled out the documents she had printed from the microfilm.

Meghan placed the copies on the table in front of Caitlin. She immediately proceeded to look over all the items. This process stirred up many emotions in people, and Meghan loved being part of this profoundly moving experience. Over seven years working at the Library, she had helped numerous families succeed, but she'd never met someone as passionate about finding family as Caitlin. She began to reflect on the story Caitlin had shared earlier. Her great-grandfather had left with his family for America, knowing he would probably never see or hear from his older brother again. She couldn't imagine losing contact with her family permanently. Despite this, Caitlin portrayed her own grandfather's desire to find a better life for his family in a strange country as admirable. Although she could understand the desire to connect with lost relatives, she seemed to have taken the responsibility upon her shoulders only to appease the rest of her family. Particularly that of a deceased grandparent. She was content to live with that decision.

"Caitlin, I'm as anxious as you to see where this adventure will take you. Who knows what the future has in store," Meghan reflected? Ireland was a land filled with exciting places as well as people. Meghan had a strange feeling Caitlin was in for an adventure of a lifetime, with the O'Malley family tagging along for the ride. Tonight would give Meghan a few insights into what the future might entail. All Meghan knew was something was about to happen. Call it a hunch. Only time would prove whether her instincts were right or wrong.

"I am rather excited about the possibilities, yet still apprehensive about getting too excited too soon," Caitlin admitted.

Something about Caitlin bred a feeling of familiarity. She just couldn't figure it out. Then Donovan came into mind as she recalled Caitlin's response to their discussion about their earlier meeting on the plane. "I keep thinking you'll return in the future if you're successful in finding family here in Ireland," Meghan explained, not entirely understanding why she'd even made her earlier comment about adventure.

The response from Caitlin came in the form of a smile. "Oh, yes, there is no doubt in my mind that I'll be returning if I find some of my relatives. My dad will definitely be buying a plane ticket the minute I have confirmation of the name and location of family members."

"That's a promise I hope you're able to keep. Regardless, I plan to continue our friendship long after your return home," Meghan said with a silly grin on her face and a wave of the hand.

Caitlin laughed. "I couldn't be happier to hear this. By the way, I'm looking forward to meeting the rest of your family tonight." A mutual admiration society had begun; both women had formed a deep respect for the other in a short time.

"I can't wait for you to meet all of my family, Caitlin, especially my two children."

"Oh, I forgot to tell you I've already met the enchanting young Liam Rafferty this morning." She began to paint a picture of her arrival and initial meeting with Meghan's son, father, and Duncan.

"Liam takes after his uncles; they know how to impress the ladies."

"Not your husband?"

"No, he is quite reserved. I did most of the pursuing in our relationship," she chuckled. "Remind me to tell you the story when we have more time."

Caitlin couldn't wait. "Definitely. In all honesty, I must confess I've already found my true love here in Ireland."

Meghan was astonished by her admission. Could Donovan have made such a big first impression on her? "And who could that be?" she asked, hoping for an honest answer.

Caitlin envisioned his red and white hair blowing in the wind and the grand greeting she'd received from her potential suitor, "Duncan."

"Oh, Caitlin! A dog does not count as one's true love. Not exactly the family member I hoped you'd fall in love with," she hinted.

Caitlin had no clue who she was alluding to. What a ridiculous notion; she didn't plan on falling in love with anyone in Ireland. "What are you suggesting, Meghan?"

"Well, I do have two unmarried brothers," she teased. "Wouldn't it be something if you ended up falling for one of them? I wouldn't mind having you as a sister-in-law. It would be the closest thing to having a sister."

Caitlin was humored by the idea, as ridiculous as it seemed. "You've got to be kidding!"

"No, I'm not. You've already met Donovan. Didn't he make a good impression on you?"

"Yes, he did. I can tell you he's great in an emergency, and he's easy on the eyes." Who was she kidding? He checked off all of her boxes. Well, maybe all except the ideal living location. But no, she didn't come to Ireland looking for love. Hadn't she learned the hard way that she couldn't trust men with her affections?

Meghan realized it would be wise to be a little less insistent about Donovan being such a great catch. "What did you think about Sheamus when you met him earlier?"

Changing the subject of the topic relaxed Caitlin immediately. "I didn't get a chance to meet him. He was out on an errand when I stopped for lunch at the pub earlier."

"Ah, too bad. Well, later tonight, we'll try again. You'll find out Sheamus is quite the charmer as well," she said with a wink.

"Really, Meghan? You are too much! You know I'm heading home at the end of the week, and I don't know when I'll be back again. I'm here to look for my blood relatives, not a husband." Meghan brushed aside Caitlin's comment, but deep inside, she truly hoped there would be a little Irish love connection between Caitlin and Donovan. Sheamus already had someone interested in him by the name of Margaret Flanagan. He just hadn't realized it yet.

Meghan couldn't resist giving her some sisterly advice, "Caitlin, you never know what will happen in the future. I think you need to take a chance and surrender to the unknown, just let things happen. Maybe you will find your true love here. You'd be amazed at how many people find Ireland calling them home, even years after their families have left."

At this point, Caitlin's mind drifted off, picturing Donovan and his intriguing smile. It would indeed be tempting to peel back the layers of Donovan O'Malley to get to the heart of who he was. She hadn't met such an endearing man in a long time. He genuinely seemed to care about someone other than himself.

"Caitlin? Did you hear what I said?"

"I'm sorry, could you repeat that?" she asked as she reengaged with reality.

Meghan laughed and opened her folder to take out another document. "Let's get back to work."

Caitlin was more than willing to return to the task at hand. "Where do we search next? I'm looking for living relatives, not deceased."

"We have the names of Brenden's children: Fionna, Anna, and Declan. I searched through marriage records at St. Mary's Cathedral, and here's what I found," Meghan held up a roll of microfilm. She explained the National Library had microfilm copies of most surviving Roman Catholic Parish registers, so the next step would be to see if there were any marriage records for Brenden's children from parishes in or near Killarney.

Overpowered by emotion, Caitlin imagined herself fulfilling her grandfather's wish, to find part of his family here in Ireland. To heal the break in their family would be a wonderful gift for her father and his siblings. She was just beginning to understand the journey Meghan was taking her on. Challenging her to think like a historian—posing the questions which would guide their research. "So, did you have any luck finding any marriage records?"

"I did." Meghan paused long enough for Caitlin to feel the suspense building. "Are you ready to see what I discovered?" Caitlin nodded enthusiastically. "I've reserved one of the Reading Rooms so we can look at the microfilm. Follow me."

A short walk down the hallway led them into a room with several carousels housing microfilm readers with attached printers. Meghan assisted Caitlin in loading the machine.

It had been over a year since she'd browsed through microfilm, a somewhat tedious job at times. Unwilling to just hand over the information, Meghan stated, "The best way to learn is by doing. I got special permission for you to handle this evidence personally."

Caitlin dropped onto the chair in front of the reader. While focusing her attention on the screen, she began her search. She struggled for a good minute to find the information desired. "I don't see any of the names I'm looking for. What am I missing?"

"Look away from the text for a few seconds, then try again. Trust me; you'll find it," encouraged Meghan. Caitlin wasn't one to give up. She appreciated a hands-on experience in her search, allowing her the chance to make some fundamental discoveries.

The second search was success, Caitlin exclaimed, "Found it! It's right here, Fiona's and Anna's marriage records!" Several people looked her way, wondering what all the excitement was.

"Sorry," Caitlin whispered to her new audience before pointing out the location to Meghan. "Fiona O'Sullivan married Killian Murphy, and Anna O'Sullivan married Daniel Cahill, both at St. Mary's Cathedral in Killarney."

Once revisiting the other church records, they noticed Fiona and her husband must have remained in Killarney because they discovered the baptismal records for one of their sons, William, born in 1939.

"I wonder if she named her son after my great-grandfather. Maybe this was Fiona's way of trying to hold on to the memory of the uncle her father had tried to forget."

"It's a possibility. Fiona would have been about 14 the year before great-grandfather left Ireland. Old enough to have developed a bond with her uncle."

"It's too bad we couldn't find any record of William's marriage at the same church."

Meghan continued to guide Caitlin in her thought process. "If William Murphy got married, his wife might have attended a different parish church. Even in the small town of Killarney, there are several Catholic Churches."

Positive thinking did not happen to be Caitlin's strength when it came to her own life, but she wouldn't let this roadblock defeat her when it came to finding her family. "So, have we hit a dead end? There has to be something more we can do to find this information."

Meghan was her ally, and she was ready to encourage her in their battle to find living members of the O'Sullivan family. They had just begun the final steps of the process. They continued their discussion as they slowly walked back to Meghan's office. "No, Caitlin, you haven't been defeated yet, but you're ready for the next part of your journey. You need to go to Killarney to see if you can track down your dad's second cousin. He might still be living in the area since we couldn't find any record of his death. He would be around 80 years old. You could also check burial records for local cemeteries."

"I agree; there is more than one way to track someone down. Taking my search to the local area would be to my advantage."

"There is a research center in the area as well as the use of a local directory to track William Murphy down," Meghan explained as she placed copies of all the documents into the file folder for Caitlin along with additional pamphlets she had on her desk. "You might want to spend some time tomorrow planning out your trip. You should be able to make some useful contacts by phone in Killarney before you leave Dublin."

"I believe in being prepared," she acknowledged. She didn't like surprises. Prior preparations seemed to waylay most of her anticipated concerns. Her mantra? Reciting a favorite quote of hers from Benjamin Franklin: *"By failing to prepare, you are preparing to fail,"* in times when she lacked self-confidence and dreaded tackling a new situation.

"One place you might want to visit before heading to Killarney is St. Andrew's Catholic Church in Westland Row. I think you'd enjoy seeing the actual church where your great-grandparents were married. Tomorrow you could stroll over to the church from the Inn. It's only a short distance away."

Caitlin felt exhilarated. It seemed as though she was riding a large ocean wave carrying her toward her final destination. She envisioned walking down the same aisle of the church where William and Johanna had been married. Aunt Mary had given her a copy of one of the happy couple's wedding photos taken a century ago. She wondered if she would ever get the chance to take a similar slow walk down the aisle toward the man of her dreams.

"Caitlin?"

Meghan's voice brought Caitlin back to the present. "I'd love to take some photos of the church. Can we talk about my plans for tomorrow at dinner tonight?" Caitlin asked.

"Of course, we'll have plenty of time to talk after the children are in bed. I decided to take up my mom's offer. We're staying overnight at the Inn since my husband is out of town."

"Oh, Meghan, fantastic! I enjoyed meeting Liam this morning, but I haven't met Grace yet. Will I get the chance to meet your husband before I leave for home?"

"I wouldn't hold your breath. The last conversation I had with my husband led me to believe he wouldn't return until late in the afternoon on Sunday." Meghan stopped to reflect on the amount of time Brian had spent traveling for work lately. It had increased over the past several months and become quite a challenge emotionally for Meghan. She could begin to empathize with single parents today. They were hoping things would change soon. However, she realized how fortunate she was to have assistance from her folks.

"Too bad, I fly home early Sunday morning. I guess I'll need to make a return visit just to meet Brian."

"I'll hold you to it, Miss Sullivan," she teased in her sternest voice. "Why don't you head back to the Inn and talk to my dad. He can help you with any other information you need for your travels."

"What time will dinner be served at your parents' tonight?"

"We're eating around 6 o'clock."

"Great! I'll still have some time to relax before we eat."

Who was Caitlin fooling? By the time she arrived back at the Inn and found the information she needed and then settled back in her room, she would be devouring the information spread across her bed in anticipation of the next stage of her adventure. She would have to plan out her time wisely regarding exploring Dublin as well. So many decisions to make and so little time to make them, she had no time to relax. She had a job to finish.

# Chapter 7

Caitlin realized how much they had accomplished at the Library in just a little over an hour. As she gathered up her belongings and prepared to leave, Meghan suggested she take a different route on her way back to the Inn.

"When you go out the main entrance, take a left and follow Kildare Street until you get to St. Stephen's Green Park. It's Ireland's best known Victorian public park," she directed.

"That sounds lovely." She realized a refreshing walk through the park might be just the thing she needed after the work they'd been doing. It was not uncommon to feel a little tense after concentrated research.

"Then head back toward the Inn by way of Grafton Street. Along Grafton Street, you'll find quite a variety of retail stores. You should do a little shopping before you leave for Killarney," Meghan suggested.

"How long is the actual walking distance?"

"Just a few minutes to the park and then about fifteen minutes from the park to the Inn."

Caitlin carefully placed the last of her research materials into a canvas bag she'd brought with her from the Inn. Just as Meghan picked up her phone to make a call, Caitlin nodded good-bye and slipped into the hallway to make her way out of the Library and onto the street.

Meghan proceeded to call her dad to let him know Caitlin was heading back to the Inn, sharing a bit about the progress they'd made during their afternoon together. "I'll keep an eye out for her, Meghan. I'm glad you had some success," her dad commented.

Donovan caught one end of the conversation as he sat sipping on a cup of tea across from his dad in O'Malley's Pub. When the call ended, he asked, "Dad, who was that on the phone?"

"Your sister, she and Caitlin just finished with their meeting at the Library. She wanted me to know Caitlin is heading back here via Grafton Street."

"So, Meghan sent her in the direction of the shops. She could be detained for quite some time," he chuckled. He predicted Caitlin would find it hard to resist stopping in more than one on the way back.

"Meghan thinks she'll arrive around 4 o'clock. I need to help her rent a car for her trip to Killarney. That's where the search for her family will continue."

"When will she be leaving?"

"Wednesday."

Donovan suddenly felt uneasy. The thought of Caitlin driving to Killarney alone had suddenly twisted his stomach into knots. He kept telling himself just to let it go. It was none of his business where Caitlin went and how she got there.

Caitlin's return trip to the Inn via Grafton Street turned out to be a rather pleasant experience. The walk through the park was like traveling through an oasis of green calm in the middle of the bustling city. She imagined traveling back in time as she passed by many important sculptural monuments to Irish history as if she were experiencing the events firsthand. She was known to have quite an imagination and thoroughly enjoyed her visions of the past, not to mention the friendly, good-natured people she met along the way. She'd been in Ireland for just a short time, but she was captivated by the character of its people.

After exiting the park, she walked down Grafton Street, adventuring into a few shops along the way. As lovely as they seemed to be, she neglected to find anything tempting enough to cause her to take out her credit card. She had a limited budget on this trip.

All along the way, to her chagrin, Caitlin kept thinking about Donovan. Something about the man had gotten under her skin. Her decision to avoid seeing him again had been reversed when Meghan mentioned he would be joining them for supper and staying overnight at the Inn. Oh fiddlesticks!

She watched the busy traffic flow by as she continued toward her destination. Meghan had mentioned Donovan would be extending his visit to attend a "pub session" later in the evening. Somehow Caitlin had let Meghan convince her to go down to O'Malley's Pub with her after the children were in bed.

"Going to the pub tonight doesn't mean I have to spend more time with Donovan," she mumbled to herself. Experiencing Irish culture would be her focus.

At the same time, Caitlin was making her way back to the Inn, Donovan and his dad were finishing up their visit and returning to the office where Sean and Bridgett had agreed to swap out duties. Donovan, ever the gentleman, walked with his mom back into the connecting building and up one flight of stairs to the room he would be staying in on the floor right above the pub.

"It's good to have you here with us, even if it's only for a night. Did you have a relaxing visit with your dad?" his mother asked.

"It was an invigorating and delightful conversation," he exaggerated with a twinkle in his eye, aware his mother had been disappointed lately by his lack of presence in their lives. He often seemed too busy to visit them, but he was trying to make light of that fact.

Bridgett was aware her eldest child loved to give her a hard time when he could, but she could give as good as she got. "My, my, that sure was a mouthful. Any problems making arrangements with your staff to stay away an extra day?"

"Not really. You've met Dana, my veterinary technician. She's highly organized and efficient. I also have a new assistant who's very capable of helping in just about any kind of situation. And, you know Finn continues to manage the equestrian center. He could run the place in his sleep."

Only one thing troubled him about delaying his return to the clinic; Dana had sounded a bit upset over the phone. During their conversation, she had mentioned how much she'd missed him, which seemed a bit confusing. She'd been working for him since he'd established the clinic five years earlier, two years before he'd lost his fiancée. Dana had comforted Donovan over his loss, always going out of her way to be helpful, but they'd never dated. Their conversation today had led him to believe she had more than platonic feelings for him.

Donovan tried to convince himself everything would be back to normal when he returned to the clinic. Presently, enjoying a visit with his family was of utmost importance.

Five minutes into their visit, signs of exhaustion started to set in, causing Donovan's mind to wander. "Mom, I'm completely knackered. Can we continue this discussion over supper?"

His mother patted him on the shoulder, "Of course, you take all the time you need to get settled in after your whirlwind of a flight and the medical emergency."

Up in his room, Donovan made the mistake of allowing himself to lay on the bed to relax. Within minutes, he'd drifted off to sleep. He dreamed he was back on the plane with Caitlin sitting beside him with her beautiful, lightly freckled face and long auburn hair draped across his shoulder. She looked so peaceful, and her lips kissable. As she opened her eyes and looked up at him loving, the phone began to ring. It took Donovan a moment to realize he'd been dreaming. He fumbled, trying to pick up his phone from the bedside table, dropping it on the carpeted floor in the process. He reached over the edge of the bed to retrieve it, then lay back on the bed and answered it.

It was his mother, as chipper as ever. "Donovan, supper will be ready in fifteen minutes. Could you go over to Caitlin's room and escort her over here?"

"Sure, Mom," he answered without thinking. Realizing he didn't know which room she was staying in, he quickly asked. Then out of courtesy, he called Caitlin's room to see when she would be ready.

Feeling refreshed by her walk, Caitlin had been browsing through the brochures Sean had given her earlier, trying to plan out the details of her trip on Wednesday. She decided Meghan and her family might recommend where to stay while she was in Killarney and might even have a few suggestions regarding the best tourist hotspots to check out. The images in the brochures made Ireland seem mystical. After lugging her professional camera along, she planned to capture all the memorable places she visited. She hoped the photos would help lure her dad into returning with her when he'd fully recovered from his back injury. It was time for her dad to make some new memories.

Lost in thought, she jumped at the sound of her phone ringing. "Hello?"

"Caitlin?"

"Yes, who is this?"

"It's me, Donovan, your seatmate from the plane."

"Oh, hello, Donovan," she stuttered upon hearing his name, struggling to formulate her next question. "Are you calling to let me know how Mrs. Murphy is doing?"

The question threw him off guard. He had almost completely forgotten about Noreen. "No... but she'll be fine. Her son joined her at the hospital, and she should be able to go home tomorrow."

"That's good news." Caitlin let the comment linger just long enough to make it awkward. "Did they figure out what caused her symptoms?"

"Uhhh, the doctor believes she was suffering from stress and a bit of a sinus infection. They were going to run some more tests before I left."

Relieved by the news, Caitlin changed the subject immediately, not being mindful of how it would change her tone. "Oh good, well, if you weren't calling to tell me about Mrs. Murphy, why did you call?"

Donovan was caught off guard. She sounded unenthused by his call. Heaven forbid she would think it was his idea to spend more time with her. "My mom wanted me to bring you up to their suite for supper. They'll be eating in about ten minutes."

"Great! Can you give me about five minutes to get ready?" she asked hesitantly.

"No problem. It's just family, so keep it casual and comfortable."

"Sure, I just want to freshen up a bit! See you soon." Caitlin immediately scrambled to the bathroom in an attempt to brush her windblown hair. She proceeded to nervously mishandle it, sending the brush flying through the air and onto the bathroom floor. What was her problem? She could feel her hands trembling. It was as though the prospect of seeing Donovan again turned her into literal mush. As for touching up her makeup, nothing she seemed to do helped hide the deep red blush on her cheeks or the dark circles under her eyes from lack of sleep. Nature had taken over.

Giving up in the beauty department, she threw on a pair of black Skinny Jeans and a white blouse with a coral crew neck cardigan, only noticing this just made her face look a deeper shade of red. She gave up entirely on looking presentable. "You're such a fool," she said to her haggard expression in the mirror. "Don't pretend like you're trying to impress someone. He's not worth it."

A few minutes later, Caitlin heard a subtle knock on the door as she put on the final touches of her makeup. "I'm coming," she called out, taking a few breaths before opening the door. She nervously looked up into Donovan's hypnotic blue eyes. They were simply mesmerizing.

"Good evening, Caitlin," he murmured, returning her gaze. It was déjà vu—the same beautiful green eyes from his afternoon dream looked back at him.

"Good evening," she returned in a whisper as she admired his casual yet classy attire. Why did this man have to be so good looking? Tomorrow he'd return home, and she wouldn't see him again. Her heartstrings began to play a rapid love song. How infuriating! *Be practical*, she told herself. *In a week, you'll be thousands of miles away.* But her internal voice also kept saying, *Enjoy his company while you have it!*

"Are you ready?" he asked with a smile, politely ignoring the fact she'd continued to stare at him. "I don't know about you, but I'm famished."

"Me, too." Caitlin walked with Donovan down to the lobby. They moved through a corridor to the stairwell in the adjoining building. An uncomfortable silence joined them as they climbed up two flights of stairs to the third floor. At the top of the steps, they simultaneously took a deep breath. Donovan placed his hand at the small of Caitlin's back, causing chills to run up and down her spine as he escorted her midway down the hallway. He knocked twice before opening the door to his parents' suite.

Stepping into a lovely sitting room, Caitlin noticed a large comfortable looking beige couch. They could both hear movement coming from behind it. Out popped Duncan wagging his tail. He rushed over to them, and to Donovan's surprise, jumped up onto Caitlin.

"Duncan, down boy!" He scolded while Caitlin just giggled. Duncan obeyed, moving immediately to Donovan's side. His tail still wagging furiously, causing them both to howl at the sight.

"Duncan and I met earlier this morning,"

"It seems like you've made a big impression on him in a small amount of time. It's hard to believe he ignored me at first, especially when I've been gone for almost a week."

"Well, I do love dogs, and we made an immediate connection." Caitlin knelt and began to pet Duncan. She put her arm around his neck, then placed a kiss on top of his head. He responded with a quick lick of the tongue to her cheek.

The room's energy level suddenly increased as Sean and Bridgett flowed in, followed by their grandchildren. Liam reached his uncle first, plowing into his left side. "Uncle Donovan, you're here!"

"Great to see you, too, Liam. Have you been helping take care of Duncan while I've been away?"

"Yes, I have. Grace helped, too!"

Donovan smiled at his four-year-old niece, who looked up at him adoringly. She had attached herself to his right leg. He bent down to fly her up to his hip before patting Liam on the head with his free hand. "I'm glad you're sharing the responsibility of helping care for him. Before you know it, your mom and dad will be ready to let you have a dog of your own."

"I heard that, Donovan! Don't you go putting ideas into my kids' heads!" Meghan abandoned her job of setting the table and joined the rest of the family. "Now that I've yelled at my brother and gotten the attention of everyone, I have something to announce."

"And..." Donovan started her off.

"Well, I wanted to wait until Brian got home, but I can't wait for another week. Keeping this secret will drive me crazy." Caitlin joined Meghan's family, waiting in silence for the news.

She smiled nervously, "Brian and I have already decided to increase the size of our family."

"So, you're ready for me to help you find a dog?" Donovan asked excitedly, the sarcasm rolling off his tongue. "It's about time, Sis."

Meghan waved her hands back and forth in front of him as she murmured, "No, no, no! Don't go bringing me one of your pups anytime too soon, dear brother. We have a different kind of addition in mind."

With a confused look on his face, Sean asked, "What are you talking about then?" A smile spread across Bridgett's face. Mothers always know these things.

"Brian and I are expecting a baby in early October," she announced, placing her hands on her abdomen.

A burst of excitement filled the air, and everyone took turns congratulating Meghan. Grace and Liam looked confused until their mother spoke to them directly. "Liam, Grace, you're going to have a baby brother or sister."

"Yeah!" they shouted.

Bridgett looked tickled pink by the news. "Oh, my, how wonderful! When Brian gets back, we'll have to celebrate properly. It's too bad this current business trip will keep him away for nearly a week."

Meghan felt relieved to share one more fact with them. "Things will be improving soon because his firm has promoted him to the quality manager position. His future travel will be no more than once a month, if at all. We decided it was the perfect time to add another wee little one to the fold."

"Does that mean we can't get a dog, Mom?" whined Liam. The adults all turned to Liam and smiled. They could understand his disappointment.

"At least not for another year, dear. In the meantime, Uncle Donovan will let you spend plenty of time with Duncan and the other animals at the farm."

Grace took her uncle's face in her two hands and turned his head toward her. "I'm glad we're having a baby."

"Me, too," agreed Donovan. "Babies can be almost as much fun as a dog," he teased.

"Oh, you're no help, big brother!" Meghan complained. Donovan liked to tease his sister, but she knew how to hold her own with him. "You know the Rafferty's wouldn't have to keep having babies if one of the O'Malley brothers would get married and start producing a few of the grandchildren."

Donovan's eyes met Caitlin's as a loud cantankerous older gentleman entered the room. "What's going on? Who's making all the racket? Did I hear something about a baby? Say, who's this pretty young lass?"

Sean started the introduction. "Dad, this is Caitlin Sullivan. Caitlin, my dad Aengus O'Malley."

Caitlin moved forward to shake his hand firmly. "A pleasure to meet you, sir."

"Say, you're the gal Meghan's been talking about," he commented before suddenly turning toward the rest of the family. "Now, what's all this about a baby?"

The entire family got a chuckle over Aengus's short attention span. Meghan stepped toward him, speaking loud enough so he could hear, "Grandad, Brian and I are expecting a baby in October!"

"Well, it's about time someone had another baby around here," Aengus spoke with sarcasm while staring directly at Donovan. His humorous interjection highly entertained Caitlin. She could already tell Aengus was quite the character. It seemed as if the sons of the O'Malley clan were being put under pressure from all directions to marry and procreate. She couldn't imagine what the delay would be on Donovan's part. He seemed to be a great catch from what she'd seen so far. She imagined women were waiting in line to audition for the role of Mrs. O'Malley.

Donovan gently lowered Grace to the ground as he snapped back, "Don't give me that look, Grandad. I'm not even dating at the moment."

"Well, it's not too late to start. There's a lovely lass in the room right now. She looks like she'd make a good candidate," he hinted, admiring their guest. Caitlin turned beet red as the entire room turned to stare at her.

Donovan came to the rescue. "We've barely met, Grandad. Now let's all sit down and eat." His response didn't prevent the flush from spreading clear across his face, signaling his and Caitlin's mutual embarrassment. While the rest of the room looked slightly amused, Bridgett tried to lighten the mood by changing the conversation's focus to the meal at hand. "Okay, everyone, it's about time we sat down for dinner. Meghan, help me serve the stew and freshly baked soda bread."

"I'm coming."

As soon as Meghan disappeared into the kitchen, Donovan took Grace's hand to escort her to the table. At the same time, Grace quickly latched onto Caitlin's hand. The three of them slowly walked toward the dining area, deeply inhaling the enticing smells that reminded Caitlin how hungry she was.

Bridgett directed everyone to their seats. She strategically placed Donovan directly across the table from Caitlin to ensure some kind of dialogue. She felt the time had come for Donovan to move past his grief over Marie's death and start living again. At 34 years of age, her son wasn't getting any younger. He deserved to have love in his life again, and she agreed with Aengus. Caitlin seemed to be a good candidate. If Duncan liked her, what more did they need to know? The dog was a good judge of character. He didn't have to marry the girl; he just needed to start to pay more attention to the opposite sex once in a while.

When everyone was seated in their places, Sean bowed his head to lead his family in prayer. "Let us pray. Bless us, O God, as we sit together. Bless the food we eat today. Bless the hands that made the food, Bless us O God. Amen."

Immediately, Bridgett began to fill bowls with stew until everyone at the table had one. They circulated the bread and butter around as Meghan took beverage orders. The meal commenced in silence, but a few minutes later, the chatter of voices filled the air.

Throughout the meal, family members shared the highlights of their week, whether it was at home, work, or school. Midway through the meal, Meghan asked Caitlin to share her family's story and explain why she'd come to Ireland.

She began with the story of the two O'Sullivan brothers and the struggles they'd encompassed raising their families in Dublin. She became emotional sharing how they'd parted and what transpired when her great-grandfather and his family arrived at Ellis Island, settling in Boston shortly afterward. "Fortunately, Meghan has been able to help me fill in some of the missing names on my family tree. I hope to help my dad reconnect with some of his relatives in Killarney and heal the break in our family caused more by fear than anger. A foolish disagreement between two brothers who loved each other."

Aengus got a little teary-eyed over the story. "Wouldn't it be lovely if you could find some of your family here in Ireland?" They were all in agreement until Aengus—in his usual way—suddenly changed the topic. "So, Caitlin, do you have anyone special back home in America?"

"Dad, it's none of our business," Sean scolded. His dad had a way of meddling in other people's business, and they'd just met Caitlin. She didn't need any of his shenanigans.

Meghan looked right at Donovan and added her opinion. "Dad, I think some of us just want to know a little more about Caitlin's personal life as a way of getting to know her better."

Caitlin wasn't offended by Aengus's line of questioning. "I don't mind sharing. At the moment, I don't have anyone special in my life, but I've been on a few dates since I moved back home."

Aengus continued to dig for information. "So, nothing serious, right?"

"Really, Dad. Enough! Let's finish our meal, and then I know Donovan wants to meet up with some of his friends at the pub." Aengus started to speak again, but Sean gave him a stern look.

Meghan jumped in to distract her grandfather from his firing line of questioning. "Caitlin, after I put the children to bed, let's join Donovan in the pub. You haven't experienced Ireland without joining a pub sing."

"I'd love to. Will Sheamus be around? I'd still like to meet him."

"Definitely. Let me wash up, and then I'll call Sheamus to confirm." Caitlin immediately offered to help Meghan.

But Bridgett, queen of her domain, complained. "I don't want any guest of mine in the kitchen cleaning."

"But I'd love to help," Caitlin volunteered. "It's my way of showing my appreciation for this wonderful meal."

"All right," she conceded, "but I have to be honest about the meal. I served a delicious Irish Stew, but it came from O'Malley's Pub. As for the soda bread, Grandad baked it." Aengus beamed with pride.

Donovan started to pick up a few plates. "Liam why don't you and Grace help me clear some of the dishes from the table. Then I'll help you get ready for bed, maybe even read you a story."

The children adored their uncle and chimed in together, "Okay, Uncle Donovan!"

They quickly helped clear the table before Donovan hustled the children into their pajamas, then to brush their teeth. He cherished this time because his busy schedule didn't allow them to be together often enough. Now and then, Meghan or his parents would bring them out to the farm for horseback riding lessons or to see some of the puppies. They loved animals as much as he did when he was a young child.

Donovan had just gotten Grace and Liam settled into bed when Meghan popped in to check on them. "I see you're ready for a story. Donovan, it's getting late, why don't you go down to the pub and join your friends. I'll read to the children."

"But..."

"It's okay, Caitlin, and I won't be far behind you. I can't wait to kick back and enjoy some music. I assume you're going to join the boys in a few tunes."

"Of course, you know how much I enjoy singing with them, especially with Brian Dunphy coming tonight. He always livens things up."

"Can Caitlin come and listen to the story?" asked Grace.

"Yah, can she?" Liam chimed in.

"Of course, she can. I'll bring her in here, and then I'll meet the two of you later," offered Donovan.

"Thanks, dear brother." He kissed both Liam and Grace on the forehead before heading off to retrieve Caitlin. He found her chatting with his mom in the kitchen. They both seemed at home with one another. He couldn't help noticing how the lights reflected off the flecks of red in Caitlin's hair. She had a glow about her, or was it just the lights playing tricks on him? He hadn't quite felt himself since meeting her.

Remembering why he'd entered the kitchen in the first place, he interrupted their conversation, "Caitlin, the children want you to join them for their Storytime. I'll show you to their room."

Before she could follow him, his mother said, "Thanks for your help, Caitlin. We'll talk again tomorrow."

She nodded before following Donovan silently down the hallway. "See you downstairs," was Donovan's simple statement before leaving her standing just outside the children's room. He wasn't prepared to have a personal conversation with her at the moment, and his abrupt departure puzzled Caitlin.

She quietly stepped into the bedroom, where she spied two twin beds covered in forest green bedspreads. Liam and Grace were lying on one of the twin-sized beds, snuggled close on either side of their mom, listening to her read a story called *A Dublin Fairytale*. Caitlin sat on the other bed. As she listened, she realized it was an Irish twist on the famous fairytale *Little Red Riding Hood*. In the adventure, a girl named Fiona encountered a handful of wildly colorful characters in Dublin city. She enjoyed hearing the story as much as the children.

As soon as Meghan finished reading, Grace begged their mother to sing them a song. It reminded Caitlin of her childhood. Her dad had an Irish lullaby he would sing to her when she struggled to fall asleep.

"Not tonight. Uncle Donovan is waiting for us downstairs," explained their mother.

"Mom," they moaned. "Please?"

Just then, Caitlin had an idea. "Do you mind if I sing them the Irish Lullaby my dad taught me when I was a young girl?" This pleasantly surprised Meghan. How could she refuse such a request?

"Of course, now Grace and Liam, into your beds!"

They flew under their covers, and Meghan quickly tucked them in bed before leaving the room. Caitlin sat on the edge of Grace's bed, facing in towards Liam. Reaching over to turn off the bedside lamp blanketed the room in darkness except for a small amount of light shining in from the hallway.

"Now close your eyes, and I'll sing to you." The children obeyed immediately. Softly she began to sing the Irish Lullaby.

*Over in Killarney, many years ago.*

*My mother sang a song to me in tones so soft and low*

*Just a simple little ditty in her good old Irish way*

*And I'd give the world if I could hear that song of hers today*

*Too-Ra-Loo-Ra-Loo-Ral*

*Too-Ra-Loo-Ra-Li*

*Too-Ra-Loo-Ra-Loo-Ral*

*Hush now, don't you cry*

*Too-Ra-Loo-Ra-Loo-Ral*

*Too-Ra-Loo-Ra-Li*

*Too-Ra-Loo-Ra-Loo-Ral*

*That's an Irish Lullaby*

Aengus slowly crept past the doorway as she finished singing. He'd overheard the beautiful music coming from the bedroom. In his heart, he knew Caitlin was a special young lady. The perfect person to help mend his grandson's broken heart. He'd already seen how Donovan looked at her during their meal together, but when he wasn't looking, she had returned the same interested glances. He decided to hustle down to the pub to help get things rolling before she left town. His wife had been a bit of a matchmaker in her days, and Aengus had learned a thing or two from her. He knew he was a sentimental fool, but something about Caitlin reminded him of the love of his life.

With the children already half asleep, Caitlin made her way into the sitting room, where she found Meghan waiting. "Great, you're here! I can't wait to get down to the pub to enjoy the music."

"Where did your folks go?"

"My mom decided to head to bed early so she could finish a book she's been reading. My dad volunteered to go downstairs to check with the night attendant at the Inn. He's a new employee working the night shift for the first time."

They were just getting ready to head out the door when Sean returned. "That was fast, Dad. Why don't you come down to the pub with us for a while? Grandad and Mom will be here if Liam or Grace need anything," invited Meghan.

Her dad couldn't help but chuckle, "Nothing will tear your mother away from her romance until she finishes the last 40 pages.

I'm on call if Liam or Grace needs anything. Your grandad is already down in the pub with Donovan.

"I can stay here if you want to go down," offered Meghan.

"No, I'll just watch some TV to unwind," he said as he physically walked them out the door.

Meghan gave her dad a peck on the cheek just before following Caitlin into the hallway. Nights like tonight reminded Meghan of her many blessings: a loving family, wonderful caring brothers, and a sweet, mischievous grandfather who was definitely up to something.

Watching Donovan tonight with her children had demonstrated his need for a family of his own. Her guess? Grandad had already realized Caitlin might be a good match for him. Meghan thought so after getting to know her during the last month, and she couldn't help meddling in the current situation. She was anxious to see what would transpire over the next few days, but she was patient enough to let nature take its course. By the looks Caitlin and Donovan were swapping, they would figure it all out sooner or later.

# Chapter 8

Caitlin and Meghan chatted as they made their way downstairs. Casually entering O'Malley's Pub, Meghan immediately began looking around for Sheamus. Caitlin's entrance was slower as she took her time to admire the beautiful dark wood interior and friendly atmosphere. Caitlin followed close behind Meghan, passing by several cozy booths filled with content customers eating, chatting, and laughing. She could hear the live music flowing out from beyond her vantage point and noticed how busy the pub seemed to be on a Monday evening.

"They sure have packed a lot of people in here tonight," Caitlin reflected.

"Yeah, some of the crowd probably came in for dinner while others came to enjoy the music. Since the band's just here for an impromptu performance, there's no charge to get in to listen tonight, which fills up the place faster."

From out of nowhere, a waitress rushed up to them and gave Meghan a big hug. "Meghan, where have you been? It's been a while."

Meghan returned the embrace. As she stepped back, a smile spread across her face. "I know, between work and raising a family, I don't get much time to myself. I'm staying at the Inn with Grace and Liam tonight. Brian is out of town for work, and I couldn't resist stopping by when Donovan told me Tommy Callaghan and his band would be entertaining tonight."

"Even the staff is excited. Sheamus posted it on our sidewalk sign by the entrance. Customers have been flowing in ever since." Caitlin silently observed the interaction between the two equally beautiful women. The enthusiastic waitress seemed rather friendly for just a mild acquaintance.

"Where are my manners Maggie, I'd like to introduce you to my American friend Caitlin Sullivan. She came along to hang out with me and enjoy the music. Caitlin, this is Maggie Flanagan. She's worked for Sheamus for several years now. I don't know what he'd do without her." Maggie's cheeks were suddenly kissed pink like a spring rose, the blooming color making her seem all the more attractive.

Meghan nudged Maggie with her elbow, causing her to squeal, "Really, Meghan." Meghan just winked at her in return.

"Welcome to Dublin, Caitlin. I hope you enjoy your visit."

Caitlin smiled at Maggie and thanked her for the warm welcome. Sometime soon, she hoped to discover the story behind the unspoken message the two had just shared. These ladies seemed to harbor some kind of secret regarding Sheamus, and her curiosity was piqued.

"Maggie, before we join Donovan and Grandad, I'd like Sheamus to meet Caitlin. Could you let my brother know we're here?"

"Sure thing, I'll have him out here in no time, even if I have to give him a kick."

"That probably won't be necessary," Meghan chuckled. "I've already given him an earful about Caitlin. I'm sure he won't need any prodding; he seemed extremely interested in meeting her." Caitlin noticed a frown appear on Maggie's face before she quickly walked off.

Once she was out of hearing range, Meghan leaned toward Caitlin and mentioned, "Maggie is sweet on Sheamus, but he's too blind to notice. So, the look you just saw on her face—pure jealousy rising to the surface. Hopefully Sheamus doesn't take too long to figure it out, or someone else will come along and sweep her off her feet. They would make a great pair. If all works out the way it should, Donovan will be the only one left sitting in the Lonely-

Hearts Club." Caitlin attempted to ignore Meghan's last remark, knowing she meant it as a subtle suggestion.

Meghan began to look around again until she spotted one of the other regular waitresses at the pub. She pointed her out to Caitlin and announced, "That's Aileen O'Connor over there. She's worked here almost as long as Maggie. She's kind of sweet on Donovan, but then there are few women I know who don't practically drool over him."

"Aren't you exaggerating a bit, Meghan? He doesn't seem to be the kind of guy looking for attention from the ladies." Caitlin found it challenging to imagine the picture her friend was attempting to paint.

"Well, all I can say is I'm glad he's my brother because I don't have to vie for his attention among the rest. The ladies say it's not just his looks they're attracted to; he's quite the gentleman. I do get tired of women swooning over him whenever he passes by." Meghan giggled as if responding to an inside joke and added, "As I said before, he'd make a great catch Caitlin. If someone took him off the market, maybe I wouldn't have to suffer any longer."

Pushy, pushy. Caitlin couldn't figure out what had gotten into her friend? "Meghan, you seem to need reminding. I'm not interested in finding an Irish sweetheart or any kind of long-distance relationship."

Caitlin's words didn't seem to deter her. "You could always move here," Meghan suggested.

"Meghan, that's enough!" Caitlin moaned as a long curly-haired man with a scraggly beard suddenly appeared. He immediately lifted Meghan off the ground and swung her around.

"Hey sis, where've you been? I've missed your nagging," he stated as he plopped her back onto the floor.

"By the looks of you, I can tell I've been gone far too long. You desperately need a haircut and trimming," she teased as she gave his beard a loving tug before kissing him on the cheek.

Caitlin immediately knew the identity of the culprit. "Aw, you must be Sheamus."

He turned toward her voice, then eyeing her up and down, asked, "And who are you, lass? I've not seen you in here before."

"My name's Caitlin, and your sister has told me all about you."

He captured Caitlin's hand and flew it to his lips. "Ah, Meghan's American friend, and what has my big sister said about me?" He tilted his head coyly, a challenge written on his ruddy face.

She played along, overtaken by his unmistakable charm. "I can't repeat it. I would not want to embarrass you."

"Ah, beautiful and smart. Well, it's a pleasure to meet you, Caitlin. I hope you have a fantastic time tonight. I'll stop by later to check and see if there's anything you need," Sheamus promised with a flirtatious grin. "In the meantime, Meghan, Grandad is saving seats for you in the back near the band."

What was her mischievous grandfather up to, she wondered? He wasn't one to stay up late. "Come on, Caitlin, let's go find the troublemaker. My dad was telling the truth when he mentioned Grandad does not come down to the pub very often in the late evening. He must be up to something. At 82, Grandad seems to need his beauty sleep, so his behavior tonight is out of the ordinary."

The band began to play another lively tune as they turned the corner. Caitlin and Meghan spied Aengus, and he immediately beckoned them to join him at a cozy corner table. Donovan had been keeping him company along with some Guinness.

Meghan's suspicions were verified the moment she laid her eyes on Aengus. He sat next to Donovan, wearing the smile of a Cheshire cat on his face. She'd have to keep an eye on the crafty old man, so he didn't get into too much mischief. The table where they sat had a curved, padded booth and Aengus patted the spot next to him for Meghan to sit on. Donovan got up and let Meghan and Caitlin slide in between him and his grandfather.

Donovan felt a little guilty for not staying around to finish helping put the children to bed. He leaned over to inquire after them, "Did you have any trouble getting the little ones to sleep after I left?"

"No, Caitlin sang them a sweet Irish lullaby, and off they went to Dreamland. What about this one right here?" she said loud enough for her grandfather to hear. "Shouldn't he be upstairs getting ready for bed as well? Right Grandad?"

Aengus turned to her with an angelic look on his face, "Who, me? I'm not going to miss out on all the fun," he stated before returning his attention to the band.

"Donovan, why aren't you singing with the boys?" Meghan inquired.

"I'm waiting for Brian. He just sent me a text message saying he'd be here shortly. In the meantime, I've been keeping Grandad company. Someone has to keep an eye on him." Meghan nodded in agreement.

"I'd like to know what he's up to," she whispered. Her brother seemed to agree. Donovan and Meghan turned their attention to the band while Caitlin observed the audience. Everyone seemed to be having the time of their lives, the band included. People were singing along. Some were clapping to the beat of the music. Thunderous applause broke out when the band finished their song.

Then, one of the band members announced a short break. "Thanks, everyone! We'll be back in about ten minutes with a few of our friends. The fun is just getting started."

Caitlin watched as Donovan stood up and followed them. He approached a relatively lean man casually dressed in jeans, a black button-down shirt, and a gray vest. He looked to be about Donovan's height. They shook hands, then pulled in to pat one another on the back.

Meghan leaned in toward Caitlin. "That's one of Donovan's friends, Brian Dunphy. He's a member of a well-known Irish folk group called The High Kings. They're back on tour in Ireland for the next few weeks. Brian had the evening free, so he found some time to come down here for about an hour. He wanted to hang out with Donovan and the band."

"So, Donovan is going to perform with them?" asked Caitlin.

"Yes, both men will join in singing with the band," she explained.

Caitlin realized Donovan had a lot of hidden talents. He didn't cease to amaze her. She knew there had to be some story behind his being single. She'd barely known him for 24 hours, yet she couldn't stop admiring him. And not merely for his good looks. What was keeping him from committing to a woman? Was he so dedicated to his career he didn't have time?

By the way he interacted with his niece and nephew, she could tell he loved children and was good with them. He was also great with animals and very gentle when it came to the elderly. Her only guess—he'd been in a lousy relationship, causing him to shy away from women and making a commitment. Caitlin realized she could relate to the experience herself. They seemed to have several things in common, and this might be one of them.

"Here they come now," Meghan announced. The men stopped and welcomed Brian enthusiastically prior to returning to their instruments.

Before Donovan could follow them, Aileen had caught his attention, and they seemed to be engaged in a friendly conversation. Caitlin noticed Aileen placing her right hand on his upper arm before leaning forward to whisper something into his ear. A smile spread across his face.

Caitlin closed her eyes and took a deep breath. *Shake it off,* she told herself. *Remember, you don't need to start pining after someone who lives clear across the ocean from you. Maybe he isn't as free as you'd like to believe.*

Upon opening her eyes, she noticed Aengus looking at her and smiling. By the time she'd returned her focus to the band, Donovan had joined them. They looked ready to start playing again.

One of the guys stepped forward to address the audience. "Hey. If you're just joining us, let me make some introductions. I'm Tommy Callaghan, and I'll be playing the keyboard tonight. To my left are Rory O'Keefe on the guitar and Gavin Maguire on the fiddle. We also have a special guest joining us who most of you know, Brian Dunphy, a member of The High Kings." The crowd broke out in a burst of applause and rowdy cheers. Then Tommy continued, "Brian just informed me they'd be performing tomorrow night at Vicar Street. There are still a few seats available, so consider heading over there for a grand time," he mentioned, followed by another round of applause.

"Last but not least, we have another familiar face here tonight. Sheamus's older but none the wiser brother, Donovan O'Malley, is in the house!" The applause started again, along with a few whistles and hoots from some women sitting in the back. "Now, let's all have a grand time. Brian is going to start us off by singing

*The Rare Ould Times.* If you know any of the songs, we're singing tonight, feel free to join right in."

The keyboard began to play, and Brian began to sing, weaving his way through the crowd, cordless microphone in hand. He encouraged others to join in when he reached the chorus. Caitlin was thoroughly enjoying the lovely tune about *Ould Dublin Town.* She'd never heard it before, but she quickly picked up on the chorus and started to sing along. Over the next hour, she joined in on the refrain of several other songs when the words were simple enough.

Time flew by quickly, and before she knew it, Meghan announced it was getting late. "I have to get up and go to work tomorrow. I think I need to go back upstairs and get some sleep. Grandad, I think you should come with me. It's past your bedtime."

Aengus began to grumble, "Wait, before we go, we should get the guys to play a song Caitlin might know." He looked directly at her and asked, "Do you know the words to *O' Danny Boy?*"

Caitlin hesitated before answering, a little apprehensive, not knowing the motivation behind his question. The band finished their song just as she answered his question. "Yes, I know the words to the song. I've sung it many times with my father and grandfather."

As quick as a leprechaun, Aengus popped up out of his seat and began waving his hands in the air. "What is it you want, Grandad?" chuckled Donovan.

"Why in our midst tonight we have a visitor from America who seems to love to sing, but I noticed she's not familiar with the songs you lads have chosen. When I asked her if she knew the song *O Danny Boy,* she said 'yes'! Can you humor an old man and play it so the lass can sing it before she goes? Maybe even invite her up there to join you?" he added with a wink.

Seized by panic, Caitlin looked around for a way to escape, but Donovan stood in front of her before she could flee. Taking her by the hand, he gently led her toward the stool where he'd been seated. Donovan gestured to her to take his place next to Brian before taking a supportive stance behind her. Brian seemed to recognize stage fright when he saw it. He proceeded to try to make her feel more at ease. "What's your name, lass?"

"Caitlin Sullivan," she stammered. Donovan placed his hands on her shoulders to help calm her. His gentle touch only made her heart beat faster.

"And you know Donovan here?"

"Yes, we just met today," she admitted rather quietly.

Interesting, Brian mused. Aengus was up to some matchmaking if he wasn't mistaken. "How did you meet Dr. O'Malley? He doesn't get to Dublin often."

The train of questioning began to distract her and slow down her rapidly beating heart. "I met him on a plane flying in from Boston. I also know his sister."

"Ah, I see! Although you've only been here a short time, I think Donovan's grandad has taken a shine to you. Are you willing to share your voice with us if we sing along? I'm sure the audience will join in and help."

The crowd started to cheer her on, "Go ahead, lass, give it a try!" shouted a man.

"With Brian by your side, you can't fail," yelled an older woman.

Donovan squeezed her shoulders again in a comforting way. "I'll sing with you as well," he assured her. "You're not alone."

Caitlin was confident in her singing voice, but she had never performed in a public place before. She felt apprehensive but no longer feared the challenge. She nodded then said, "Before we sing, I'd like to dedicate this song to the memory of my grandfather, who was born in Dublin."

One of the band members passed an extra microphone over to her. "What a beautiful dedication," acknowledged Brian. "Thomas, can you start us out on the keyboard, then Rory and Gavin can join us after Caitlin seems comfortable with the melody. Everyone else, I'll have you join us partway through the song because I know it's a favorite for most of us here. Just watch me for your cue," encouraged Brian.

Everyone sat back quietly as the keyboard played an introduction to the familiar tune, then Brian led Caitlin and Donovan into the song. The fiddle began playing softly in the background. Memories of singing this song with her grandfather invoked strong emotions within Caitlin, and she was transported back in time, slowly forgetting strangers surrounded her.

When the song ended, the crowd broke out in thunderous applause while a tear trickled down Caitlin's cheek. Donovan, purely mesmerized by her beautiful soprano voice, stood almost frozen in time. Brian took Caitlin's hand and pulled her to a stand, encouraging her to take a bow with the rest of them.

Immediately following the applause, Donovan stepped forward and wrapped Caitlin in his arms as the band stood back and simply smiled. They hadn't seen Donovan moved by anything on two feet since Marie. The entire crowd watched as he placed a light kiss on her forehead. "Simply beautiful, Caitlin. Thank you for sharing your beautiful soprano voice with us tonight."

Brian turned to them both and spoke softly enough for just the two of them to hear. "Donovan, the High Kings are performing tomorrow night. You have to bring Caitlin to the show and to meet the rest of the band."

Donovan looked directly at Caitlin and asked, "What do you think? How about being my date to the concert tomorrow?"

"Yes," she whispered without hesitation. "I would love to go." Then she turned back to Brian to extend her thanks. "If your other band members are anything like you, I'm in for a special treat."

"You haven't heard anything yet! Donovan, you'll have to prepare Caitlin for the rest of the crew. They can be quite the handful!" he told her. Then Brian addressed Donovan, "Come early and bring her backstage to the Green Room before the show. I'll let management know to expect you."

Donovan hoped he wouldn't regret spending even more time with Caitlin, but he remembered an Irish proverb that made him rethink his doubts. *A good friend is like a four-leaf clover, hard to find and lucky to have.* As apprehensive as he felt about getting to know Caitlin better, he knew one could never have enough friends. What was he so afraid of?

Meghan made her way through the crowd surrounding the band. All the excitement had taken a toll on her grandad, and he needed to get some rest. But it didn't seem to prevent Aengus's smile from beaming back at her—tears filling his eyes.

Caitlin felt a hand rest on her shoulder as she watched Aengus. She turned to stare right into Donovan's eyes. "Things are wrapping up here, but I'm going to take Duncan for a short walk before I go to bed. I'd love to have your company so we can talk over our plans for tomorrow. I have an idea you might be interested in," he said somewhat mysteriously.

Meghan, overhearing his offer, agreed a walk in the fresh air would help Caitlin sleep better. She prevented Caitlin from responding by loudly shouting over her shoulder, "She'd be happy to join you!" Caitlin silently agreed by nodding at Donovan.

"Good. Here's my cellphone. Can you enter your number so I can text you if it's going to take me longer than 15 minutes to help the band load their equipment?"

She hesitated momentarily, wondering what she was getting herself into. "Sure." Once finished, she and Meghan escorted Aengus out of the pub.

Caitlin wished them goodnight before passing through the double doors into the Inn's lobby, slowly making her way up the stairs—a feeling of floating overtaking her. Quietly singing O Danny Boy, visions of the evening danced through her head.

Once inside her room, she sat down in the nearest chair and let the tears flow freely. She felt emotionally overwhelmed. Tonight, she felt as if her grandfather had been standing alongside her as they sang. Being here in the city of his birth had emotionally touched her to the core. Although she had traveled to a foreign land, she felt like she had come home. Now to get her act together and calmly try to wait until Donovan picked her up for their walk.

Caitlin stood up to move into the bathroom to fix the damage the tears had done to her make-up when her cell phone rang. Seeing her sister's number pop up, she answered immediately, "Hello, Abbey."

A perturbed voice grabbed at her throat through the phone, "Caitlin! Dad and I are anxious to hear how things are going. I couldn't wait any longer for you to call us," she rambled on.

"Slow down, Abbey, and take a breath. Everything's great here!" She began to break down the events of the day: the medical emergency on the plane, meeting Donovan and the rest of the O'Malley family, her successful first day of research, the "pub sing," and her tentative plans to drive to Killarney on Wednesday.

Abbey couldn't believe Caitlin had packed so much into her first day in Dublin. "Wow, it sounds like you had a productive first day! What are your plans for tomorrow? Do you have more research to do?"

"No, I'm finished with my research at the Library. I'm going to stop at St. Andrew's Church tomorrow, where our great-grandparents were married, and Grandpa Pat was baptized. I'm not sure what I'll do afterward, but I'm considering a little sightseeing before I go to a concert in the evening with Donovan." Caitlin was greeted by silence on the other end of the phone. "Abbey are you still there?" she asked.

Her sister tried to take in everything Caitlin had just shared. On top of everything else, she already had a date her second night in Ireland. "I'm here," she responded.

"Look, Abbey, I don't have much time."

"Wait, Caitlin, before you say anything else who is Donovan?"

"He's Meghan's oldest brother. Now I don't have time to talk, he's stopping by in a few minutes. We're going on a short walk before turning in for the night. He has something he wants to talk to me about."

"So, let me get this straight. You've been in Dublin for less than a day, and now you're going on an evening stroll with an unmarried man who's already asked you out on a date tomorrow evening?" *Would wonders never cease*, Abbey thought to herself?

"Abbey, you just said it yourself. I've known him for less than a day. We're just going to take his dog for a walk, and we'll discuss our plans for tomorrow evening at the same time. And might I add, he did not ask me out. One of Donovan's friends is in a band and has invited us to his concert."

Abbey knew her sister well. No matter what, she wouldn't have accepted the offer if she didn't want to go out with the man. "Fine, deny it. We'll see what you're saying a day or two from now."

Caitlin glanced at her watch and realized Donovan would be picking her up shortly. "We'll have to finish this disagreement another time. I need to get ready to go out. I promise we'll talk again sometime tomorrow."

"All right, you're off the hook for now, but I want to hear more details later. Remember, we're six hours earlier than you, so even if you get back to your room after midnight tomorrow, it's still early enough for you to give us a call. Love you."

"Love you, too, Sis. I'll talk to you tomorrow. Give Dad my love. Please let him know I'll be calling."

"Okay, Caitlin. Goodnight."

Caitlin was amazed at how many times today someone had suggested she and Donovan would make a lovely couple. She struggled with the idea. Just six months earlier, she had believed herself head over heels in love with Jeremy Fisher. But there was no denying it; Caitlin felt an intense attraction toward Donovan, but not just because of his good looks. After spending just a few hours in his company, he had managed to make an emotional connection with her through his kind and caring ways. She understood why his family wanted to see him married and with children. He would make a great husband and father by the look of things, but why her? Why were people so eager to suggest she was a good match for him?

As Caitlin tried to make sense of her feelings, she heard a dog whimper, followed by a gentle knock. Knowing who waited on the other side of the door, she slowly opened it. The sight she beheld instantly put a big smile on her face. Donovan held fast to Duncan's leash to prevent him from jumping up on her.

She immediately dropped to her knees to pet his head and fondle his soft ears. "Are you ready to go for a walk, Duncan?" His tail began furiously wagging in response, and he lifted one paw onto her thigh. She chuckled as she stood back up.

"Come on, you two, let's go before we wake up the other guests on this floor. Grab a warm jacket to wear. The night air is on the chilly side," informed Donovan.

Caitlin grabbed her gray mid-length coat from the nearby chair. A warm wave of heat passed through her as Donovan helped her put it on. She turned her back to him as she donned her hat and gloves, embarrassed by how easily he could make her blush.

They took the short walk down the hallway and then slowly descended the stairs to the lobby. Donovan greeted the desk clerk as they passed by, then held the door for Caitlin as she stepped out into the cool night air. He took the lead, and Caitlin noticed they seemed to be taking the same path she'd walked earlier to the National Library.

"College Park is just a short walk from the Inn, and it will be a great place to let Duncan run off some steam and take care of his business before spending the night at the Inn," he explained.

As they continued to walk toward the park, Donovan began to reveal his ideas for the day ahead. She listened intently. "Since you haven't planned much for tomorrow other than your morning visit to the church, maybe you'd be interested in coming on a short road trip with me tomorrow."

*Here we go again,* she feared. *Just when I try to avoid spending more time with Donovan, he is asking just that.* "I don't know," she hesitated. "What were you planning to do?"

"First, I thought you might like to see my clinic before visiting my home and the O'Malley family business. There are so many things we could do there. Besides, I think you'd enjoy the experience of seeing some of the Irish countryside. We would have plenty of time for a little fun before driving back into the city for dinner and the concert. What do you think?"

*Let's see,* Caitlin contemplated as she began to weigh the pros and cons of spending an entire day alone with Donovan. The pros: She would be with a charming, polite, and intelligent man who would probably be good company and a lot of fun if she gave him half a chance. Major con: The more time she spent with Donovan, the more she felt emotionally involved in an impossible situation. A vast ocean separated their daily lives. What should she do?

"Well," she hesitated, "I came to Ireland for some adventure, but I have to finalize my arrangements for my trip on Wednesday to Killarney. I'll probably be staying for at least two nights. To avoid wasting time, I need to map out those plans tomorrow."

A feeling of uneasiness rushed through Donovan at the mention of Caitlin's travel plans. She was going off on a road trip in a foreign country with different driving rules and road conditions. What if something were to happen to her?

Visions of Marie's accident started flashing through his mind. Donovan knew he shouldn't get more involved with Caitlin than he already had, but something in his heart told him a few more days with her might be all he would ever have. He had to push past his fears.

Donovan didn't want to miss out on time with Caitlin, even if the memories later brought him heartache. Besides, if Donovan were honest with himself, he would admit that he'd become a better person having known Marie. Why should he deny himself the privilege of getting to know Caitlin better?

"Caitlin, I'd hate to see you driving around Ireland alone. You'd enjoy it so much more if you had some company. It so happens Mrs. Murphy lives in Killarney. If I were to travel with you, we could personally stop in and check on her. I know she would love to see you again due to her abrupt parting."

"But you've already been away from your work for over a week now. Can you afford to be away two to three more days?" True to her nature, Caitlin was putting him first above her own needs. And he knew she needed him, if not for assistance in her travels, then for the company in a foreign country. He hoped she wouldn't fight the connection they'd made thus far.

"Please, Caitlin. You aren't going to force me to beg, are you?" he pleaded.

A thrill of excitement coursed through Caitlin's veins at the idea of seeing some of the countryside. Besides, the chance to travel with Donovan to Killarney and see Mrs. Murphy would be priceless. Who would have known her search would take her to the very place where Noreen lived? It certainly was a small world. She didn't have to think long, "How can I say no?"

"Excellent! It looks like Duncan is ready to head back." On the return trip they discussed their plans for the next day, including meeting for breakfast in the morning.

Upon reentering the Inn's lobby, they said their goodnights and went in opposite directions—Caitlin realizing her heart was beating fast in her chest. She had forgotten the thrill of starting a new relationship and she had to admit it felt good.

# Chapter 9

Upon waking the next morning, Caitlin felt surprisingly refreshed. Anxious to spend a day in the countryside with Donovan, she jumped out of bed and put on her most comfortable pair of blue jeans and a dark lavender sweater. She felt confident a light jacket would be the only other thing she would need to keep warm while visiting the farm. Last night Donovan had suggested a change of clothes would be necessary as they would be trekking through the mud at times and potentially pick up a few strong animal smells. Caitlin decided to bring along the beautiful dress her aunt had bought for their evening out. She couldn't think of a better opportunity to show it off.

As she got her clothes ready for the evening, a feeling of guilt began to spread over her. The reason? She had neglected to communicate with her father on Monday, only passing him a message through her sister the night before. She pictured his furrowed brow as he contemplated the idea of his oldest daughter traveling alone in a foreign country for the first time. He'd always been the worrier of the family, whereas their mother had been the one with nerves of steel.

Caitlin contemplated whether she should text him now or try to call him sometime in the evening, as Abbey had suggested earlier. *Text him now*, she told herself. *You know how he'll worry about you if you don't.* She slowly picked up her phone and unlocked the screen. Immediately she noticed a text message from her Aunt Mary.

"One more person I need to connect with," Caitlin sighed. She reflected on the events of the past day and giggled at the cause of her absent-mindedness.

She immediately sent brief text messages: *Dad, wonderful first day. I'll call tonight.* The second message to her aunt. *Arrived safely. Research going well. Will call in the next day or two.* When she finished, she began to freak out when she noticed the time. Donovan would be waiting for her.

Feeling slightly jet-lagged, Donovan made his way slowly down the hallway to the breakfast nook. Due to haunting nightmares, he woke up several times during the night. The first dream was about Marie's accident and funeral. In the second, he pictured Caitlin cruising in his car down a twisting road—when out of nowhere, a horse appeared—causing her to crash. If he were to interpret these dreams correctly, he seemed to be connecting his feelings about Marie's accident somehow with Caitlin and subconsciously worrying unnecessarily about her upcoming trip to Killarney. It was a bad sign—Donovan was forming an attachment to her. He didn't want to get emotionally involved with Caitlin, nor any other woman right now. He needed more time to grieve, but his family didn't seem to understand. No one did. They continued to pressure him to date, marry, and start a family.

Donovan caught a glance at his reflection in the hallway mirror. The bags under his eyes reminded him of the lack of sleep he'd had over the last few days. Looking directly in the mirror, he began to give himself advice. "Donovan, you need to focus on just being a polite host today. And remember, your main reason for wanting to go to Killarney tomorrow is to double-check on Mrs. Murphy," he tried to convince himself.

The pep-talk continued in his most convincing tone, "Driving Caitlin to her destination is just a kind gesture on your part." Warning bells went off inside his head. He had failed to persuade himself. Would this extra time together really lead to just a casual friendship? *You're such a fool!* he scolded himself before continuing with Duncan in tow on his journey to the breakfast room. After seating himself at a corner table for two, he tried to compose himself. Still a little off-balance from the thoughts running through his head, he took three cleansing breaths.

"Good morning," came a cheery greeting, snapping him out of his head. Startled, Donovan turned sharply to his left to capture a glimpse of Caitlin's quirky smile, pixie nose, and soft, long flowing red hair. He closed his eyes momentarily as he envisioned his fingers taking a walk through it.

"Morning," he responded softly, wanting to kick himself for being so drawn to Caitlin's physical attributes. It wasn't like him to be distracted so easily by a woman's looks. Then, remembering his manners, he jumped up and pulled out the chair for her. She sat down as Duncan managed to move his furry head within reach of Caitlin's right hand.

"Good morning to you too, Duncan. Did you sleep well?" Duncan responded by licking her hand. "You're such a sweetheart," she remarked with a smile as she continued to pet him. When Caitlin looked up to meet Donovan's eyes, she saw a somewhat confused look staring back at her. She flushed when she realized Donovan might have gotten the impression, she'd been talking to him, not his dog. Duncan settled next to her on the floor as though he were giving his stamp of approval.

Oblivious to the other people around them, they were both startled by a question seeming to come out of thin air. "Are you two hungry this morning, or are you just going to sit there staring at each other all day?" Donovan recognized his mother's voice immediately and joined Caitlin in redirecting their attention toward her.

"Yes," they answered, almost comically in unison.

Bridgett wondered what had transpired between her son and their guest since supper the night before. The room seemed steeped in nervous energy. "I suggest you both get up then and fill your plates at the buffet—the food won't be serving itself."

Donovan nodded, then gestured to Caitlin to precede him. By the time they sat down, they had both lost their appetites. They appeared to have been fueled by some other source and found themselves picking at their food in response.

Half an hour later and several cups of calming tea, Donovan just happened to check the time and realized they had to get moving if they were going to walk the short distance to the church. "I've already loaded my luggage in the car," he informed Caitlin. "We need to leave now if you don't want to be late for your appointment with the church secretary."

"Oh my, I lost track of time. I'm all packed and ready to go."

"Great!" Donovan stood quickly, anxious to get started on a walk in the fresh air. He needed to clear his head and Duncan could use a little exercise before they drove to the clinic. The morning rush hour kept the roads and sidewalks buzzing with traffic. Walking certainly helped speed up their arrival at the church just a few minutes' walk away.

Once there, Caitlin enjoyed hearing a little bit about the church's history from its secretary, as well as receiving an informational brochure. Before leaving, she paused to take several shots of the church's interior, including the aisle leading to the altar. Distracted by the location, Caitlin envisioned a faceless groom standing at the foot of the altar waiting for her. She wondered: Would she find someone kind and compassionate like Donovan once she returned home? A man who would sing with her and make her laugh? The uneasiness these visions stirred up in her caused butterflies to flutter around inside her stomach. Maybe she'd be better off continuing to date someone predictable like her boss Jonathan. They'd gone out a few times. He was reliable, someone to do things with, and practical. She didn't need a relationship that made her feel so confused and vulnerable, she told herself.

She imagined what her grandfather might say to her. *When you get back home, you can be practical, but since you have come all the way across the ocean, you might as well have a little adventure while you're here!* She closed her eyes and pictured him winking at her. It was comforting to cherish this image for a short while.

She kept her visit at the church brief, stopping to take a few more photos before exiting. Ending her tour at the majestic double doors, she walked outside to find Donovan and Duncan waiting patiently for her.

She came to a jolting stop at the top of the steps, suddenly brought to life by her family's history in this place. "Donovan, would you mind taking a picture of me in front of the church? It would be the perfect photo to help me begin to tell the story I've learned about my family here in Ireland."

Caitlin held up her phone—Donovan appearing to hesitate at her request. He glanced up at her. His clear blue eyes revealed the admiration he felt for the subject of this impending photo. Then seeming to snap out of it, he bowed gracefully, stating rather ridiculously, "Your wish is my command."

Before leaving, Donovan placed an arm over Caitlin's shoulder, convincing her to pose for a picture with him. His nearness caused her senses to intensify when she caught a fragrance like the earth itself, a woody element to it that conjured up timeless masculinity.

"You have to remember to save the memories not only of the interesting places you see in Ireland but the people you meet as well. For it's the people who truly make it the special place it is." Silently, Caitlin winced in agony, feeling overpowered by the essence of this man. He seemed to know just the right thing to say.

Fifteen minutes passed by in the blink of an eye, and Caitlin found herself enjoying the sunshine caressing her left cheek gently as she sat in the passenger seat of Donovan's Pacific Blue Kia Sportage. The traffic had slowed a bit, but she didn't care. Caitlin had never before seen such lush and green countryside as on the drive to Donovan's clinic. She beheld the glorious scenery and its quirky but charming appeal. She realized Ireland was a land where history and myth intertwine. The lines between Druids, Celts, and Saints blurred throughout the centuries—hidden among the grassy fields and rolling hills. These thoughts, and the picture-perfect pastures had a calming effect on her. She began to dream of their adventure ahead in Killarney, and before she knew it, they'd arrived at their destination.

"Ah, here we are," announced Donovan as they pulled into a small parking lot off the main road. A large sign posted outside read O'MALLEY'S VETERINARY CLINIC, in bright, bold letters. On the shingle, hanging below it were the clinic's hours. Caitlin noticed they were closed on the weekends. She wasn't surprised since it was such a small community, but she couldn't resist teasing Donovan about it.

"So... no weekend hours?" she mused, her attention moving in his direction.

Donovan's answer seemed to the point. "I like to give my staff the weekends off to revitalize themselves. In case of an emergency, I can quickly get to the clinic because my home is just down the road. Equine specialists never sleep, especially if we have to make house calls." He seemed to have taken his answer straight out of the handbook of a workaholic, Caitlin acknowledged. He gives his employees the time off while he picks up the slack.

Instead of being honest about her opinion, she instead rewarded him by saying, "It sounds like the people in this area are lucky to have a clinic like yours. If your staff is half as devoted as you, your patients are in good hands."

This praising remark caught Donovan off guard. "Thanks for your vote of confidence, Cait. I'm sorry, is it okay for me to call you Cait?"

"Most people usually call me Caitlin, but my dad calls me Caitie. I've seldom been called Cait," she responded honestly. She briefly paused to reflect on how she felt about him calling her by a nickname. It seemed rather personal, but she couldn't help smiling at him when she responded. "I'm not opposed to it, though," she found herself admitting.

"Cait it is then," he smiled in return with a lift of his right eyebrow.

As the day progressed, Donovan found himself more and more intrigued by Caitlin. There was just something so magnetic about her. Every time he tried to distance himself, something Caitlin said or did pulled him right back to her.

"Let's bring Duncan in with us," Donovan said, refocusing on the task at hand. "If you hang onto him, I can take care of my business as quickly as possible. I'd like to get to the farm in less than an hour."

Caitlin took the dog by its leash and followed slowly behind Donovan, briefly pausing so Duncan could relieve himself before entering the clinic. A rather slender brunette with her hair pulled back into a ponytail seemed to fly on her invisible broomstick toward them. Even in her teal scrub top and matching pants, she looked attractive, but there was something intense in the way she looked at Caitlin. Before Donovan could introduce her, the woman unceremoniously threw her arms around him.

"Donovan, you're finally here!"

"Hello, Dana. It's good to see you, too. I didn't realize how much I'd be missed after just one week away," he remarked stiffly, not returning the embrace.

She reluctantly released him. "Of course, I missed you," she said sweetly. "We all did. Are you ready to get back to work now?

We've been so busy lately the owners of our patients have started to comment on your absence. They've had longer wait times than usual."

Donovan knew an exaggeration when he heard it. Besides, he'd been in close contact with the clinic since he'd left. "Dana, I talked to Aidan just yesterday afternoon. He said the clinic was running smoothly, and there were no surgeries scheduled this week. He even complimented you on your efficiency. There's no need for all of this drama."

Dana didn't like being challenged by Donovan in front of a stranger. She cast a few daggers in Caitlin's direction. "Who's your friend here?"

"Dana, meet Caitlin Sullivan. She's visiting the area to research her family history. My sister is trying to help her find some of her relatives here in Ireland. She heads to Killarney tomorrow, where we hope to locate some of them before she returns to America." Perplexed by this information, Dana just continued to stare at Caitlin while Donovan finished his introductions. "Caitlin, this is my veterinary technician, Dana Gallagher."

Caitlin's cheery disposition was like fingernails on a chalkboard to Dana. "A pleasure to meet you. I hope you don't mind my asking, but what does a veterinary technician do?"

Donovan answered the question, ignoring the rude look on Dana's face. "Her responsibilities are like that of a nurse to a doctor; only our patients are animals. Dana works alongside me during physical exams, surgical procedures, and consultations. She also assists with laboratory duties, anesthetizing animals, and x-rays. Dana is a jack of all trades and manages the clinic when I'm away."

"It sounds like you have a lot of responsibilities here," Caitlin directed at Dana before turning her attention back to Donovan. "Is Dana your key assistant?"

"Yes, we make a good team," Dana emphasized as she stepped toward Duncan in an attempt to pet him. Duncan pulled away from her and closer to Caitlin. "I see you've made a friend. I've never known Duncan to prefer any other human over Donovan."

Feeling an uncomfortable tension growing, Caitlin quipped a little uncharacteristically, "Really? That's interesting. I hope he'll be just one of the many friends I make while I'm in Ireland." Caitlin directed a smile at Donovan. For some reason, she didn't care for the negative energy coming from Dana, not the warm welcome she'd come to expect since she'd arrived in Ireland.

Donovan realized Caitlin and Dana reminded him of two dogs marking their territory— him being the territory. It made absolutely no sense to him. Maybe he'd missed something along the way. Dana had always been there by his side, helping at the clinic, but they weren't dating. Well, maybe they'd gone out for dinner a time or two, but he hadn't thought of them as a couple, just co-workers enjoying each other's company. As for Caitlin, they'd known each other for less than 48 hours.

"I also oversee our veterinary assistant, Aidan Kelly," she interjected. "Here, he comes now." Dana directed Caitlin's attention to a young, stocky man walking toward them.

"Welcome. I overheard Dr. O'Malley giving you Dana's job description. He left out the part of her job where she constantly bosses me around while I try to provide compassionate medical care to all the animals. I'm the heart of the service we provide," he jokingly bragged. Dana gave him the evil eye. Caitlin couldn't help but chuckle. The man had a great sense of humor next to his co-worker carrying the "green-eyed monster" on her back.

"Really, Aidan? Now look who's being overly dramatic!" complained Dana.

Caitlin stepped forward and introduced herself. Aidan took her hand in his, holding it a little too long for Donovan's comfort. "Enough of the introductions. Dana, can we talk for a few minutes about the schedule for the rest of this week? My plans have changed, and I won't be available at the clinic until the start of next week."

"But…"

"Aidan, would you give Caitlin a short tour of the clinic while I discuss a few things with Dana?"

"Sure, Dr. O'Malley. It's quiet here this morning. We don't have any scheduled appointments until the afternoon, and we have volunteers cleaning the animal pens and cages right now."

Interesting, thought Caitlin. Dana had been lying to Donovan after all.

"Great. Be back here in about 15 minutes. We've a busy day ahead of us. Caitlin, are you okay keeping Duncan with you?"

"Of course," she replied immediately. Caitlin noticed Dana didn't seem happy with Donovan as they walked toward what looked like an office. His nonverbal response demonstrated extreme impatience, and he didn't strike her as an impatient individual.

Aidan couldn't help enjoying this unexpected entertainment. It wasn't often Dana got the short end of the deal around here. "Follow me, Caitlin. I'll show you around while Dana tries to convince Dr. O'Malley that we can't function here without him."

Aidan proved to be a charming tour guide as they walked through the clinic. He began his tour by explaining their use of a specialized veterinary software system. Caitlin only half-listened to all of the jargon, "These records are always available on-site to the vet treating one of the animals, whether it's a routine visit or an emergency vet consultation. It makes it easier for our part-time vets to cover when Dr. O'Malley's not available."

*Interesting.* "How often do you have other vets filling in?" Caitlin asked.

"Once in a while, when the doctor is away on business." Aiden began walking her toward the kennel area, where they housed a few smaller animals.

Not knowing Donovan well, she felt uncomfortable asking him personal questions. Aiden was a different story. "What does Dr. O'Malley do when he's traveling? He mentioned he attended a dog show in Boston. Why travel such a far distance for a dog show?"

Aiden could tell an interrogation had begun by the intensity of her questions. "One of his passions is breeding Irish Red and White Setters. He traveled to Boston to see one of these dogs compete in an American Kennel Club competition. He continues to mentor owners after they've purchased a puppy from one of the litters Duncan has sired."

"What got him started breeding dogs? I'd think a vet would be more focused on finding homes for stray animals or rescues," she asked.

Up went the red flag. "Dr. O'Malley only breeds Red and White Setters, but it's his story to tell, not mine," he concluded. He knew where to draw the line at answering questions.

Caitlin backed off at Aiden's request. "I can see working with these animals is your passion as well. It must be personally fulfilling to work here."

"Yes, animals have a way of bringing meaning to my life. I'm happy anytime I can help relieve an animal from pain or discomfort. Working with Dr. O'Malley and the rest of the staff is a bonus. I feel fortunate to have my job."

Moved by his response, Caitlin reached forward to squeeze his forearm. "You're a special man, Aiden. Dr. O'Malley is fortunate to have you working here."

"Thanks, I appreciate your kind words."

Donovan noticed their exchange from a distance, and it made him feel uncomfortable. He hurried to finish his conversation with Dana. "Everything looks like it's in order. We have a pretty quiet schedule this week, and you're doing a great job overseeing everything. In case of an emergency, call either Dr. O'Neill or Dr. Kavanagh. I appreciate all your hard work and dedication to keep things running smoothly while I'm away. Until next Monday then."

"But, Donovan, I...."

"You'll be fine. Before you know it, I'll be back here, and you'll be wishing otherwise. You know how bossy I can get, and a little crabby, too."

"Never!" she denied, placing a hand on his arm.

"Good-bye, Dana," he sternly responded.

Not easily irritated, today his assistant was getting on his nerves. At the risk of thinking too deeply about the reason, he quickly turned his attention to several other staff members before leaving. Donovan felt rather pleased about Caitlin seeing his home and family business. For some reason, he wanted her to love it as much as he did.

# Chapter 10

Caitlin scanned the grounds as they pulled up in front of Donovan's colossal two-story brick house. Numerous outdoor buildings surrounded the expansive area in front of her. After slowly stepping out of the vehicle to survey the area more closely, her host enthusiastically gave the overview of his family-run Equestrian Centre and outdoor recreational facility.

Caitlin noticed several people riding on horses of a variety of sizes near a large stable and couldn't help smiling and sharing her feelings aloud, "It's been a long time since I've been on a horse, but I love horseback riding. Would it be possible to go for a ride today?"

"We'll start there, but you've a few more choices available." Donovan went on to describe the variety of activities to choose from for guests who came to visit. She felt like a kid in a candy shop, not knowing what delightful decadence to select.

"Many people like you come here just to ride horses while others take horseback riding lessons. We even have ponies for younger children. Grace and Liam both take riding lessons here."

"I hope they know how lucky they are. Riding can get quite expensive back home. I haven't had the time or funds to enjoy such a guilty pleasure since my youth."

"That's too bad."

"What's one of your favorite memories of your time here? What makes this place so special?"

"What I love most is when we hold pony camps for our young riders. Seeing the smiles on their faces brightens up my day." Donovan pictured Liam on his first pony ride. He was only one example of the many children who had experienced the thrill of their first time on a horse on his family's property. "I remember when Liam had just turned five and my birthday gift to him was to attend his first camp. He had the time of his life."

"I can just imagine."

He couldn't help himself and began to brag a bit. "I still remember how afraid he seemed at first to even get on his pony. But with a little coaching from me, once he mounted and began moving around, his grin stretched from ear to ear for the entire ride. The funniest part was we had to bribe him with candy to get him off the horse. He had so much fun."

Donovan went on to describe some of the other activities available to guests. Caitlin tried to visualize the variety of things Donovan was describing. Amazed by the diverse options, she couldn't wait to get started. "So how much time do we have this afternoon before we head back to Dublin?"

The look on her face told Donovan the whole story; this lass was ready for a little adventure. She seemed like someone who seldom took the time out of her busy schedule just to let her hair down. "It's almost noon now. I'll arrange to have a picnic lunch made that we can take with us on the horseback ride you've requested. Afterward, we'll still have time to shoot at some targets. Have you any experience with shooting: clay pigeons, archery, or air rifles?"

"When I was a teenager, I did some competitive trap shooting, but I've never shot an air rifle. I'd love to try it today. Oh! I'd also like some time to practice on the archery range."

Donovan couldn't help but chuckle, "We can do both of those things. We have plenty of time. It won't take me long to pack for our trip to Killarney and for us to get ready for our date tonight."

His comment caught her attention. "Is it technically a date if Brian asked you to bring me to the concert?" she wondered aloud.

He grinned at her; a devilish smile Caitlin had a feeling he'd used to melt many a heart in the past. "Maybe not, but a guy can dream, can't he?"

"Now, I know you're just teasing me. Let's just agree we're going to enjoy the evening out as friends." She felt determined to keep their relationship on simple terms.

"Friends," he agreed wholeheartedly.

So engaged in serious dialogue, Donovan hadn't realized he'd left Duncan in the car until he abruptly began barking. Donovan quickly opened the vehicle's back door, and Duncan bounded off like a bolt of lightning, racing past and almost knocking Caitlin over. Donovan grabbed her by the arm in the "nick of time" before she took a header, pulling her toward him. Startled by his touch, she quickly regained her balance.

Caitlin looked up at Donovan hesitantly. "I'm fine, thank you," she responded, his nearness increasing her discomfort. She tugged on her arm, and he released her abruptly. They both stared at each other, short of breath and a little shaken. As they proceeded to gather their wits about them, Donovan began to move in the direction of the stable.

Still a little stunned, Caitlin ran to catch up to him. As they entered the building, she couldn't help asking the question that remained on her mind. She rather bluntly just came out with it, "Donovan, when Aidan and I were talking earlier, he mentioned you breed Irish Red and White Setters. I'm curious. Why do you breed dogs instead of helping rescues or strays find homes? Do you need the money through the program to help fund your clinic?"

He calmly responded to her questions. "Absolutely not, Caitlin. This breed became nearly extinct at the end of the 19th century, but in the 1920s, a renewed interest began to help their numbers increase again. In the 1980s, they were imported to Great Britain, where they are still considered vulnerable. In 2009 the American Kennel Club fully recognized them for competition."

Facts, facts, and more facts, Caitlin wanted to know about his reasons, so she continued to press the issue. "That's all very interesting from a historical perspective, but what got you personally involved?"

"When I was a kid, my family had a Red and White Setter as a pet. We named him Harrison. He and I went together everywhere on the farm. As I got older, I learned more about this endangered breed of dogs and wanted to make a difference. They have a good temperament, perfect for a younger, energetic family like Meghan's." The look in his eyes revealed the love he felt for these dogs. Caitlin decided to back off.

"Oh, Donovan, no wonder you were teasing Meghan earlier about their family getting a dog."

"I'm guilty of wanting my sister's kids to have what we had growing up, a loving pet. Grace and Liam love Duncan and enjoy his company. I work hard to ensure the dogs I breed find the right homes and receive the best care. Their family would be the perfect fit for one of Duncan's pups."

Seeing the large smile on Caitlin's face demonstrated she was beginning to understand the motivation behind his breeding these elegant, lovable creatures. He relaxed a bit. "I do want to assure you my clinic spends a lot of time caring specifically for farm animals, with my specialty being horses. We have a partnership with the local animal shelter, too. We offer free medical services for their sick and injured animals before they find their new homes."

A large smile had found its way onto Caitlin's face, which only seemed to distract Donovan. His breathing quickened, which annoyed him, but only because it confused him.

They entered the horse stable through a wide-open doorway where over half of the stalls were empty, typical of a busy day. Donovan waved his hand at one of the older men in the stable area and hustled over to him. Caitlin followed closely behind.

"Welcome back, Donovan," greeted the man with a firm handshake. "I see you've brought the guest we spoke about on the phone."

"Yes. Caitlin, meet Finn McCarthy, my manager," he introduced. "Finn, this is Caitlin Sullivan. She's come from America to experience the beauty of our Irish countryside. We'd like to take a country trek. Could you saddle up two horses for us? Caitlin hasn't been riding for a while, so I'm sure she'd appreciate a gentler ride today."

Nothing got past Finn. He eyed her feet briefly. "No problem, helmets, and safety gear are over there along the wall," he pointed out to Caitlin, "but by the looks of it, you'll need a pair of boots to replace your shoes. I'm sure you can find a pair up at the house that you can use."

"We'll be back shortly, Finn," warned Donovan.

Before Caitlin could respond, Donovan took her hand in his and started walking out of the stable toward the main house, pulling her along behind him. He opened the large front door for her, allowing her to gain access to the large entryway. Stopping abruptly, he pulled two pairs of boots out of the large hallway closet.

"Here, try these on," was all he said. Then before Caitlin knew it, he'd disappeared through a hallway, leaving her alone to make a footwear choice. The newer black boots were a little tight, but the well-worn, tan pair fit like a glove.

Donovan returned to slip on a pair of his boots. He carried their lunch in a large leather bag slung over his shoulder as they made their way back to the stable.

Once back inside, they donned their helmets. Caitlin struggled to fasten hers, so Donovan stepped in to assist. The light brush of his hand against her cheek sent fire scorching through her veins. She had no control over her emotions when he stood so close to her. She hoped he hadn't noticed her intensifying attraction to him.

Finn surveyed the interesting interaction between his boss and the American. When they looked his way, he stood expressionless, quietly holding the reins of two horses who patiently waited to be mounted. Donovan took one set of reins from him and led the larger horse out into the open. Finn followed with the smaller mount, Caitlin trailing behind.

"Finn, what breed of horses are these?"

"They're Irish Sport horses. They have great personalities and incredible jumping abilities." He noticed his rider tense when he mentioned the word jumping. "Don't worry, the horse you'll be riding is rather gentle and a good fit for inexperienced riders. You'll be doing no jumping today."

Caitlin sighed. "They are beautiful horses."

"Donovan has begun to breed these horses here on the farm," Finn seemed to brag. "Interestingly enough, they are a product of crossing Irish Draught Horses with the majestic Thoroughbred."

"It sounds like Dr. O'Malley knows a lot about breeding animals," she commented.

Finn responded, "Yes, he's one of the most responsible breeders in these parts, and he cares deeply for all his animals."

Caitlin heard respect and admiration in his voice. "Thanks for sharing Finn."

"Now, let me help you up onto your horse. I think you'll find Penny here to your liking." Finn proceeded to hold the horse steady to assist Caitlin in mounting.

"Penny, what a nice name. What's your horse's name, Donovan?"

Before answering, he stepped into the stirrup and gracefully mounted his horse. Caitlin couldn't help but stare at the strength of his movement. Both horse and rider were physically fit. "Don't laugh. His name is Ruffian."

She was confused, "Now, why would I make fun of a name like that? By the looks of him, it's a good fit."

"The kids think it's a funny name because he is the gentlest horse around, nothing of a ruffian."

"Oh, I get it. The name fits his looks but not his personality." Before she could say another word, Donovan started to ease Ruffian into a steady walk. Fortunately, her past training on horses kicked into gear, and she lessened the tension on the reins, gripped the horse with her legs to cue it to go forward, and pushed her hips forward in the saddle. Soon she'd caught up to him, following close behind.

The sun shone down upon them, making the temperature in the mid-50s still a pleasant one for horseback riding. Donovan soon learned Caitlin didn't need much instruction to help her remember how to ride a horse, especially one as mild-mannered as Penny. They traveled side by side along a quiet country lane before coming across a rutted field, a trail of some sort. They turned off onto it, and before long, they arrived at a large, bare, ash tree near a fence. Some of the trees in the area had already stepped out of their dormancy and come into leaf earlier in the month, but the ash tree seemed to be taking its time.

Donovan dismounted Ruffian and tied his lead rope to the fence post. Next, he came over to Penny's left side, holding the horse steady while he watched Caitlin lift her right leg back over the horse in an attempt to dismount. She lost her footing as she tried to step down, catching her left foot in the stirrup. Before she could call out for help, she had fallen back into Donovan's waiting arms.

"Hold on, I'll have your foot free in just a moment," he assured her.

Donovan made quick work of it, and once he'd set her foot free, he lowered her feet down gently onto the ground. Embarrassed, Caitlin turned around a little too quickly to thank him, bringing them just inches apart. She lifted her chin to look up at him. To someone standing off in the distance, they might have looked like a pair of statues posed for an intended kiss. And Donovan was tempted to kiss her. He began to lower his face toward hers when Penny whinnied and placed her head right between theirs, preventing him from acting on impulse.

They laughed nervously. Then Donovan grabbed the horse's reins and tied her next to Ruffian by the fence posthaste. Both horses began grazing on the lush green grass of the meadow. "I guess we should take a hint from our horses and eat our lunch," Caitlin suggested, moving further away from temptation.

Donovan reached to retrieve a rolled-up blanket Finn had placed behind his saddle earlier. He tossed it to Caitlin, and she stretched it out on the ground under another beautiful tree, just beginning to bud. They sat down, and Donovan pulled ham and cheese sandwiches, carrots, apples, and some bottled water out of the canvas bag.

"How long has your family owned this land?" Caitlin asked curiously.

Donovan leaned back against the large shady sessile oak tree and began to tell the tale. "Well, my grandfather was born in the northwestern part of Ireland, County Mayo. When he turned 18, he left home and went looking for work with a friend of his. The owner of this farm hired them. Grandad worked here for many years and became the right-hand man of the owner after years of hard work and dedication."

"How did your grandfather come to own the place?"

"The owner had no sons, just one daughter named Shannon. She fell madly in love with Grandad and they got married. When her father passed away, she inherited the farm. My grandfather enjoyed horses more than anything and loved to ride. His interest led my grandparents into thinking it would make a great equestrian center. A place for other people to come and enjoy horses, especially those who lived in larger cities like Dublin."

So, Aengus O'Malley was an adventurer, risk-taker, hard worker, and a dreamer all wrapped up into one enchanting human being, Caitlin realized. No wonder she liked him at first glance. "When did you add the other activities, people come here to enjoy?"

"As Grandad's family grew, their interests turned into what you see today. My dad is the only sibling who remained in the area and had the desire to manage things around here. Since he was the oldest sibling, the farm passed on to him and is one reason Grandad continues to live with my parents. I guess along with the farm; they inherited him as well."

Caitlin chuckled at the thought. "I don't think they mind. Aengus seems to be happy living with your parents, even though they've moved into the city."

"Our family always seems to make smooth transitions, even when they're big life changes. Sheamus, Meghan, and I each found our niche in the world, and our family continues to have close ties to one another. We're fortunate. Family is everything to us, but there is nothing like good friends, even though I appreciate my loving family. Cait, have you considered our friendship to be destiny?" he asked endearingly with a slight tilt of his head.

"Why do you ask?"

"Well, if we had only met by chance in the airport terminal," he reminded her, "and then again on the plane, it might have just been insignificant and forgettable. But the fact you already knew my sister and are now staying at my folks' Inn, well, it feels as if us being friends is, pure and simple, fate."

She had trouble denying she felt the same. "I guess anything is possible when you're in Ireland."

"'Tis true, Cait. I've lived here my whole life and am no longer surprised by such things."

Caitlin paused for a moment, wondering whether she should ask the next question or not. "I know I'm asking rather personal questions, and we've only just met, but I'm curious why you never married? You're a rather handsome man and somewhat likeable," she teased.

Immediately Donovan's smile turned upside down, and his face paled as if someone had sucked the life out of him.

She couldn't help but notice the change in his demeanor. "I'm sorry, did I say something wrong?"

"No, Cait. I was engaged at one time, but an accident killed my fiancée."

"Oh my, I'm so sorry. It's OK if we don't talk about it."

For some reason, Donovan decided it might be somewhat therapeutic to share, work through his feelings with someone other than family. For some unknown reason, Caitlin made him feel emotionally safe.

"Marie worked for us, training horses, and giving riding lessons. She had a way with animals. The staff called her the 'Horse Whisperer' and loved every second with her. I fell for her like a ton of bricks, and it was only a short time later, we became engaged. Then a few months before our wedding, her mother became ill and needed surgery. Marie planned to fly home to be with her, and I had promised to drive her to the airport, but something came up." Donovan sighed, running his hands through his hair. Caitlin could tell he was struggling to retell the story.

"That day, one of our mares was getting ready to deliver her first foal. She had gone into labor in the late afternoon, right as I was about to leave with Marie. I was the only vet near enough to assist with what could be a difficult delivery, so I had to take back my offer." He paused for a moment; his eyes slightly glassy as he re-parsed the events through his mind.

"I remember Marie stepping into the stable and her sweet understanding voice saying, 'Don't worry about me, you're needed here.' The weather hadn't been the best, so I pleaded with her to change her plans. She insisted on leaving so she could be present for her mother's surgery. In hindsight, but ultimately out of respect to Marie's independent nature and self-confidence, I let her win the argument."

"She left?"

"Yes, she kissed me goodbye with her final words etched into my memory. 'Now do what you have to do, Donovan O'Malley,' she said. 'Before you know it, I'll be back, and we'll be husband and wife. Then you'll be complaining because you can't get rid of me.'" Caitlin listened with her eyes half-shut to the strained control of his emotions.

"Of course, I told her no matter what she did; I'd always love her. Then we embraced for the final time. I hadn't realized the weather had changed. The temperature had dropped, and rain had fallen. Black ice and the curve of the roads around here can make a dangerous combination. Marie never made it to the airport. She lost control on a patch of black ice and hit a tree, dying soon after."

Silence followed his final words. Placing her hand briefly on his for comfort was the only way Caitlin knew how to respond to the story of his loss. By the expression on his face, it was all he seemed to need.

They quickly finished the rest of their lunch in silence. Thankfully, Donovan had packed two extra apples to share with the horses. Offering them to Penny and Ruffian was a pleasant distraction. Caitlin giggled as Penny took a bite out of her apple, but she was so apprehensive she almost dropped it. Penny's teeth were so large she feared the horse would take a bite out of more than just the apple.

"Relax, Cait. Here, let me help you." Donovan stood behind her and gently placed his hand under hers. "Now keep your hand wide open and let the apple just rest in your palm."

Caitlin tried to relax and listen to his directions as he gently lifted her hand closer to Penny's mouth, waiting there until the mare picked the rest of the apple up. Donovan handed Caitlin the second apple as they moved toward Ruffian. Again, standing close behind her, Caitlin could feel Donovan's warm breath upon her neck as he spoke softly into her ear, giving her the courage to offer the treat up to the larger horse. She couldn't resist leaning back against him, momentarily wishing she could fill the void in his life. Ruffian practically inhaled the treat, startling Caitlin backward and into Donovan's arms. He held on tight until she could regain her balance.

Startled at first, they both took a moment to get their breath. Feeling a little embarrassed, Caitlin stepped forward to give herself some space. As she slowly turned back around to face him, all she could say in response was, "That was fun." Donovan broke out laughing, shortly followed by Caitlin.

Once their laughter had ceased, Donovan untied the horses from the post. He helped Caitlin remount, then off he took her on a different trail through taller grassy fields. Feeling more comfortable on her horse, they slowly galloped up and down a few countryside hills before slowing to a walk—an opportune time to discuss their upcoming trip.

"Cait, I've reserved the hotel rooms for our stay in Killarney, and I suggest the first thing we might want to do is visit the church your great-great-grandparents were married at."

"That sounds great," she said absentmindedly. *Do not get too used to it,* she told herself. She liked having someone else take charge now and then, even though she was a reasonably independent individual. When she'd been dating Jeremy, he had never taken responsibility for anything. She had to make all the arrangements whenever they went somewhere together. Maybe it was a sign of his immaturity and not being ready to commit himself to their relationship. Lately, she tended to absorb her time and energy in her work to compensate for her more recent single status, not something she had expected at this point in her life.

Donovan looked at her a little dreamy-eyed while explaining the rest of his plans. "We'll need to take some time while we're in Killarney just to have some fun and act like tourists. I thought one thing we should do is take a jaunting cart ride through Killarney National Park."

"What's a jaunting cart?"

"OK, this is quite an obscure reference, but have you ever seen the old John Wayne movie called 'The Quiet Man' with Maureen O'Hara?"

Immediately visions of the feisty pair appeared. They had such great chemistry on screen. "Yes! It was one of my great-grandfather's favorite movies, and I watched it with him more than once. I think it reminded him of his homeland and my great-grandmother."

"Well, if you remember, there's a scene where they're courting, and they are seated in an open two-wheeled one-horse cart. The actors had a driver in the front who drove them around town to make sure nothing improper went on during the process. On the jaunting carts used for tourism today, benches are still on the opposite sides of each other; but they're on the inside of the cart facing one another."

"I'd enjoy riding in one. It would be a great way to see the countryside."

"One of the trips they take is actually to a large mansion called Muckross House. It's beautiful," he said with a whimsical smile.

Caitlin loved anything historical and experiencing the history of Ireland piqued her interests.

"If the weather cooperates, we could also take a bike ride to Ross Castle. It isn't far from our hotel. I want you to experience the beauty of the land, especially in the area where your great-great-grandfather was born."

"A bike ride sounds heavenly," she admitted.

"Then it will be the first thing on our agenda. A little exercise after the long car ride would be refreshing."

"Just lead the way, and I'll follow you anywhere," she suggested coyly.

"Be careful what you promise, Cait. I could easily lead you astray." Donovan smiled enticingly at her when she glanced his way.

As they continued to ride side by side, she remembered her manners and added, "I hope you realize how thankful I am to you and your family for your hospitality."

"It's our pleasure. Don't think anything of it. I know I don't mind giving you a little of my attention."

"More than a little, you're taking time off from work to escort me…"

"Ah, I don't take enough vacation time as it is! Besides, traveling across the country is much more enjoyable in such beautiful company. Don't lose any sleep over the fact that I'm willing to chauffeur you around. It's purely selfish."

"Fine, I won't!" Caitlin played along.

Their conversation ended just as they arrived back at the stables. Finn seemed to be waiting for their return, and after they dismounted, he took their horses back into the stable for grooming.

Caitlin had forgotten how refreshing horseback riding could be. As a young girl, she'd spent time on a friend's farm. Her friend Kathy was an only child. Frequently she would invite her to go riding. Caitlin loved the feel of the wind whipping through her hair when they broke into a gallop, racing each other along the gravel road on the property. Today's ride had brought back some of those fond memories.

"Let's stop in the stables for a few minutes so you can see Duncan's puppies."

After putting their equipment away, they walked back toward Finn's office. Caitlin could hear high-pitched barking. She made her way toward the sound. Donovan opened a half-door, and Caitlin was amazed at the affectionate scene she beheld. Duncan lay on the ground near another Red and White Setter. Caitlin counted nine puppies in all, running around and chasing each other. Now and then, they'd stop and play with their rubber toys. One even tried to climb up Duncan's leg.

Donovan gave a little whistle, and the puppies suddenly came running over to him. He sat down on the floor and picked the closest one up and began petting it. Caitlin plunked down next to him. Before long, the puppies were climbing all over their legs and begging for attention. They were the most adorable puppies Caitlin had ever seen.

"I can see why you'd want to make sure this breed continues to grow in population. They're such beautiful dogs and absolute sweethearts, too." Donovan nodded in agreement.

"All right, let's get a move on before I have to drag you away from their puppy dog eyes. We still have a lot of things for you to experience, friend," he emphasized.

They stopped next at the archery range, where Caitlin met Will, one of the archery instructors. He held out a quiver holding 50 arrows. Typically, he would advise guests as they shot them one after another, but today he realized he'd have an easier job with Donovan around.

"This should be enough shots to allow you time to improve your aim. Will and I will give you some pointers along the way," Donovan volunteered.

Her first few shots landed far from the bullseye. With a little coaching from the two men by her side, she began to hit closer to the center of the target halfway through emptying her quiver.

At one point, Donovan decided to position himself to the left of Caitlin. She momentarily tensed up when he suddenly wrapped his arm around her to assist in the process of loading the bow and guiding her through the next shot. Although his nearness proved to be a significant distraction, she scored a bullseye.

"Nice job, Cait! Try it again on your own," he encouraged.

She had to regain her composure first. Then once she had refocused her concentration, the rest of the arrows sailed one after another. Hitting close to the center of the target without any help.

"Great job, sharpshooter. You're turning out to be fairly good at this."

"You're not so bad yourself. I mean, all ten of your arrows hit either the bullseye or were just off the mark."

"I've had a little practice. Remember, I grew up here. Who knows how many of those arrows flew past the entire target over the years?" Donovan admitted before thanking Will for his valuable time. Will nodded at Donovan. The past few years since Marie's death, Will had seen too few smiles on Donovan's face. Caitlin seemed to have somehow changed that.

"Will, thanks for coaching me today," said Caitlin.

He responded politely, "It was an honor. I hope you continue to enjoy your time here today and on the rest of your visit in Ireland."

She gave him a big hug, which threw him off guard. "I had so much fun! Thank you, Will."

"You're welcome, Miss Caitlin."

Confusion set in for Donovan for the second time that day. He knew he was starting to have some feelings for Caitlin, but she seemed to show affection toward all the people she met, especially men. Maybe she was just a friendly person, and friendship was all she truly wanted. He felt like a balloon filling up with air; the happier he got, the larger his balloon. Then pop! Something she did caused him to burst and deflate.

The air rifle shooting range ended up being their final stop for the afternoon. Donovan and Caitlin finished shooting almost before they started. Caitlin's history with rifles made her such a sharpshooter.

"I'll never forget this day!" Caitlin spoke as they began to pack up their things to head back to the house. "I can see why people pay money to come here."

"I'm glad you think so. Maybe next time, I'll charge you for my services."

As usual, she was motivated to punch him in the arm, but she managed to refrain from doing so. All in all, she had a feeling of contentment from the day's activities. She found it hard to believe it was already time to head back to Dublin. She couldn't help but let out one long sigh.

"What is it, Cait?"

"Nothing, I'm simply happy. Thanks for today," was Caitlin's final response as they continued to walk back toward the house. She knew the photos she and Donovan had taken throughout the day would help preserve her memories for years to come. She hated to lose this feeling of peace and calm.

# Chapter 11

After retrieving their things from the car, they re-entered Donovan's house. Caitlin admired the elegant decor of the two-story home as they made their way up the carved oak staircase to the second floor. Donovan directed her to the first room on the right at the top of the stairs, a large guest bedroom. "When you're ready, head down to the living room near the entryway. I'll meet you there. Give me about 30 minutes since I have to pack my bag for tomorrow's trip."

"Sounds good. It's plenty of time for me to get ready," Caitlin responded.

Donovan sent a friendly smile in Caitlin's direction as he began to casually stroll away. She couldn't resist watching him until he disappeared into another room at the end of the long hallway. "That's a picture I'll just have to store in my memory bank," she muttered to herself, briefly hesitating before entering the bedroom. Layers of patterns and textures in green filled the cozy, traditional country bedroom. Its showstopper, a beautiful, canopied bed. She felt very much at home in her surroundings. She shut the door behind her and carried her bag over to the bed. She gently pulled out the dress her aunt had bought her—spreading it out gingerly on the bed—followed by her clean undergarments, leggings, and black dress boots. She leisurely removed her soiled clothing and moved into the large ensuite bathroom to shower.

It was apparent to her this older farmhouse had been recently updated, and she admired the beautifully tiled bathroom with its white porcelain claw tub and large walk-in shower. The temptation to take a long soak in the tub immediately vanished when she glanced at the time. Instead, she walked into the shower and relaxed as steady, tepid water streamed down her body, washing away any residue from the day's activities on the farm.

An available blow dryer sped up her process of getting ready. With just the final touches on her make-up left, she finished preparing for her so-called "date" within the 30-minute window of time. A wave of excitement washed over her in anticipation of what lay ahead. She planned to enjoy herself.

Down the hallway, Donovan started a little apprehensive regarding the upcoming evening. He quickly showered before donning a pair of black trousers, a standard white button-down shirt with the top two buttons left undone, and a sporty gray jacket. When ready, it left him barely ten minutes to pack for the 3-day getaway. No problem, he was an efficient packer. On the other hand, he had no clue what he was getting into where Caitlin was concerned. Going to the concert together was not a big deal but traveling cross country to Killarney with the lovely American lass he now called Cait, well, that could spell trouble.

He couldn't understand how he'd convinced himself to take her to Killarney in the first place. What about Caitlin had wreaked havoc in such a short time on his determination to keep his distance? At first, he thought something about her reminded him of Marie. Not possible. They looked nothing alike. Yes, they were both beautiful and intelligent women, but he'd known many in his lifetime. That couldn't be it. They also had different personalities and mannerisms; he couldn't figure it out. Only time would unveil the connection he'd already internally made.

"Just go with the flow," he mumbled. "Relax and enjoy the evening ahead in the company of a charming woman. No strings attached." Once he'd changed and finished packing, he grabbed his small suitcase and confidently made his way back downstairs to join Caitlin.

Donovan, surprised to find he'd beaten Caitlin to their meeting spot, sat in a comfortable large stuffed chair and let the sunlight from the large windows bathe his body in warmth. Before he could become too preoccupied with his earlier thoughts, a sound of movement caused him to jump to his feet. Caitlin stood in front of him. He took the time to appreciate the vision before saying, "You look breathtaking. I'll be the envy of every man at the concert tonight."

"Thank you. You don't look so bad yourself," Caitlin returned, slightly embarrassed by the fact they were standing and staring at one another. A habit they seemed to have been forming over the past two days. To break up the silence, she added, "Hadn't we best be leaving, so we aren't late?"

"Yes," he agreed.

Caitlin only paused a moment before turning to head into the front hallway. She could feel her cheeks start to redden, and she didn't want to give away her true feelings about Donovan.

Once outside, they walked briskly to the car, loading their things into the trunk before heading back on the road. They shared a friendly conversation on their ride back to Dublin, entering the outskirts of the city just as Caitlin got to the climax of one of her favorite childhood stories. Their destination, Arthur's Pub, was a short three-minute walk from Vicar Street on the west end of the city where they would be attending The High Kings concert.

"Tell me more about this restaurant you chose for tonight's meal," Caitlin requested.

"Oh, yes! Arthur's Pub has been around for over 200 years and has a rich history. Uniquely enough, they light a real turf fire every day, play an eclectic mix of Irish music, and have live music sessions in the evenings."

Caitlin listened intently, stopping the conversation to clarify something Donovan had said. "What's a turf fire?"

"You may know it as peat in your part of the world. It looked like brown earthen blocks and was a primary fuel source for Irish people for thousands of years. It's still being used today in open fire cooking."

"Interesting." Caitlin loved the historical knowledge Donovan continually shared with her. For a lover of history such as she, it was quite an attractive quality in a man.

"One thing I like best about eating there is how relaxing it is. Upstairs they have a room that is a restaurant during the day, but it becomes a Blues and Jazz Club at night. They host some high-quality, live music too. "

Once parked, Caitlin noticed Donovan seemed to kick into some kind of "date mode," turning on the charm even more than before. He opened the car door for her and held out his arm to escort her inside. Even though Brian had preordained this date, Donovan seemed to be taking it rather seriously.

Donovan wanted Caitlin to fall in love with Ireland in as many ways as possible, but he wasn't about to admit to himself the real motive behind his desire for his homeland to capture her heart.

At first sight, Caitlin was in awe of the elegant charm the restaurant possessed. They were seated almost immediately, and Caitlin felt the need to clear the air before settling into their meal. "Donovan, I don't usually use my phone when I'm on a date. But with me being so far away from home, I just want to make sure I'm available if one of my family members gives me a call. Do you mind?"

"No problem. I'm old school and still carry my pager in case an emergency call comes from the clinic." Donovan laughed, showing off his well-worn device.

"Then, we agree. Those are the only kind of messages we are responding to?"

"Absolutely."

"Once we're at the concert, we both ignore all messages?"

"Yes! We'll be so busy listening to the music we won't notice anything else."

As if on cue, Caitlin's phone vibrated, and her aunt's photo popped up on her screen. They both laughed at the timing of the call. "It's my aunt. I'll keep it brief."

"Go ahead. I'll double-check to see if I have any messages from the clinic."

To Caitlin's surprise, it wasn't her aunt's voice on the opposite end of the line. "Caitlin, it's me, Jeremy. I just found out you stopped to visit your aunt last weekend. Now don't say anything yet, and please don't hang up. I convinced your aunt to let me contact you and explain my feelings. We never had a chance to talk following our breakup."

Was he kidding? Was Jeremy Two-Timing Fisher kidding!? "You think we should talk? What do you think we need to discuss?" she tried to respond in a quiet, stern voice.

"I made a mistake, a BIG MISTAKE! I never really stopped loving you. Please, won't you consider giving me a second chance? We spent two wonderful years together; you know we're a good fit. What do you have to lose?"

"I don't have time for this conversation right now, nor are you making a convincing argument."

"Later then, I could come to visit you when you return home. I feel like such a fool; I'm miserable without you."

"I have to go. This isn't the time for a conversation, nor do I care to have one. My date is waiting for me."

"Your date?"

"Goodbye!" The nerve of the man, she fumed. She could feel her blood pressure rising, and she desperately needed some fresh air. She laid her phone on the table before excusing herself.

Stepping outside into the cool air, she took a few deep breaths as she tried to clear her head. She didn't need any more confusing relationships commanding her attention right now.

Back inside, Donovan could tell Caitlin had been upset by her conversation with her aunt. He decided he'd wait until she returned to see if she wanted to talk about it. Just then, her phone vibrated, and a text message appeared on her screen. Thinking it might be one of her family members, he glanced at the text that popped up. He didn't mean to read it, but his reflexes weren't fast enough to avoid being sucked in by the first four words.

*I love you, Caitlin. Please forgive me. I want to marry you.* The screen went dark. Donovan felt as if a knife had been stabbed into his heart. Of course, Caitlin had a significant other. Better to know this now before he let himself get too attached. He didn't need to take another risk after losing someone he loved dearly. Unfortunately, there was no Band-Aid for broken hearts—but there were ways to ease the pain. He wanted to avoid experiencing heartache again at any cost.

Once Caitlin returned, they resumed a friendly yet safe conversation. Caitlin commented on her tasty Shepherd's Pie and how excited she was for the show.

With dinner finished, they found themselves stepping out onto the sidewalk as a gentle breeze blew past them. Caitlin and Donovan huddled together and hurried the short distance to Vicar Street. Caitlin allowed the crisp night air and the brisk walk to clear her thoughts.

Once they arrived, they had to wait in line in the alleyway until the doors opened. Although the evening air had cooled things down a bit, Caitlin had planned ahead. Digging into her bag, she immediately pulled out the golden-colored wrap she'd brought along to keep herself warm. The constant sound of chatter filled the air around them as the line began to move, stopping just once at the box office to pick up their tickets. Inside the lobby, they decided to stop at the bar first to pick up their drinks, chatting along the way to kill time.

Caitlin, taking a sip of her white wine, couldn't help pumping Donovan for information about the band. "So, tell me more about The High Kings. Have they been together for a long time?"

"Over ten years, all except Paul are original members of the band formed in 2008." Donovan shared a few more specifics about the group until the venue's concert hall door opened, and people started to enter. As they walked into the performance area, Donovan announced, "Our seats are upfront thanks to Brian."

"You're lucky to have such a nice friend," she reflected.

"I don't think our friendship had anything to do with it. I think your singing captivated Brian last night."

"I rather doubt it," Caitlin denied, scanning the room as they moved toward their designated seats.

She was amazed at how they'd managed to fit so many small round tables and chairs throughout the venue. They'd only placed their drinks on the table when Donovan whisked her away toward a door to the right of the stage. "Come on, let's go backstage now before it gets too close to the start of the concert. Brian is expecting us."

Caitlin followed Donovan, and a concert attendant stopped them briefly to verify their identity and permit them to go backstage. They followed him through the door and down a long hallway. When they rounded the corner, they saw a door labeled "The Green Room". The attendant knocked on the door, and Brian opened it.

"Hey, glad you found your way back here. We're just rehearsing a few songs before our show." He rejoined the other band members as they finished running through one of the songs they'd be singing on stage. Once they finished, Brian introduced Caitlin to the band members.

"It's nice to see you again, Caitlin. Guys, this is Caitlin Sullivan from the fine state of Minnesota in the good old U.S.A."

"Hi, Caitlin!" they chorused.

"And, of course, you all know Donovan O'Malley." The men all shared a greeting; then Brian continued the introductions. "Caitlin, to my left is Darren on the mandolin, Finbarr on the guitar, and our newest member, Paul."

"You all sounded great when we walked in here. I enjoyed singing with Brian last night, and I can't wait to hear the band play tonight."

Darren couldn't help himself; he had to ask. "So, did you sing one of our tunes with Brian?"

"No, this is the first time I'll be hearing any of your music, but last night Brian and Donovan helped me sing a popular Irish tune instead," Caitlin felt as if she'd just stuck her foot in her mouth. "Oh, not that your tunes aren't popular, I mean we sang one that most Americans know. I bet you can't guess its name," Caitlin added facetiously.

Finbarr jumped in quickly, "O'Danny Boy?"

"We've got a winner!" Brian announced. They all got a good chuckle from that.

Donovan knew the show had to go on, so he gave a none too subtle reminder, "Well, we better get a move on and let you finish your preparations. Thanks for inviting us tonight, Brian. Break a leg everyone!" Donovan opened the door to exit.

Caitlin turned to say a final thank you. Donovan, half-way out the door, overheard her say something about Irish folk music being soothing to her soul. That made him smile. After her experience at O'Malley's Pub the night before, he knew she would enjoy herself tonight.

Shortly after they took their seats, The High Kings' concert began with background bagpipe music playing. Toward the back of the stage, a screen hung from the ceiling with The High Kings' banner. Darren stepped onto the stage, first making his way to the keyboard, followed closely by Finbarr with his guitar, Brian with the bodhrán (an Irish drum), and Paul with his flute. The crowd cheered them on, and soon they were singing their opening song *Rocky Road to Dublin*. The audience joined in singing on the chorus, as well as many of the songs that followed.

"Are you having a good time?" Donovan asked near the end of the concert.

"A fantastic time!"

"I'm glad," he placed his hand on hers as the band started playing their next song. Darren sang lead, the lyrics rooting deeply into Caitlin's heart: "*O Maggie give me one more chance, I swear I'll make everything right...*"

When the song ended, Donovan looked into Caitlin's eyes, and he could see tears resting at the corners.

*How am I ever going to leave this place?* she wondered. Donovan looked at her and squeezed her hand. Caitlin realized she seemed to be falling in love with this music, this place, and this man.

When the band moved into their final song, the crowd flew to their feet in a standing ovation. The concert was ending, but after thunderous applause, The High Kings were encouraged to play two additional encore numbers ending with the song *Friends for Life*. Caitlin thought it an appropriate close to the evening and an enchanting day packed full of adventure.

When they returned to the Inn, Donovan escorted Caitlin back to her room. "I had a wonderful time tonight," she shared as she rummaged in her purse for her room key. When she found it, she smiled up at Donovan, "The music will be playing in my head for the rest of the night. I envision myself singing in my dreams."

"You're not the only one. Singing along with the High Kings has a way of filling one's heart with so much joy you feel it might just explode."

"I'll never forget this evening, this music, and you."

He stopped talking, letting his eyes wander first to her face, then her eyes, then her mouth. There, his gaze stopped. He wondered what it would be like to kiss Caitlin.

She raised her eyes to his, and he saw his question reflected in them. "Cait."

Her answering expression offered the silent permission he needed. Donovan slowly lowered his head, his hands gently resting on her shoulders. Their lips met. Soft. Sweet. Warm.

He could feel the softening of his heart despite the text he had read earlier on her phone. He wanted to surrender to the emotions flowing through him. Whomever Jeremy turned out to be, Caitlin couldn't feel strongly about another man when she so freely kissed him. He was here—now. He didn't want to let her forget that.

When their lips parted, he didn't pull away, couldn't pull away. He embraced Caitlin in a hug, one hand cradling the back of her head, the other arm wrapped around her, not wanting this moment to end.

Caitlin dropped her forehead then eased back. "Thank you for the lovely day. I'll remember it long after I return home."

Donovan felt disappointed. Why did she need to remind him she'd be leaving in the not-too-distant future?

Once on the other side of the door, Caitlin leaned against it for support. She'd had a great day and an even better evening. Then the kiss, an unforgettable kiss. She would later describe it to her sister as a gentle kiss with a powerful punch. She knew she wouldn't be able to fall asleep right away, so maybe now would be the best time to make a call home.

She noticed she'd received two text messages during the concert. The most recent from her sister mentioning their dad wanted to talk to her before she went to bed. The second text came from her Aunt's phone, and when she pulled it up on the screen, it displayed Jeremy's proclamation of love and his proposal. How ridiculous! Without hesitation, she called her sister.

"Hi, Caitlin! Before I ask you a million questions, Dad is anxious to hear from you. Can I put him on?"

"No, wait, not yet! I am so angry right now, and I need to vent."

"What's going on?"

"It's Jeremy!"

Abbey felt confused. She knew Caitlin hadn't seen nor heard from her former boyfriend in at least six months. What could he have done to make her so angry? "Go ahead. I'm listening."

Caitlin told her about the phone call she'd received earlier in the evening and the follow-up text message. "I can't believe he had

121

the nerve to tell me he loves me and wants to marry me in a text message. Does he think I am going to take him back? How desperate does he think I am?"

"Relax, Sis. My advice to you, ignore the text. You're in Ireland to enjoy yourself, don't let him mess with your head."

Caitlin broke down, crying. "Abbey, I'm so confused."

"What are you confused about?"

"When Jeremy called, it irritated me, and when I read his text message, it made me mad."

"What are you trying to tell me?"

"I'm irritated because he dated someone else behind my back, but when things didn't work out in his new relationship, he decided to profess his love for me. He told me the other woman had all been a big mistake on his part. I can't believe he has the nerve to think I'd drop everything and marry him just because he said the words 'I love you' and 'will you marry me?' The nerve of the two-timing man!"

"Are you sure you don't still have any feelings for him? You dated for over two years," challenged Abbey.

Caitlin lay face down on the bed and began to cry. Her phone still in her hand but off to the side, away from her mouth.

"Caitlin, what's wrong. I can hear you crying. Talk to me."

Caitlin rolled onto her back and positioned her phone near her ear. "Abbey, I kissed him."

"Kissed who? What are you talking about?"

"I kissed Donovan tonight. Why would I kiss him if I still had feelings for Jeremy? Does this mean I'm over Jeremy for good?"

"I don't know, you tell me. How did you feel when Donovan kissed you?"

"Wonderful, simply wonderful."

"Then I think you can give yourself permission to move on."

"I know, but…"

"No buts, just take one day at a time while you're there and make the most of it. You don't need to feel guilty. You don't have any commitments back home. Now tell me about the rest of your day, everything before the kiss."

An hour later, they were still talking. "Abbey, I don't feel up to speaking to dad tonight. Can you share the information I gave you with him? About the research, I mean, nothing else. Once I get to Killarney and learn more, I can call and talk to him directly. "

"Sounds good to me. Now get some sleep and remember, take one day at a time." Exhausted, Caitlin fell into a deep and fortunately dreamless sleep.

# Chapter 12

Caitlin and Donovan left for Killarney shortly after eight the next morning. Bridgett had packed them a light breakfast to eat in the car. They munched on what Donovan called Irish *Jambon*, bits of ham and cheese baked into a pastry. His mother had also thrown in some warm blueberry scones and a variety of fresh fruit.

"Your mom sent way too much food with us. There's no way we can eat all of it," complained Caitlin.

"I could try, but I agree with you. My mom tends to overdo it sometimes. The good news is we'll have leftovers for the next day or two," he suggested.

"I'd eat another *Jambon*, but I'm saving room for a few of those succulent looking strawberries."

Donovan didn't think they were the only tempting things in the vehicle. "They do look tasty. I'm personally enjoying this tea. How's yours?" Donovan asked, raising his cup.

"I'm not much of a tea drinker. I consume my daily quota of caffeine in the illustrious form of coffee." She held up her disposable cup as if to make a cheer. "Thanks to your mom, I have what I need to start the day outright."

Entertained by her enthusiasm, he couldn't help sharing his thoughts. "Thankfully, my mom knows I prefer my tea, although the Irish are becoming quite the coffee drinkers."

Caitlin chuckled. "How far do we have to travel to get to Killarney? Didn't you say it would take about three hours?"

"Actually, Miss Sullivan, it will take about 3 ½ hours to go the 303-kilometer distance to Killarney. That's approximately 188 miles for you Americans who still haven't quite learned how to use the metric system like the rest of the world." Donovan turned slightly toward Caitlin and winked to let her know he was only teasing.

"Okay, Mr. Precision, what do you mean 'us Americans'? Are you picking on me, Doc? Is that how Irish tour guides treat their American tourists?"

Suddenly, Donovan's mood changed. Only one woman had ever called him Doc—Marie.

Noticing his abrupt shift in demeanor, Caitlin adjusted her weight in the passenger seat to look more intently at Donovan. "Donovan, are you okay?"

"I'm sorry. You just took me off guard. Marie is the only woman who has ever called me Doc. It was her term of endearment for me. I must still be a little sensitive when someone else uses it."

Caitlin didn't know how to respond, quickly ending their flirtatious and light-hearted conversation. Thirty minutes later, the silence between them began to destroy Caitlin's earlier peace of mind. The quiet music playing on the radio was a reminder of her inability to respond to him comfortably in the enclosed space. Finally, she got the courage to start up another conversation.

"Please tell me more about Marie. How did the two of you meet?" Silence followed. Caitlin immediately regretted her decision. "It's okay if you'd rather not tell me."

"I'm sure it wouldn't hurt to reminisce. Marie was a lovely woman, just 22 years old when she came to work at our Equestrian Center. She loved horses more than anything else in the world, and they loved her. She was our most skilled horse trainer, and riders came from far and wide to learn from her. She loved to challenge herself and excelled at training horses to move through the obstacle courses with accuracy and speed."

Caitlin glanced over at Donovan, intently watching as he continued to share the intimate details of the woman who had captured his heart.

"I didn't notice her at first, but word got around. Several people told me a fair-haired lass working on the grounds had hypnotized all the horses. They followed her every command. I laughed at the rumors and continued to ignore all the chatter until one day when I happened to see her in action. Less than two years later, we were engaged and planning our wedding, and then, you know, her funeral."

"I'm so sorry. It must have been a challenging time for you."

"Caitlin, I still struggle daily. I've avoided dating because I'm still grieving. My family doesn't seem to understand, and they constantly try to push women into my path."

"Oh," she felt unnerved.

"I don't mean to sound rude. You're a lovely woman, and I can see why some of my family has already taken a liking to you, particularly Grandad."

Caitlin remembered the kiss they had shared the night before. "So, our kiss last night?"

He sighed. "I'm sorry, Caitlin. A lapse in good judgment on my part. I became wrapped up in the moment. I apologize if I mislead you in any way. Even if I was interested in something more, you're leaving in a few days. I won't overstep the boundaries of friendship again because I'm determined to be your friend, Caitlin."

Was he speaking the truth? Could he keep his distance for the next few days? He didn't want to, but he knew it would be best for both of them if he did.

"Of course, with thousands of miles separating us, it makes the most sense." She wanted to cry. Turning her head toward the window, she tried to hold back her tears. She knew Donovan made perfect sense, she'd told herself the same thing several times since they'd met, but it still hurt. Drawn to him like a strong magnet, she didn't know how long they could continue to fight their obvious attraction for one another.

More time passed in silence, and Caitlin couldn't help but notice a multitude of wildflowers growing in vibrant yellows, pinks, blues, and purples along the roadside. Being a passenger had allowed Caitlin time to enjoy the artistry of Mother Nature. The spring rains had brought the trees to life and covered them in multiple shades of green. The countryside depicted one long canvas she'd skillfully painted.

Again, bothered by the silence, Caitlin spoke up. "Thanks for offering to drive me to Killarney. Once we arrive, where did you plan on taking me first? We never really discussed our final plans."

"To St. Mary's Cathedral, where your great-great-grandparents were married, and your great-grandfather was baptized. It's only a short bike ride from our hotel. Maybe we can dig up a few more clues about your family."

"You make us sound like a pair of detectives."

"At least we only have a missing person's case to solve and not a murder."

Caitlin punched Donovan's left shoulder. "What a morbid thought."

"Ouch! That hurt!" Donovan moaned. "Why'd you hit me? I said, at least it wasn't a murder."

"Why do you have to keep saying murder? I don't think it's necessary, and I didn't hit you that hard." She took her right hand and began to rub the spot where her punch had landed. Donovan continued to steer with his left hand while reaching over with his right hand to pat hers.

"I'm fine. I was just teasing." Donovan let his hand linger a little too long on hers. Despite what he'd told Caitlin earlier, he didn't want to let go of her hand, and he felt a strong urge to take her in his arms and press his lips against hers once more. Luckily, he couldn't follow through on his desires and drive at the same time. Besides, it was best not to say one thing and do another. Oh, was he in trouble!

With that, their conversation ended once more. Other than the music playing on the radio, and the decision to make one quick pit stop, Caitlin and Donovan didn't speak until they arrived at their hotel. The check-in process turned out to be painless, yet the conversation between them remained stilted until they reached their floor.

Their rooms were just across the hall from each other. Before entering them, Donovan suggested Caitlin change into more comfortable clothes for the bike ride they would take after they had a few bites to eat.

During lunch, they discussed some of the attractions in the area they might want to visit. Caitlin found herself fascinated by the delightful city. The only thing she regretted was the short amount of time they had for their visit.

Donovan couldn't contain his excitement for Caitlin. He hoped she would enjoy the time in one of his favorite cities. "You'll get a chance to see Ross Castle this afternoon. The bike rental shop is just across the street from here, and it's only a 15-minute bike ride to the castle. We'll stop at St. Mary's Cathedral on the way," he rattled on like a little kid listing all of his favorite activities.

"That sounds wonderful! I'm looking forward to it."

After lunch, it didn't take long to rent bikes and helmets. Caitlin's enthusiasm to take off on her bike showed by the way she hopped on with her backpack in tow, her camera carefully stowed within it. "It isn't often I get to have such a variety of adventures when I'm on vacation. First horseback riding and now biking."

"And we're in luck. The weather is cooperating today, so we might as well take advantage of it."

The direction they took to get to St. Mary's Cathedral did turn out to be a short 5-minute bike ride. As they neared their destination, the Cathedral seemed to tower amongst the clouds with a backdrop of Killarney's glorious lakes and mountains. The view captivated Caitlin. She noticed its location seemed unusual for a Cathedral. It stood in a vast field on the edge of the city, not more centrally located as you would expect of most churches.

She dismounted her bike and gazed at the unbelievable structure built of brown and grey limestones, in a Gothic revival style of architecture. Caitlin found it hard to believe she was standing in front of the church where family members had attended services. Some of her ancestors had even been baptized and married here.

"Do you think the church is open? Can we go look inside?" she asked.

"Let's check." They immediately found access to the church. In the entryway, they picked up a brochure welcoming visitors and describing the work done on this historic church over the years. Caitlin learned the original interior features were removed or damaged during renovations in 1973, and only a few small areas remained from the original construction. From a historian's perspective, she found this disappointing and immediately pointed this misgiving out to Donovan.

"Caitlin, it doesn't change the fact that your ancestors worshipped here," he assured her.

"I suppose." As a public historian, one of Caitlin's pet peeves was the razing of older buildings to make way for newer, more modern ones. Thinking about it had a way of emotionally charging her system, causing her to overreact.

"Besides, for all we know, some of your family may still attend mass here."

"So true. What am I getting myself so worked up about?"

"Let's walk around for a few minutes to look at the church," Donovan suggested.

Caitlin nodded, pulling out her camera to prepare to take photos. The church had an extremely high wooden ceiling supported by massive stone pillars. Beautiful stained-glass windows allowed light to stream into the building. Local people were praying in unison in the chapel where they entered, and a few spoke softly near bulletin boards plastered with information. They spotted several other visitors flowing through the alcoves and side altars.

Caitlin paused briefly at one end of the aisle and focused on the path leading to the altar, thinking of her great-great-grandparents. It certainly would be a lovely place for a wedding, she acknowledged. Caitlin imagined herself slowly walking down the aisle toward a faceless groom. A journey she knew she longed to take one day.

"What a beautiful place for a wedding," were the words from Donovan interrupting her thoughts. It was almost as if he could read her mind. She nodded in response as the faceless groom near the altar suddenly looked a lot like Donovan. She blinked twice to erase the image just as a hand lightly touched her shoulder.

"Are you ready to bike over to the church office building to see if we can access some of the church records? I'm anxious to see what we can find there." Caitlin turned and began to move with Donovan toward the exit, leaving her dreams of the perfect wedding behind her.

At the Diocesan office, they were able to find the marriage record of her Great Uncle Brenden's daughter, Fiona. She'd married Killian Murphy. Their son William had also been baptized at St. Mary's Cathedral. Unfortunately, there wasn't any record of him getting married there or even in the diocese.

"Donovan, I'm so frustrated. Just when we think we're hot on the trail, our lead turns stone cold."

"Caitlin, detectives don't let their emotions get the best of them, even history detectives. Who do we know that lives in or near Killarney?"

Caitlin looked at him with a puzzled expression, "I have no clue. I don't know anyone who lives in Killarney."

"Yes, you do, think hard," he prodded.

"I'm not getting anything. Could you at least give me a clue?" Caitlin asked in frustration.

"Airplane" was his short response.

"Airplane, hmm. Wait, Mrs. Murphy?"

"Yes, Noreen Murphy." For the second time in one day, she punched him in the shoulder, harder than the last time.

"Hey! Stop hitting me! What did I do now?"

"You neglected to tell me Mrs. Murphy lived in Killarney. At least I don't remember you telling me. Do you think she might be related to our William Murphy? I still feel like we're at a dead end. Do you have her address?"

"Slow down, Caitlin!" Donovan laughed. "I don't have her address, but I do have her phone number. I called before we left Dublin to tell her we'd be traveling this way, and it slipped my mind."

"What!? How could something like that just slip your mind?"

"Maybe the company I'm keeping," he playfully suggested. "Noreen's going to meet us at her son John's pub tomorrow evening around six."

Caitlin found it hard to believe Donovan had neglected to inform her of such an important meeting. "Do you think there's a possibility Noreen knows William Murphy?"

"Possibly. Maybe Noreen's husband is even related to you. Wouldn't that be something?"

"It certainly would, but with my luck, I find it highly unlikely. We can only hope."

"Anything is possible, Caitlin."

"I think I'll say a little prayer tonight. I'd have a better chance with that than relying on my luck."

"You do that. Now, let's get back on our bikes. Your castle awaits!"

Ross Castle was a typical example of the stronghold of an Irish Chieftain during the Middle Ages. It sat on the edge of Killarney's lower lake. Fully restored and furnished with period oak furniture, Caitlin found it fascinating. She had a great love for things of the past, and the thought of life here during the 15th-century was intriguing. They were in luck. When they arrived at the castle, the next guided tour for the day was scheduled to start in five minutes and still had room for them.

As their tour began, Caitlin quickly became engrossed in the story being told of Sabina, the Black Baron of Ross Castle's daughter. She wanted to marry her love, who was an O'Neill and archenemy of her father. One night they tried to escape to elope, but while crossing the river, the boat capsized, and her love died. Afterward, Sabina locked herself in the castle tower. She refused to eat or drink and thus perished. With that, the guide went on to tell some elaborate stories about potential castle hauntings.

"Do you think this castle is really haunted, Donovan?" Caitlin asked, eyes full of wonder.

"It's considered one of the most haunted locations in Killarney. I've heard the Black Baron and his daughter are among the spirits still roaming the castle. One never really knows what is folklore or fact here in Ireland. We're a superstitious lot," he quipped.

They purchased beverages and snacks following their tour, then found a quiet bench outside the castle to sit for a while. Ross Castle overlooked Lough Sheelin, one of Ireland's preeminent midland lakes. Today it looked magnificent. The clouds' reflection on the lake's surface had a mesmerizing effect on them. Caitlin captured several beautiful images on her camera.

As they sat, still in a moment of calm, Donovan reminisced back to the kiss he'd shared with Caitlin the night before. It had affected him like no other kiss ever had. Even as much in love as he'd believed himself to be with Marie, something powerful had happened during their brief exchange. But for some reason, he couldn't ignore the text message he'd accidentally read the night before. Could a moment seem so special when Caitlin had another man proposing marriage to her? Maybe that's why he had acted so strangely earlier, trying to build an emotional barrier between them. He did like Caitlin. He just wasn't sure how to process his feelings.

Donovan realized he needed to get to the bottom of things and find out who this Jeremy guy was. "So, we've discussed my love life. I think it's only fair you share a little with me about yours."

"There's nothing to tell," she replied almost too quickly.

"Come now, a beautiful lass like you? You must have a sweetheart back home in America."

"I've gone out on a few dates with someone I work with, but it's nothing serious."

"What's his name?"

"Who?"

"The man you work with?"

"Jonathan, he's the curator at the museum where I work. Honestly, he's no one special."

That didn't match the name of the man who'd proposed to her last night. Donovan was getting tired of beating around the bush. He wanted the truth. He knew Caitlin's text message had come from her aunt's phone. He wasn't going to give up that easily. "So, no one close to your heart?"

"Why do you want to know?" Could he be interested in her after all, she wondered.

"I'm only curious. Didn't you say you've only been on your job for a few months?"

"Yes, I stayed in Boston after attending graduate school and worked as a public historian for a short time in a local museum before moving back home."

"So, why did you fly out of Boston instead of an airport near where you live now? Did you go there to visit with friends?"

"Oh, didn't I tell you my Aunt Mary lives in Boston? I went to visit her before coming here. She had some old family photos and information regarding our ancestors that I wanted to examine before coming to Ireland."

"So, you only visited your aunt? Do you still have friends back in Boston?"

Caitlin, confused by the questioning, asked, "Yes, on both accounts. Why do you want to know?"

"I'm just curious," was his brief response before asking one last question. The one Caitlin had been trying to avoid. "Did you date anyone when you lived in Boston?"

Caitlin wasn't one to lie, so she gave him a brief answer. "Yes, but we broke things off before I left to go back home."

"And his name?"

"Donovan, why all of these questions?" He stubbornly folded his arms and waited for her answer. Caitlin didn't like feeling forced to respond, and with a huff, she reluctantly answered. "His name was Jeremy. We had a pretty serious relationship, but I discovered I'd been wrong about his true intentions, and I've moved on."

Donovan exhaled. The resonance of her voice confirmed the conviction behind her statement, but by the indication of Jeremy's text message, he certainly hadn't left the past behind him. Donovan decided to drop his line of questioning and change the subject. "I didn't mean to upset you in any way. I just wondered..."

"Wondered what? Does this have anything to do with our kissing last night? We seem to keep coming back to this topic. I certainly wouldn't have allowed you to kiss me if I were in a relationship with another man," she defended herself. "I don't think we should make a federal case out of an impulsive act on your part. Besides, haven't we already agreed it isn't something we plan on repeating?"

"I agree, but I appreciate you sharing a little of your story with me. We are friends, aren't we?"

His barrage of questioning hadn't seemed friendly, but she was understanding. She wouldn't let a few moments of discomfort work against the start of what could be a good friendship. "Umm, yes?"

"And as your friend, doesn't it make sense we'd want to learn more about each other to strengthen our relationship?" He knew he was swimming in circles instead of just coming out and admitting what he'd discovered earlier. If he had, he could've gone straight to the point and just asked her about Jeremy. He didn't want to give the impression he was too interested, though.

"I suppose."

"Good. I think we should head back to the hotel now; it's almost five. Let's have a relaxing meal together and then take a walk around the town. It'll help you get a feel for the atmosphere of this charming city."

On the bike ride back to the hotel, Caitlin couldn't help replaying their conversation in her head. What had been the real purpose behind all of Donovan's questions? His emphasis had been on strengthening their friendship, but she couldn't figure out why he wanted to know anything about her relationship with Jeremy. Was he interested in being more than just friends but too afraid to admit it? Oh well, she didn't plan on losing any sleep over it. She had more important things to do, namely looking back over all the information she'd collected thus far that might help them find some of her family. They had limited time on their hands.

When they stopped to drop their bikes off, she mustered the courage to make a request even if it meant spending more time together. "Hey, later this evening, do you think you'd mind helping me go over the information I've already collected before we continue our search tomorrow? A second pair of eyes might catch some detail I've missed."

"Sure, what are friends for?" came his brief response. In Caitlin's mind, she was curious to see what kind of friend he would be and if the first kiss they'd shared indeed had been their last.

# Chapter 13

Disappointment had set in. After working with Donovan to review the data stored on her laptop. Caitlin still hadn't made any further progress. She had some birth, marriage, and death records compiled in her family tree database, but moving forward in time was the challenge. They had William Murphy's birth date but no evidence of his death.

Brenden's other children were daughters who'd been married at the Cathedral but then moved elsewhere before having any children baptized there. Another dead end. They'd learned that most of the local Roman Catholic parishes didn't permit research on their original records at the Diocesan Offices. Usually, they referred people to heritage centers.

"So, the two questions I have at this point are... Did William continue to live in Killarney into adulthood, and did he eventually marry and have children? We know he was born on April 8, 1939, so he's in his early 80s if he's still alive," Caitlin explained.

"Maybe he got married at another church and remained in the area," was Donovan's response.

"Sure, but maybe the sad reality is he's already dead, and we are at an impasse."

Donovan tried to cheer Caitlin up. "There's still a chance Noreen Murphy and her husband know something about your relatives. I think Noreen's in her 70s."

Donovan returned to his room, leaving Caitlin to think about her next steps. With no additional vacation time to lengthen her stay, she had limited time to find her family. She sat and contemplated her dilemma. What were the chances that Noreen would be able to help them?

Caitlin bowed her head and prayed a simple prayer of surrender. She wasn't ready to give up. Could Noreen be the key? Did marriage connect her to one of Caitlin's relatives? She had so many questions.

The next morning, they were standing outside the hotel when a driver and his large brown and white draught horse arrived, pulling a four-wheeled blue cart with wooden panels and seats behind it. Caitlin noticed it had a covered roof with transparent plastics rolled up, which could be dropped down in case of rain. Very appropriate for the climate in the area.

Donovan waved at the driver as he came to a stop in front of them. Immediately hopping out of the cart, the driver went around to the back to open the gate. It would allow them to step up into the cart from the street.

"Good morning to you," the man greeted as he tipped his hat. "Are you Donovan O'Malley?"

Donovan stretched out his hand for a welcoming handshake. "Yes, and this is Caitlin Sullivan."

The spry white-haired man gently shook her hand, then introduced himself. "I'm Paddy, and I'll be your jarvey today. That's what the driver of a jaunting cart is called. I brought Charlie with me to help us on our journey. He's a very gentle horse who especially likes it when we have company riding with us."

Caitlin couldn't resist walking up to Charlie and gently stroking his neck and front left shoulder. "What a handsome horse."

"Why, thank you, lass. He was foaled, raised, and trained by myself."

She was amazed at his size. "He's rather large. What breed of horse is he?"

"He's an Irish draft horse. Kind of like a mini-Clydesdale, a Bud Light," he joked.

"Good one, Paddy," Donovan appreciated someone with a good sense of humor. "Caitlin, they're the national horse of Ireland, developed primarily for farm use."

"They seem like mighty powerful animals."

Paddy added, "These horses work very well with a harness and saddle. Are you ready to see what Charlie can do?" Caitlin nodded at him, and he winked back. "Now Donovan, I understand you'd like to make your way down to see Muckross House while seeing some of Killarney National Park at the same time?"

"Yes, and if time allows, I'd like you to swing by Torc Waterfall. Would that be possible? We need to be back to the hotel no later than 5 o'clock."

"Yes, it isn't far from Muckross. I'd be glad to take you there."

"Great! Let's go, Cait." She gently patted Charlie one last time before moving to the back. Donovan helped her on board. Two benches sat facing each other. She sat on one, and when Donovan stepped up into the cart, he slightly hesitated before sitting on the opposite side.

Paddy shut the gate on the back. "I see you know the rules we follow around here when a couple is courting. No sitting next to each other because absolutely no touching is allowed."

Donovan noticed Caitlin immediately became uncomfortable by the comment. "We aren't courting, we…" she stuttered.

"We're just good friends sightseeing together," Donovan finished for her. "Paddy, Caitlin has come here all the way from America to find family living in Killarney. Her great-great-grandparents lived here long ago."

"Ah. So, lass, do you have a husband back home in America?"

"No," responded Caitlin.

"A sweetheart?"

"No, she doesn't," Donovan responded abruptly, even though he doubted his answer.

"And what about you, Donovan?"

"No, no wife or sweetheart of any kind."

"So, what you're telling me is neither of you are married or have sweethearts." They both nodded in response.

"Well then, maybe this ride will take you places you never thought you'd go." Paddy quickly moved toward the front of the jaunting cart with a twinkle in his eye. Stepping up onto the bench, he picked up the reigns, then slowly moved into the traffic on the left side of the road.

Despite the gray skies, Caitlin's disposition was a sunny one. She felt relaxed and happy to be here. A slight breeze was blowing, but the covering above their heads gave them confidence they'd stay dry if it rained. To ward off a chill, Paddy had given them each a blanket to place on their laps.

For the first part of the ride, Paddy seemed to concentrate on the road ahead. They shared it with numerous motorized vehicles, and he had to pay close attention to the flow of traffic. Charlie moved at a steady clip down the street.

When they slowed down for a stop sign, Caitlin asked, "Paddy, how long a workday does Charlie have? He's a strong animal, but it must be quite a big job to pull a loaded jaunting cart."

"Horses like Charlie can pull about 8,000 pounds alone, and by the look of our load today, you don't even come close to that. We take good care of our horses and don't work them too hard." Charlie started to move again, and Paddy began to point out some of the sights along the way. "On the right, you can see the McGillycuddy Range. It's about 12 miles long and Ireland's highest mountain range. It includes most of the highest and sharpest ridges in Ireland and is nearly 3,400 feet high." Whenever Paddy was taking Americans around, he avoided giving details in metric measurements. It was like Greek to them.

"I wonder if the naming of the mountain range has anything to do with my great-great grandmother's family, her maiden name was McGillycuddy," Caitlin wondered loud enough for Paddy to hear.

"Why then, your family must have come from this area," was his reaction.

"Yes, most definitely."

Today the tops of the mountains were hidden by a mass of low hanging gray clouds. Caitlin appreciated the beautiful view as Charlie trotted quickly down the road. Cars passed on the right every so often, speeding up and slowing down depending on the traffic.

"To your right, you can see Cahername House Hotel," Paddy turned toward it, then immediately to the left onto a paved pathway parallel to the highway. "It's an upscale seasonal hotel which originally started as a grand 1870s mansion. Now folks, the rest of our trip today will be on a non-motorized pathway, so hold on to your bladders," Paddy warned. They slowed down as they moved onto a narrower path. Young oak trees stood on the pathway's left side and to the right, a stonewall and grassy fields.

"Those all-black cows in the field are Kerry cows." Paddy pointed out.

Donovan, quite knowledgeable regarding large farm animals, went on to explain more. "Caitlin, the Kerry Cattle are a rare breed of dairy cows native to Ireland, and they are one of the oldest breeds in Europe. There aren't many left in the world, a few herds in Ireland and the UK, even some in North America. Gratefully, American breeders often collaborate with Irish owners to help protect the breed."

"So, in a way, they're similar to the Red and White Setters you breed? They're also a vulnerable breed people are trying to save," Caitlin acknowledged.

"You're correct and quite smart, my friend!" They silently exchanged a knowing look as Donovan realized she seemed to have begun to appreciate the reason behind a need to breed animals to preserve their existence.

Paddy seemed impressed by the knowledge his passenger had. "You know a lot about animals, Donovan. Why is that?"

"I'm a vet in County Kildare. I specialize in the care of horses and other large farm animals."

"Ah, so you're an animal expert." Just then, the cart took a little veer to the right into a more wooded area. The path narrowed, and they rode between trees of various sizes.

"Killarney National Park contains 25,000 acres of preserves. It's home to many kinds of wildlife, and the last surviving indigenous herd of red deer in Ireland lives in Killarney Valley." Caitlin got excited. She loved animals and hoped they'd see some of these large deer.

A few minutes later, they rode into a clearing. To the right of the path, they could see a lake. "What lake is that?" Caitlin asked.

"Lough Leane, the largest of the three lakes of Killarney," Paddy began to explain. "It's five miles long, three miles wide, and full of trout and salmon."

"It's so beautiful around here. Oh, look at the lovely lavender blossoms." Caitlin pointed to some flower-covered trees nearby.

"Those are evergreen rhododendrons, first introduced to the Valley in 1865. They usually bloom from April to July in this area. They grow like weeds in the park and are a highly invasive and destructive plant. They may seem pretty to you, but they threaten the areas of oak wood in the park."

"It's sad something so beautiful can cause problems for other plant life."

Paddy quickly changed the subject. "Look, you can see The Lake Hotel there on the other side of Lough Leane. It's a perfect place for a honeymoon," Paddy hinted. "You can honeymoon and fish out your window for salmon and trout at the same time."

"That would be some honeymoon! I love to fish," informed Donovan.

"You're lucky I'm not sitting next to you right now, Donovan."

Gripping his left shoulder, he chuckled as he read her mind. "I've already got bruises on my arm from you. Control yourself, Miss Sullivan."

She glared at him, making it more challenging for him to keep from busting a gut. In the end, it was Caitlin who couldn't help snickering. "I'm a little disappointed. I honestly believed any honeymoon you would plan would be more on the romantic side."

"Ah, so you find me charming, then, do you?"

"Sometimes," she admitted before spotting a large structure. "What's that building up ahead on the left?"

Paddy, who'd been listening to their banter earlier, realized she was talking to him now. "That's Muckross Abbey. What you see ahead are the ruins of a Franciscan friary founded in the 15th century. The buildings have held up fairly well over time, with the Cloister walls and its associated buildings still in their original and complete state."

"Are you sure we can't stop just for a few minutes?" she pleaded.

Donovan was quick to interrupt, "The next time you're in Killarney, you can stop and get a better look at it. If we're going to stop at Muckross House and Torc Falls, we need to keep moving. We have plans to meet Noreen for dinner tonight around 6 o'clock, and we'll need a little time to freshen up and change before we head out for the evening."

She conceded to her one real enemy—time—by responding, "I know, I do hope to come back another time."

As they continued on the path toward Muckross House, there was silence once again. The time in Killarney seemed to be passing by so quickly, and Caitlin hated the idea of leaving for home in less than three days. She glanced at Donovan momentarily, saddened because she knew it would be difficult to say good-bye to this man at the end of the week.

"Here we are at Muckross House and Gardens, one of our most popular tourist spots," Paddy announced.

"How enchanting!" exclaimed Caitlin as she surveyed the enormous mansion and its surrounding meticulously landscaped grounds.

"It's a magnificent Victorian mansion, one of Ireland's leading stately homes. Elegantly furnished, the rooms portray the lifestyles of the gentry. At the same time, downstairs in the basement, you can experience the working conditions of the servants employed in the house in the past."

"My kind of historical adventure. I love museums that allow me to step into the past by bringing history to life."

Paddy called back to them. "I'll find a good spot to pull over so you can get off. Let's plan on meeting back here again when you're finished. Charlie and I will take a nice rest until you're ready to head on to Torc Waterfall."

They picked up a map of the grounds from a nearby kiosk. Browsing through the pamphlet, Caitlin pointed to a bolded paragraph, "It says here the Muckross Farms aren't open during the weekdays until May. That's disappointing. We won't be able to see that part of the estates."

"But..."

"I know, I can always come another time of year when they are. I think you're just determined to get me back to Ireland sometime in the future."

"Maybe," he subtly agreed. He guided Caitlin up the steps toward the main entrance. A few minutes later, they were ready to tour.

"I'd love to see the house first, then have a little lunch before visiting the gardens," suggested Caitlin.

"Your wish is my command," he pleasantly responded.

Caitlin wondered how familiar Donovan was with the area. They hadn't discussed it previously. "Have you ever visited here in the past?"

"I've stayed in this area before, but never as a tourist." As they walked into Muckross House, they noticed a tour had just started, so Caitlin quickly paid for their admission. Donovan knew better than to argue with her. She'd been adamant earlier about the cost of this trip. He'd already taken time off from work to drive her to Killarney and paid for his hotel room. She insisted on paying for any of their expenses today.

They could hear the tour guide nearby begin speaking. "Hurry, Caitlin, they're starting," prodded Donovan as she put her credit card back into her purse.

"Muckross House is a 65-room Tudor-style mansion designed by Scottish architect William Burn," began the guide. "In 1843, it was built for Parliament member Henry Arthur Herbert and his wife, the painter Mary Balfour Herbert. The Irish government now owns it. You'll be amazed because this 19th-century mansion contains all original pieces of furniture, artwork, trophies, and many other furnishings from that period."

Caitlin and Donovan had joined the group by the time the tour guide had finished sharing this initial history of the house. They enjoyed the 45-minute walking tour. Smiling and nodding at each other now and then throughout the presentation. Even though they didn't speak of it, they both knew they were enjoying their time together. Neither understood the force behind their feelings—they just felt at peace in each other's presence.

When the tour ended, they made their way to the conservatory area of the Garden Restaurant. They could see Killarney National Park's scenic surroundings from their table through the sizable expansive windowpanes. The Torc and Mangerton Mountains stood tall in the background as they enjoyed a light lunch of soup and sandwiches.

Caitlin wished they had time to enjoy all that the eye could see. "Wouldn't this be a beautiful area to take a long horseback ride?"

"Oh, it would, wouldn't it? But Caitlin, we don't have much time to play the part of tourists."

"I know, but I can dream, can't I?"

"Personally, I believe I'd much rather take the time to get to know you better before you have to leave."

"Why?"

"Just curious, I guess. I haven't felt this relaxed in a long time. Just watching you explore the country I love dearly puts a smile on my face. And you make me laugh. Something I haven't done for quite some time," Donovan admitted.

Seeing she had finished eating, he suggested they head to the gift shop before exploring the gardens. The minute they walked in, Caitlin immediately went into overdrive. She strolled over toward a display of colorful scarves and began to rifle through them until she had found a few she liked. Her second stop was the hat display. She tried on a green Irish Newsboy cap and turned to model it for Donovan.

"Great choice, Cait. It compliments your amazing hair color."

She immediately turned back toward the hats as her face turned about the same shade of red. Her hunt continued until she found a cap and scarf for her dad and a beautiful blue plaid Mary Hat for Abbey. All fit nicely in the shopping basket she carried.

When she turned back to check on Donovan, she found him eyeing some beautiful Irish sweaters. "What do you think?" he asked as he held one up in front of him.

"It's a beautiful cable knit pattern. I think you'd look rather handsome in it."

"It is a lovely pattern, but I'm rather partial to the O'Malley clan pattern. I think I'd rather place an order for a sweater today and have it sent to me," he replied. Caitlin wondered if there were any in the pile of sweaters with the O'Sullivan clan pattern. She wasn't interested in buying one today, but she would undoubtedly order one down the road.

They browsed around a little longer until Caitlin found the perfect wedding gift for her sister—handmade dishware she decided to order and have shipped. She hesitated for a moment, wondering if it would arrive back in the states in time for the wedding.

Donovan noticed her hesitation. "What's the problem?"

"I'd love to order this as my sister's wedding gift, but I'm worried it won't make it in time."

"When is it?"

"The second weekend in June."

"It should be fine. Just let the clerk know, and they may be able to rush the order."

"Thanks for the suggestion," she acknowledged before heading over to the counter. With purchases in hand, they spent half an hour leisurely walking through the estate's gardens before meeting back up with Paddy.

"Well, I see you spent some of your time in the gift shop. It seems to be a popular tourist trap," he declared. "I hope you had good luck finding something special."

Caitlin pulled out her new hat and placed it on her head. "Good choice, lass. I don't think you could've made a better choice for yourself!"

She batted her eyes at him and said in response, "Don't make me blush, Paddy. Now let's get moving. I'd like to see this waterfall in the daylight."

Paddy hastily made his way around to the back of the cart to help her up. Then Donovan handed Caitlin a few packages to place on the cart floor before he hopped in. She sat down and immediately started rubbing her arms as if she were cold. Donovan, noticing his opening, quickly sat on the bench next to her. Caitlin leaned against him without hesitation as he covered their laps with one of the blankets before putting his arm around her for additional warmth.

"We're ready to go, Paddy."

Paddy looked back at them to make sure they were securely seated. "Wait a minute; you're breaking the rules," he dramatically grumbled.

"But, Paddy, we're not courting, so the rules don't apply to us. We're just trying to keep warm. There seems to be a slight chill in the air," Donovan defended himself.

"That's right, Paddy, we're just feeling a little cold back here," agreed Caitlin.

"Well, just this once then," he answered back, before expertly guiding Charlie slowly back onto the pathway toward their next stopping point.

As Paddy pulled out of the parking area, Donovan leaned over and whispered in Caitlin's ear, "I think your hat suits you, too, Miss Sullivan," causing a wave of heat to spread throughout her entire body.

They continued to enjoy their scenic ride as Paddy shared more of his local knowledge. Caitlin, the forever note-taker, almost wished she'd been writing this all down to share back at home with her family. Now she was content to enjoy the view along the way with Donovan's arm draped around her instead.

At the next stop on their journey, Paddy pointed in the direction they'd need to take to get to the waterfall. "Just follow the gravel path, and you'll come to the base of Torc Waterfall. It's a bit of a climb up a stone stairway to the top for a view; the falls stand about 20 meters high." Caitlin had a puzzled look on her face. For most of the trip, Paddy used standard measurement when speaking to them, not metrics.

Donovan lifted Caitlin out of the cart, and as he lowered her to the ground, he whispered, "It's about 70 feet high to you Americans." She rewarded him with an elbow to his ribs. He overreacted by grabbing his side to fake an injury, even though he'd hardly felt a thing.

Caitlin looked directly at Donovan. Then, placing her hands on her hips, she declared, "That joke is getting old, Donovan." His first response was to laugh, but then he had a better idea. He picked her up and swung her around, cutting off any further explanation Paddy planned on making.

"Put me down, Donovan!" she demanded, trying not to laugh. He lowered her gently to the ground before suddenly turning to stride off down the path in front of them.

"Wait for me! I'm coming."

Donovan stopped and turned toward her, extending his hand. She took it, then quietly walked with him the short distance down the path to the foot of Torc Falls. It wasn't the largest waterfall, but the view was such a picturesque scene, so picture-perfect Caitlin felt an impulse to reach for her camera. Sadly, she'd forgotten it back in the cart. She used her phone instead to take several photos, including a snapshot of the two of them.

"Just follow the rocky path to the left of the waterfall. I'm right behind you. We'll be able to get a better view of the park and all the lakes from above."

Donovan had her take the lead up the stone path to the top of the waterfall just in case she lost her footing. Sure enough, about halfway up, she slipped off one of the stones and stumbled backward. Of course, Donovan had been prepared and caught her. He held on to her almost too long because she felt she needed to say, "I'm all right, Donovan. You can let go of me now."

The steps lead to another viewing point at a higher altitude providing a view over the Middle Lake. It had been worth the journey. Unfortunately, it was getting late, so they didn't linger. Quickly they returned to where Paddy and Charlie were waiting for them.

As the cart began to head back to Killarney, Paddy started to entertain them with a story. Caitlin didn't hear a word as her mind began to drift. She thought back to several of the conversations she and Donovan had shared earlier. He'd complimented her and suggested he'd like to get to know her better. Did Donovan believe her when she said she was single? Might he be interested in a long-distance relationship? She knew it would be futile to attempt it for all practical reasons, but her heart refused to listen to her head. She looked over at Donovan as he laughed at something Paddy had said. She sighed. In her mind, he was the total package. She would be foolish to resist.

# Chapter 14

Back at the hotel, Caitlin hurried to change for their dinner date with the Murphys. She eagerly anticipated the reunion with Noreen that could potentially reveal the missing piece to her puzzle. It's funny how life sometimes brings you full circle.

It was a short drive from their hotel, and they arrived at the pub just a little before the agreed meeting time. Upon entering, Caitlin appreciated the casual and friendly atmosphere. She could hear the chatter of conversation and light laughter coming from every direction. Caitlin felt assured that all the patrons would be leaving with full bellies and lifted spirits when she spied the large portions of food heaped on their plates and drinks at every table. In the background, she could hear traditional Irish music softly playing while several TV monitors hanging around the room displayed the latest sporting events. It looked to be a home away from home.

Donovan immediately asked to speak to the owner, and in less than a minute, a sandy-haired man with a ruddy face and scruffy beard ambled toward them wearing a huge smile. As he approached them, he stretched out his hand toward Donovan, his Irish accent thick in the air. "Good evening, I'm John Murphy, the owner of this lovely pub."

"Nice to meet you! I'm Donovan O'Malley, and this is Caitlin Sullivan."

"Donovan! So great to finally meet you. My mom hasn't stopped talking about you since she left the hospital."

Caitlin stepped forward to extend her hand in greeting as well, "Happy to meet you, John. Your mom is such a sweet lady, and I'm so glad she's doing better. We're anxious to see her again and to meet your dad. We're hoping they can help us solve a family mystery of mine."

"Sounds intriguing. Follow me, and I'll take you to them."

They fell in line behind John, passing a crowded table where an animated older gentleman entertained with what seemed to be a lively story. Just beyond his gesticulating hands, Caitlin caught a glimpse of Noreen waving at them. The last time Caitlin had seen Noreen, she'd been so pale, but today she had a natural color to her face and jumped in delight at seeing them both.

John spoke first, "Mom, here are your guests. I'll try to take a break and join you a little later in the evening when things quiet down. It looks like we're going to be busy tonight."

"No problem join us if you can," she encouraged.

As John walked away, Noreen spoke up, "Why it's so lovely to see you again."

"And you, Noreen," Donovan leaned down to greet her with a quick peck on her cheek.

"Ah, my knight in shining armor. I can't believe you two were able to manage a trip here to see us so quickly."

Caitlin stepped forward and gave Noreen a big hug. "You look wonderful! I'm so glad you're feeling better. I've been worried about you ever since I watched them cart you off the plane on that uncomfortable looking gurney."

"Yes, the good news is my symptoms were not heart related, which is why I panicked that day on the plane. I thought I was having a heart attack. But all is well! My doctor gave me some medication and some good old-fashioned advice on the best way to deal with my stress. Now here I am, feeling fit as a fiddle."

"I'm so glad. Now, where is your husband? I'm anxious to meet him."

Noreen turned her head to the right and then to the left before beckoning to someone across the room. A short, relatively thin man with a balding head slowly moved across the room. He looked quite fragile, but he had a lively glimmer in his eyes that spoke of mischief.

"Darling, come here. I'd like you to meet Caitlin, the lass from America who sat by me on the plane." He reached toward her and shook her hand. "And this is Donovan, the vet who took such good care of me in my time of need. If it weren't for him, I would have lost my wits."

"You're too kind, Noreen." He held out his hand to her husband, "A pleasure to meet you, Mr. Murphy."

"Call me William, all my friends do. I think you're my new best friend, Donovan. I appreciate you helping to take such good care of my Noreen."

Caitlin stood and stared at him, searching his face looking for hints of familiar family features. She wondered if this was her dad's second cousin. He seemed to be about the right age.

Caitlin tried to remain calm, restraining herself from blurting out the main reason for their visit. But she couldn't help herself. "Oh, I can't wait any longer, Mr. Murphy! We're in Killarney to solve a mystery."

"Oh, a mystery, you say. Do tell, my dear!" He leaned in toward her for her revelation.

Caitlin took a deep breath and began, "Noreen, do you remember when we were on the plane, and I told you I came to Ireland to track down some of my family?"

"Yes, dear. Have you had any success?" Noreen asked calmly.

"Yes and no," the words sputtered out of her.

Donovan, realizing Caitlin felt a little overwhelmed by the situation, decided to give her a hand with the explanation. He hadn't quite got the hang of the relationships on family trees—they had a way of getting complicated—but he owed this to Caitlin after venturing with her this far.

"Let me help explain what we've learned," he offered, looking directly at Noreen. "After Caitlin finished her research in Dublin, we learned the name of her dad's second cousin. We discovered his baptism had taken place at St. Mary's Cathedral, and that's what led us here to Killarney. After discovering that key fact, the trail went cold. The funny thing though—which is what brought us to you—is he has the same name as your husband, William Murphy."

"I was baptized at St. Mary's Cathedral. Do you think it's a coincidence?"

"Let me tell you the rest of my family story," Caitlin continued. "My grandfather traveled to America with his parents in 1927. He was only seven at the time. His family had decided to leave Ireland in search of a better life. My great-grandfather's name was William O'Sullivan. He had two older brothers, Ryan, who died at the age of 14, and Brenden, seven years older than him."

"Your grandfather's name was William O'Sullivan?"

"Yes."

William placed his elbows on the table and leaned forward. "It's unbelievable. My grandfather's name was Brenden O'Sullivan."

Caitlin was stunned. Had she found one of her Irish relatives?

William continued, unphased by Caitlin's increasingly animated expression. "My mom's name was Fiona O'Sullivan, and she had a sister named Anna and a brother named Declan. My dad's name was Killian Murphy."

"That's amazing! That matches the information I found perfectly. The only family I had success tracing in this area was yours. I found out Anna married Jack Cahill, but it doesn't look like they stayed in Killarney. Declan O'Sullivan wasn't married at St. Mary's Cathedral like his sister. The only other record I could find was your baptismal record. That's when I came to a dead end."

William and Noreen listened carefully, trying to let the information sink in to make their own connections. Before they could get any further, one of the servers stopped at the table to take their drink and food orders. Immediately after, William began to fill in the blanks.

"Caitlin, while Anna and my mother were married at the Cathedral, Declan had married at his wife's parish in County Cork where they lived and raised their children. We saw them occasionally, but I have to admit I lost track of my cousins over the years."

Caitlin pulled out a pad of paper to take a few notes as William detailed names and ages. "So, it's your side of the family that I tried following. Did you have any other brothers or sisters?"

"Yes, my parents had three boys and three girls. We were a lively bunch, us Murphys."

Donovan finally spoke up for the first time since they had started their in-depth conversation, "And are any of your siblings still alive?"

"My two older brothers are gone as well as my youngest sister. We buried them in the Old Kilcummin Cemetery northeast of Killarney along with most of the other Murphys and O'Sullivans from here."

Caitlin felt frustrated but oddly vindicated at how close she'd come. If she'd only spent more time searching local cemetery records, she would've found just the information she'd needed.

"My two other sisters, Colleen and Molly, still live in the area."

"What about your children? We've met John, but does he have any siblings?"

"Yes, William and I were lucky enough to have three children. John is our youngest. He has two older sisters, Cathleen, and Ilona. We also have nine grandchildren and six great-grandchildren."

"Oh, this is fantastic!" cried Caitlin.

"Cait, and I have to head back to Dublin sometime tomorrow, but is there any way we could meet with some of your family before we leave town?"

William and Noreen conferred for a moment before agreeing. They believed they could arrange a family gathering with just a few phone calls. Their son John had been busy most of the evening, but he did stop by briefly and promised to bring his wife Erin over to his parent's home the next day.

"Now, as soon as we get home, I'm going to try to call my children to let them know you'll be at our house tomorrow for lunch. They'll be so excited."

"Cait, it's getting late. We'd better head back to our hotel to get some much-needed sleep," Donovan suggested. "Tomorrow will be another busy day." She nodded in agreement, and a few good-byes later, they were on their way.

Before entering their separate hotel rooms for the night, they stopped just outside Caitlin's room. She turned, and with her back to the door, she found the courage to share what was on her heart.

151

"Donovan, thank you for everything you've done for me these past few days. Your patient assistance throughout this process has meant so much to me."

He watched her lips intently as she spoke, mesmerized by their movement. "It's been my pleasure. Who would've ever imagined how our lives would intertwine the day we boarded the airplane in Boston?"

"It's amazing, that's for sure. I've never had much luck before in any part of my life," she admitted aloud. "Having you with me on this adventure has made this trip more enjoyable than I could ever have imagined. I can never begin to repay you."

He took a step closer to her. "Cait, you don't owe me anything. I wouldn't have missed this experience for anything in the world. Besides, when you are the boss, you should be able to give yourself a vacation now and then."

"I suppose that's true."

"There is one thing I'd like to ask of you," he began, placing his hands on her shoulders.

"What's that?" she asked, looking up into Donovan's eyes. He leaned in closer, causing her to become weak in the knees, the door becoming her support system.

"Don't ever forget the wonderful time we've had together this week. I know I won't." He paused for a moment, looking for a sign her feelings had moved beyond that of just friendship.

Caitlin seemed to relax just before Donovan's face moved in slow motion toward her. Like a dream, his face blurred, then disappeared, as she closed her eyes to the feeling of his hot mouth pressing against hers. Caitlin couldn't resist wrapping her arms around his neck to draw him nearer, unwilling to put out the fire. In the end, it was Donovan who released himself from the hold she had on him. He slowly stepped back, taking a deep breath in the process. Caitlin opened her eyes slowly, standing dazed and speechless, her senses reeling.

Donovan found he still held both of her hands in his. He suddenly released them and straightened up, trying to get his emotions in check. Unsure of what to say, he merely uttered, "Well...Good night, Cait. I'll meet you in the morning for breakfast at around 8 o'clock."

Still confused by the feel of his kiss still lingering on her lips and her unexpected reaction to it, she managed to ask, "What time tomorrow do we need to leave for Dublin?"

"By 4 o'clock at the latest. Now try to get a good night's sleep." Donovan leaned in once more, causing Caitlin's heart to race in anticipation, but this time he gave her a brief kiss on the forehead before adding, "and pleasant dreams."

"You, too," Caitlin blurted out as she quickly turned and attempted to unlock the door with her key card, fumbling at her first attempt. The second did the trick, and once inside, she shut the door firmly behind her.

Caitlin could still feel the memory of Donovan's lips imprinted on her own. Touching her fingers to her mouth, she wondered how their feelings had so rapidly gone beyond the boundaries of friendship? Oh, how she longed for more of the passion. It was a tempting feeling, and like any fire, it could quickly get out of control. Perhaps she owed Donovan her thanks for pulling back. Someone had to be rational about their situation. She would be getting back on a plane for home early Sunday morning. Any more kisses like tonight's, and she would find leaving a struggle.

For Donovan, being rational was the furthest thing from his mind. Their kiss had only whetted his appetite for more, and it had taken all he had to restrain himself from taking advantage of the situation and the receptive emotions he felt flowing through Caitlin. It would have been easy to lose sight of the bigger picture and take their relationship past the point of no return, but he knew he needed to keep focused on the purpose of their trip. Soon Caitlin would be heading home and out of his life. At this point, he didn't know what to do to make their situation any easier other than treading carefully.

Before going to bed, they both made quick phone calls home to check in with family members. Caitlin called her dad and filled him in on the past few days in Killarney and details about the next day's visit with the Murphys. She promised she'd take photos of all of their relatives and jot down some key facts about their Irish family members. Her dad told her they needed to plan a trip together to Ireland soon.

Donovan chose to talk briefly to his sister. After listening to the progress of their trip, Meghan couldn't help but question him,

"So, you're coming home tomorrow? What are your plans for the weekend? Are you going to stay in town until Caitlin leaves?"

"Oh, Sis, are you up to your matchmaking again?"

"No," she hesitated as she tried to find the best way to word what she wanted to say, "but it sure would be nice to have an excuse to keep you in town with the family one more weekend. Once Caitlin leaves, you'll go back to your daily routine, and we won't get to see you for a long time. You always have excuses for not hanging out with the family," she complained.

Even when he knew it would be wiser to head back home, Meghan succeeded in making him feel guilty. "I'll check in with the clinic tomorrow morning. If things look quiet for the weekend, I'll stay in town."

Meghan, humored by his last statement, realized Donovan complained too often about her matchmaking. She knew he was trying to hide his feelings for Caitlin. She could hear it in his voice. With a sigh of relief, she responded, "Wonderful!"

He hoped he wouldn't regret volunteering to stay in town. "Don't push your luck. Let's see how things go. I will admit one thing, being with Caitlin this week has stirred up feelings in me I haven't felt since Marie passed away."

"So, you do like Caitlin?"

Immediately he regretted his honesty with his younger sister. "Meghan don't go there. Caitlin will be leaving on Sunday, and we may never see her again. Now I must get some rest before morning comes, or I'll fall asleep on the drive home, and you wouldn't want that."

"No, dear brother, I wouldn't," she admitted. "Now, off to bed. And remember, where love is concerned, anything is possible. I love you, big brother."

"I love you, too, Meghan." They ended the call, and Donovan couldn't help deliberating over his conflicting feelings for Caitlin, so much so it was several hours before he finally fell asleep.

# Chapter 15

Anticipation filled the air Friday morning in Killarney as William and Noreen planned their big family gathering. Noreen had been able to contact all of their children by phone. John and Cathleen planned to come over for lunch with their spouses. And several of their grandchildren had decided to pop in for a short visit.

Caitlin couldn't wait to meet them. It had been a blast the night before at John's pub. What a tremendous experience, meeting some of her Irish relatives. She still had trouble believing God had placed Noreen in the seat next to her on the plane and Donovan as her back up, ensuring her mission's success. She didn't believe in coincidences. By the grace of God, she had found William.

She mostly felt grateful she'd come to Ireland now and not a year or two down the road, as William was already in his early 80s. The timing meant everything. Caitlin was looking forward to continuing to bond with him and this long-lost side of her family.

Caitlin tried to focus on the experience that lay ahead and not be distracted by the man seated next to her as they neared their destination. She needed to keep her eyes on the prize. The minute their paths had crossed that morning, Caitlin had been trying to avoid thinking of last night's exchange. Donovan O'Malley might tempt her with his stunning blue eyes, beguiling accent, and casually messed up looking hairstyle. Still, she could no longer afford to dream about things she knew deep in her heart were bound to turn out disastrously for her in the end. The realization was causing her to feel a little testy.

"Are you sure they don't mind us arriving a couple of hours before lunch?" asked Caitlin as they made their way toward the Murphy's home.

"Relax, Noreen assured me last night it wouldn't be a problem. We can do some additional visiting before the rest of the family arrives. I talked to her again this morning, right after breakfast."

"I'm sorry, Donovan. I'm feeling rather irritable this morning. I didn't sleep well." He reached over and took her right hand in his, giving it a light squeeze. She looked at him, but he kept his eyes on the road.

"Don't worry. I'll survive. I understand how you're feeling. Is your stomach all tied up in knots?" Donovan asked, releasing her hand before returning it to the steering wheel as they rounded a bend in the road.

"How did you know?" she wondered aloud.

He smiled knowingly, "I've learned a thing or two about you in the past few days, Cait. You like to have control over things, and you don't like surprises." He couldn't help pestering her a little further, "Come on, I know you like to plan everything down to the minute detail. Admit it, letting me take control of our time in Killarney has been a challenge for you, hasn't it?"

She pouted, "Yes, but it isn't really about having control. I just get a little anxious when I'm anticipating something. Going to new places, meeting new people, and waiting for time to pass are all things that make me a little uneasy. If I ever get married, I won't be the bride patiently waiting to see the groom and our guests for the first time when I walk down the aisle. I'll be in full view in my bridal gown, greeting them as they come walking through the door of the church. I won't miss one minute of the celebration waiting in a back room alone. That's the only way I'll prevent having a major meltdown."

The fact the reference point of her explanation was a potential future wedding highly amused Donovan. Did it have anything to do with their visiting St. Mary's and last night's heated kiss? He knew he couldn't get it off his mind. When he glanced in her direction, he could see by the arms folded across her chest and the stare ahead that she was bound and determined to put up a few walls of defense against her true feelings and what was really behind her current moodiness.

Donovan envisioned her description, right down to Caitlin in a beautiful white lace wedding gown as she greeted his family members. Finally snapping out of it, he realized he had neglected to respond and blurted out, "I think that's more information than I needed, but good luck convincing your future groom about those plans." True to her nature, Caitlin punched Donovan in the arm. This time he couldn't hold back the laughter.

"Stop! It's not funny!" she whined, slugging him once again.

Caitlin and Donovan continued the last mile in silence. Their journey had taken them to the edge of town, where they pulled up in front of a charming two-story Irish cottage with a white stucco exterior—the gravel driveway wrapped around the front of the house in an arch. Smaller trees on the grassy lawn lay between it and the road. To the right of the house stood a stone wall with a gate leading into the backyard. Positioned in front of the wall were a variety of colorful flowering shrubs.

Drawn to a large oak tree in the front yard, Caitlin envisioned the Murphy family members sitting together at the picnic table positioned under it, eating and conversing. She imagined what the tree would be like when its new leaves had grown larger to provide a beautiful, shaded summer escape.

A wooded area made up of a few flowering shrubs, and several large trees lay to the left of the house, completing the lovely setting. It gave her a homey feeling.

As if on cue, Noreen appeared at the front door the minute they'd parked, greeting them as they hustled across the gravel. They followed her inside to a lovely sitting room where William sat patiently, staring at photo-filled boxes stacked on the coffee table in front of him.

"Hello, William! What have you got there?" Caitlin greeted.

He splayed his hands out in front of him, a grin exploding across his face. "Just a few photos I thought might jog my memory and help me tell some of my family's stories."

"Only a few?" Donovan jokingly challenged.

"Well, maybe more than a few, but when you get to be my age, you need all the help you can get just to remember where the toilet is." Caitlin and Donovan were humored by his answer.

"You're something else, my dear," chuckled Noreen. "Now Caitlin, let's see what we can find for you to take home for your dad's enjoyment. Some of the photos include dates and names scribbled on the back."

"Which is only helpful if you can read the scribble," William added.

"While you're telling the stories I've heard a hundred times already, I'm going to go into the kitchen and finish preparing lunch," Noreen announced.

"How many family members are you expecting, Noreen?" asked Donovan.

"About ten beside us. I hope Caitlin won't get overwhelmed meeting so many new family members all at one time."

"That's amazing! You just called them last night, and they were all willing to come over today?" Caitlin exclaimed.

"Yes," continued Noreen, "much of our family lives nearby, and it's a special occasion. Some are even coming during their lunch break from work so they can meet you."

"Besides, how often do they get a call announcing an American relative they didn't know existed had arrived in Killarney?" William chimed in from his corner of the room. "Who knows, many of them may show up later on your doorstep looking for a place to stay when they suddenly decide to visit America themselves."

"You're so right, William," agreed Noreen. "Our daughter Colleen asked us where you lived. We told her near Minneapolis, Minnesota."

"Our Colleen reacted by saying, *'Why isn't that where the Mall of America is?'"* William added.

The remark struck Caitlin rather funny. "It's amazing how many people around the world have heard of the Mall of America. If any of your family wants to visit, they're more than welcome to stay with our family. My father and I have homes in the area, and my sister and her husband will be living not far from us after their wedding in June."

"I wish we were a little younger, William. Wouldn't it be nice to go and visit your family in America? Even attend Caitlin's sister's wedding?" Noreen got a little teary-eyed. She realized their days of traveling overseas had come to an end after her last trip to visit family in Boston. Both of them had health issues, and it wasn't going to get any easier.

Donovan realized by her comment that she could probably use some of his help. "Where's your kitchen? I think I'll help you finish preparing lunch. I'm sure you could use some assistance."

"I'd love to have some help from a handsome lad such as yourself. Just follow me."

Before they'd even left the room, Caitlin and William had started to look through photos. Noreen and Donovan carried their conversation with them into the kitchen as they prepared a simple lunch of potato soup and ham sandwiches, with all the fixings on the side. Meanwhile, Caitlin began placing photos into a large manila envelope she planned to take home with her.

Before noon, other Murphy family members began to stream in through the front door, each introducing themselves and divulging a few details about where they lived and what they did for a living. Caitlin shared information with them in return. Many of the family members mistakenly believed Donovan was her husband. He had a way of hovering near her and casually touching her now and then before sweeping off to get her something at a moment's notice.

They brushed off the idea, then explained how they had just become good friends due to unusual circumstances. At one point, William winked at Noreen during one of their explanations to a newly arrived family member. Even if Caitlin and Donovan hadn't noticed it, everyone around them saw the chemistry between them. At times Noreen noticed a little underlying tension between the two. It was spring. She wondered if romance was blooming between the two of them. She could feel Caitlin's pain. Donovan was about as charming as a fellow could be.

Time seemed to fly by as they continued to share family stories. Soon it was late afternoon. Donovan and Caitlin made their final farewells, both promising it wouldn't be the last time they heard from them.

"Now Donovan, you'll come back and visit, won't you?" Noreen pressed.

"I promise I'll return, and next time I'll even bring my mom and dad with me for a mini-vacation. They could use a break. It's been a long time since they last visited this area, and I know they would enjoy the beauty of the surroundings."

Noreen was tickled pink, "I'd like to meet your parents, Donovan. We even have enough bedrooms so you can stay here as our guests."

William hugged Caitlin, "I hope someday soon you can bring your dad here to visit us as well. It's hard to believe, after all this time, our families have finally reconnected. How old did you say your dad was?"

"He's 62."

"Why, that's 18 years younger than me. Your dad's more fit to travel than I am. Just don't wait too long to come and see us," he hinted.

"Don't worry. I'll be sure to bring my dad for a visit as soon as possible," Caitlin vowed.

"Come now, Cait," Donovan urged as he glanced again at his watch. "We need to be on our way. We still have almost four hours of driving ahead of us."

Noreen packed up some leftovers for them, "Here's some food for the road."

Donovan graciously took it from her, "Thank you, Noreen. We appreciate it."

It was a struggle to say good-bye, but finally, they were on their way back to Dublin. Caitlin talked nonstop on the return trip, sharing stories she'd heard about her Great-Great-Uncle Brenden's side of the family.

Only a few miles outside of Dublin, Caitlin felt a wave of sadness wash over her. She had to think for a moment before she realized the cause. "Donovan, before you know it, I'll be flying home. I'm going to miss you and your family," she finally allowed herself to admit.

Yes, they would miss her, too. Donovan's chest tightened at the thought of it. "We'll miss you as well. I feel as if I've known you for a lifetime instead of less than a week." He honestly didn't know how he was going to deal with her leaving. He was well on his way to becoming quite besotted. Every moment he spent with Caitlin only increased his desire to extend his time with her. She fascinated him on so many different levels. He liked everything about her, from the way the sunlight caught in her auburn-colored hair to her love for Irish music and devoted interest in anything history related. "I didn't tell you this, but my sister convinced me to stay in Dublin through the weekend. I suggested I might even drop you off at the airport before heading home on Sunday. What do you think?"

Caitlin could feel tears welling up in her eyes. She blinked them back. "I'd like that," came her reserved response. "It's going to be so hard to say goodbye to your whole family."

"It's settled then. Everything's fine at the clinic, and there's no reason for me to head back home until Sunday. So, maybe you'd like to see a bit of Dublin with me tomorrow?"

She glanced over at him, "Are you offering to be my tour guide? Again?" she questioned.

"Yes, I'd like to spend as much time with you as I can before you leave." He reached over and found her hand, pulling it toward his chest.

Her heart skipped a beat, "I'd like that." Who was she kidding? Only herself. And if she couldn't admit wanting to spend every waking moment with him before she had to get on the plane, she was only trying to fool herself.

Donovan found a parking spot a block from the Inn. Friday nights always seemed to bring plenty of people into O'Malley's Pub. Neither of them felt hungry after snacking on food Noreen had sent with them for their journey back to Dublin. They agreed it would be nice to just unwind for the rest of the evening, maybe spend an hour down in the pub or meet up with Donovan's parents for a short visit. If they got a good night's rest, they'd have plenty of time to enjoy seeing a few of the sights around Dublin the next day. He truly felt blessed to have one more full day in Caitlin's company. Before he knew it, she'd be gone. The notion of her leaving seemed to weigh heavy on his heart.

As they entered the lobby of the Inn, Donovan's phone began to ring. He recognized the clinic number. "Hello?"

Aiden's voice answered back, "Donovan, we just got an emergency call from Jack Kelly's farm. One of their horses is in a great deal of pain. Dana drove over there to check on it."

"Give me the details," ordered Donovan. Aiden wasted no time describing the situation. "I can leave immediately and be there in less than an hour, have Dana stay with the horse and tell her I'll meet her there," Donovan promised.

"Sure thing, I'll get everything ready for surgery in case we need to operate."

"Great! Now call Dana and tell her I'm on my way."

Caitlin overheard Donovan's side of the conversation. She knew an emergency at the clinic would prevent them from spending the rest of the evening together as they had planned. He looked at her, and she could already see the apology forming on his lips.

"I'm sorry, Caitlin. There's an emergency at one of the local farms back home, and I need to rush there to evaluate the situation. There's a good chance I'll need to do emergency surgery."

"What's wrong?" she asked in a concerned voice.

"A horse at the Kelly farm may have colic."

She'd heard of babies having colic, but not horses. "I've heard that word used before, but only where babies are concerned."

He began to explain, "Colic simply means pain anywhere within a horse's gut. It has many causes, from a gassy build up to a more serious blockage or twists in the intestines. The problem is colic is the number one medical cause of death in horses."

Caitlin gasped, "Oh, how awful."

"Dana's evaluating the situation, but I need to leave now to join her as soon as possible. I guess my vacation is over."

Caitlin placed her hand on Donovan's arm for reassurance. She understood that he didn't have a choice. "Just go and do what you need to do. I'll be fine."

She wasn't aware of the thread of sadness twisting through her voice, but he heard it and fought the urge to hug her as regret seeped through him like water through limestone.

"You don't leave until Sunday morning; that should give me enough time to get back here," he promised. They stood, staring longingly into each other's eyes. He felt overwhelmed by emotion, fearing their time together had come to an end. Donovan placed a tender kiss on her forehead as if trying to implant memories of him and their last few days together in her mind.

Caitlin wrapped her arms tightly around him before he could step away, feeling his firm muscles against her. He made a low sound in his throat that seemed to slide down her spine, making her shiver. She didn't want to let go out of him, for fear it would be the last she'd ever see of him. Several guests entered the Inn behind them, causing Caitlin to loosen her hold on Donovan and step away reluctantly.

"Goodbye, Donovan. Thank you so much for all your help over the last few days. It was priceless." A tear slowly began to make its way down her cheek. Donovan reached over and gently wiped it away.

"Cait, I'll call you as soon as I can, and rest assured, I plan on seeing you before you leave. I promise."

As he turned to rush out the door, tears flooded her eyes, breaking like a bursting dam to overflow onto her pale cheeks. She felt awful. She reached up with her hand to wipe the other tears off her face. She needed to snap out of it. Whether Donovan came back or not, she'd be heading home Sunday, not knowing when she'd return. She needed to get her emotions under control. Maybe calling home was what she needed. Talking to her sister always had a way of calming her spirits.

She quickly wiped away any remaining tears before moving towards the check-in desk. Caitlin noticed Bridgett exiting her office. Bridgett caught sight of her at the same time and casually walked in her direction, greeting Caitlin with a big hug.

"Where's Donovan? He told Meghan he'd be staying the weekend and would be willing to drive you to the airport on Sunday morning. I have your rooms ready."

Trying hard to mask her emotions, Caitlin forced a smile before responding in one breath, "He just got an emergency call from the clinic and had to leave."

"Well, if Donovan doesn't make it back to town, Sean or I will be available to take you to the airport," she volunteered. As kind as Bridgett's offer of a ride was, it wouldn't be the same as Donovan escorting her.

"Thank you. I think I'm going to go upstairs now and relax a bit before I turn in for the night."

"No problem, here's your key. I'll see you at breakfast. I can't wait to hear about your trip. Have a good night's rest."

As Caitlin slowly walked up the stairs, she suddenly felt emotionally exhausted, dragging her feet every step of the way. Once inside her room, she shut the door and immediately laid down on the bed. Caitlin closed her eyes, letting her thoughts go blank.

Within a few minutes, she'd fallen fast asleep, forgetting her intended phone call to Abbey.

On the other hand, Donovan had been thinking of Caitlin on the way to Jack's farm. He prayed the horse didn't have a severe colic case so he could turn right back around and return to Dublin, where he had some unfinished business.

Upon entering the stable, he could see Jack pacing the floor. Dana stood not far away from him, trying to calm the agitated horse. She noticed movement from the corner of her eye and turned to see Donovan approaching. From what he'd witnessed already, it didn't look like he'd be making a quick return to Dublin after all.

Dana rushed toward him, "Donovan, we were waiting for you to arrive before loading Jack's horse for transport to the clinic. Aidan's been in close contact with me, and the entire surgery team awaits our arrival. Our patient, Daisy, has been in excruciating pain."

"Thanks for taking care of things until I could get here, Dana. Let's get moving." He turned to Jack to assure him the mare would get the best of care.

He gently cooed the horse's name as he approached her. "Hey Daisy, I hear you aren't feeling so well. Let's get you some help." He slowly led her the short distance to the horse trailer that awaited them outside.

After loading Daisy for transit, Donovan instantly sent a text to Caitlin, letting her know he needed to perform surgery, and he'd give her a call sometime on Saturday. He had high hopes of joining her for at least part of the day, but he couldn't let himself dwell on the future. He needed to focus on saving Daisy's life. She had to be his number one priority now.

Caitlin, awakened by the sound of the arriving text message, rolled over to tap on her screen. She read the text before rolling over and falling back to sleep with a smile on her face because although tonight had been hard on her heart, there would always be tomorrow.

# Chapter 16

Caitlin felt exhausted the next morning as she lay in bed. She'd fallen asleep quickly, but all through the night, she repeatedly tossed and turned. Donovan's abrupt departure had left her feeling unsettled. After reading his text message the night before, she was anxiously awaiting a follow-up call. The lack of closure between them was nerve-racking.

When she finally convinced herself remaining in bed would accomplish nothing, the bedside phone began to ring. She sat up immediately and reached for it. In anticipation, she answered, "Hello? Donovan?"

"I'm sorry, Caitlin, it's Meghan. Are you all right?"

"Yes, I'm fine. Good morning."

"I'm calling to tell you Brian won't be home until later this afternoon, so I brought the children over to hang out with their grandparents. I hoped we could spend some time together this morning unless you already have plans."

"No, Donovan wanted to show me more of Dublin, but a sudden medical emergency popped up last night." Caitlin's voice had a clear tone undercut by a choking heaviness, which forced her to pause several times.

"I see, but you still got your hopes up when the phone rang, didn't you?"

"Wait a moment. I was waiting for Donovan's call, so I didn't think to look for another text. Can you hold on a minute while I check?"

"Go ahead. I'll wait." Caitlin's anxious voice humored Meghan. She was curious as to what had transpired between her brother and Caitlin over the past few days and if they'd had any success cracking the O'Sullivan mystery.

Caitlin had several text messages: one from her sister, one from her father, and the last one from Jeremy, but no new messages from Donovan. "Nope, no text message. Just your luck, I'd love to spend some time with you, Meghan."

"Why don't I pick up some breakfast and bring it over to your room. I'd like to talk to you in private. I have some news you might be interested in. After lunch, the children and I can take you on an adventure."

"Sounds like a great plan. I'll get dressed while you rustle up some food. Why don't I just meet you in the Breakfast Room?"

Meghan couldn't take a chance on anyone listening in on their conversation, especially her mother. "No, Caitlin. What I want to discuss with you needs a little privacy. I wouldn't want anyone overhearing our conversation, especially someone from my family."

Caitlin couldn't begin to imagine what Meghan had to say that she didn't want anyone else to know. "Okay, no problem. See you soon."

She dressed quickly in a pair of comfortable jeans, a yellow buttoned-down shirt, and a full-zip University of Minnesota hoodie before carefully reading her other text messages. Abbey's pertained to her final wedding plans. Before they knew it, the wedding would be upon them, and Ireland would be a distant memory. Caitlin could feel her heart twinge at the idea of leaving.

The second message had been from her dad. He was anxious to hear about her time in Killarney.

The final text had been sent by Jeremy, begging for an opportunity to talk. Unwilling to take the chance of ruining her last day in Ireland, she decided any conversation with Jeremy was going to have to wait until she got home. Hopefully, she could convince him to move on. As far as she was concerned, after meeting the more mature Donovan, there was no looking back. Jeremy couldn't begin to compare to a considerate and trustworthy man like him. The intense feelings she felt for Donovan versus Jeremy were like comparing a fiery inferno to a dying ember.

Lost in her thoughts, she jumped at the sound of a knock on her door. "Caitlin, it's me, Meghan."

"I'm coming!" Caitlin opened the door to find Meghan standing behind a rolling cart full of a variety of delicious smelling breakfast foods. The aroma from the coffee forced her to realize how desperately she needed some caffeine. That would kick start her brain!

"Did you leave anything for the other guests?"

"I'm sorry, I didn't know what to bring, so I brought a little of everything," Meghan confessed. "Most of our guests were done eating."

Caitlin glanced at the vast array of delicious food. "You're forgiven. I'm so hungry I could eat a horse!"

"Oh, Caitlin, that is the wrong thing to say to someone in my family," scolded Meghan.

Realizing her misfortunate choice of words, she apologized wholeheartedly, "I'm sorry, I didn't think before speaking. You realize we don't eat horses where I come from, don't you?"

"Of course, you don't. I just couldn't help pulling your leg. We have a similar saying here in Ireland, 'I'm so hungry I could eat the horse and chase the jockey'. I forgive you this time, but remember, we all avoid saying such things around the children." They both broke out in spurts of laughter, then hugged each other. "It's so good to have you back with us, even if it's only for one more day."

A frown spread across Caitlin's face. "Meghan don't remind me. You'll make me cry. Now, why are you so anxious to talk to me privately? Trying to figure it out has been driving me crazy." Meghan encouraged Caitlin to fill her plate with food before she divulged her news.

*Here goes*, thought Meghan. She knew her idea was a little farfetched, but what did she have to lose? "Now, Caitlin, you know Brian and I are expecting our baby in early October. I've been talking to my boss at the Library about taking maternity leave in the fall. While you were in Killarney, I spoke with Brian, and we decided it would be so much nicer if I could take an extended child-rearing leave."

"I'm sure it would make the transition to caring for three children much easier," Caitlin agreed. "How much time did you plan on taking off from work?"

"About a year, starting in September and going through the end of the following August. The Library Board agreed on one condition; they would need to find a person willing to cover the position for the year with no guarantee of a job at year's end." Meghan paused, waiting for Caitlin to react to the news.

"And you're telling me this because…"

"Because I believe you'd be the perfect person to apply for the job," she stressed.

What did Meghan expect her to say on such short notice? She was puzzled. "But I already have one. I can't leave a good steady job for a temporary one. I don't know how it would be to my benefit. Surely someone around here would be interested in an opportunity to work at the National Library. The experience they'd gain might later help them find their next job opportunity."

Meghan took a deep breath and prayed her words would convince her friend. "Caitlin, I've seen how you and Donovan look at each other. I just spoke to him yesterday morning on the phone. He has feelings for you. I know it. If you came here to work for a year, there would be time for you to get to know one another better. Then you might discover whether or not you had a future as a couple."

"Meghan, while working at the National Library would be my dream job, I'd find it difficult to quit the one I have now and move here for a year even if I were starting to have feelings for your brother. It would be foolish on my part." Her head began to spin while her heart pounded loudly inside her chest. She couldn't believe she was feeling tempted by the thought. *Be realistic*, she told herself.

"Maybe it is a crazy idea, but I scheduled an interview at 11 o'clock this morning for you at the Library, just in case you might be interested."

"But Meghan…"

"Before you say no, listen to me. You're the most qualified person for the job. You're also someone who would personally benefit from living in Ireland for the year. You'd have time to connect further with your own family here and be able to spend more time getting to know Donovan. You'd even be able to continue your research in more depth and connect with other family members," she surmised.

"It sounds crazy, Meghan, but it would be a wonderful opportunity," Caitlin admitted. "How much time would I have to think about this?" Caitlin felt torn over what to do, but if she were honest with herself, the thought of leaving Donovan behind would break her heart. She was overwhelmed by her feelings for him, but she feared the unknown—the risk of uprooting herself to live in a foreign country, not knowing what lay ahead in the future. Did Donovan feel the same way about her? Was he interested in seeing whether their relationship would evolve into something more than pure friendship? She could only hope.

"My boss will pass her top three recommendations for the job on to the Library Board. They will make the final selection. They plan to have my position filled no later than the end of June. The person hired would start in August or September, depending on how my pregnancy is going."

Silence filled the room as Meghan waited for a response from Caitlin. The waiting seemed unbearable. Then she came up with one additional advantage Caitlin would gain by applying for the position. "Just think, if you lived here for a year, it would be much easier for your dad and other family members to join you for a visit. What do you say, Caitlin? Are you even somewhat interested?"

Caitlin closed her eyes and tried to listen to what her heart was telling her, not her head. Her mother would have encouraged her to do just that. She slowly opened her eyes and took a deep, cleansing breath before answering. "Yes, I'll go for the interview this morning. What do I have to lose? It'll only take a few minutes to update my resumé and e-mail a copy to your boss."

"Yes!" Meghan shouted out with glee, pumping her fists in the air.

Caitlin felt she needed to give her friend a little reality check after that reaction to her answer. "Now remember, Meghan, going for an interview doesn't mean I'll accept the job if I get the offer. Do you understand?"

She nodded slowly in response, and despite Caitlin's warning, it was apparent she was elated. "Yes, but at least you'd have the ability to make the decision. If you didn't go for the interview, you'd be closing the door to a fantastic opportunity."

Quite right, she agreed. "You're a wise woman, Meghan Rafferty, but you have to make me one promise."

"What's that?"

"Under no circumstance are you to tell Donovan about this interview or the possibility of me considering coming here to work."

"I promise," she agreed, with fingers crossed behind her back and a twinkle in her eye. "There's no pressure from anyone in our family for you and Donovan to be more than friends, but we would be the first to stand in line to congratulate you if you did," she admitted honestly.

Caitlin did not know what to think about that revelation, but regardless, the thought of spending a full year in Ireland was very tempting. "Meghan, promise you'll keep it a secret if I tell you something?"

Meghan looked directly at Caitlin and spoke in a serious tone, "You can trust me with your life."

"I already consider your brother my good friend. But I think I'm starting to harbor much stronger feelings for him. It's hard to ignore his endearing personality…"

"And good looks?" Meghan added.

"I suppose he isn't too hard on the eyes. Now, it's too early to say whether we have the makings of a lasting relationship, but he has a way of making my heart do flip-flops," Caitlin admitted.

"Ah, I know the feeling. When Donovan comes too close, your heart feels as if it skips a beat, and at other times the nearer he gets, the faster your heart begins to beat, almost as if you're running in the race of your life." At least that had been Meghan's experience with her husband.

Caitlin could only nod, rendered speechless by the overwhelming emotions swirling around within her. Donovan could stir such intense feelings in her that the effect was not only emotional but physical. The last few days had been the most alive she's felt since her break-up with Jeremy.

"Oh, Caitlin. I'm so glad we had this talk. Now let's finish our breakfast before we get you ready for the most important interview of your life."

"Meghan, you're going to make me nervous. Let's look at it this way. If it's God's will for me to get this job and move here for a year, it'll happen."

"Agreed. I won't say anything more."

The morning flew by swiftly, including her interview. Caitlin felt satisfied by her performance under pressure. She got the impression she had as good a chance as anyone else to get the job but waiting to find out would be the most challenging part of the process.

Shortly afterward, Caitlin and Meghan hurried to pick up Grace and Liam from the Inn. Both children were over the moon about going out to lunch and for their trip to The Irish Emigration Museum. Caitlin had also promised to update Meghan on her trip to Killarney and its success.

As they were leaving the restaurant, Caitlin's cell phone began to ring. "It's Donovan's number," she informed Meghan. "Hello? Donovan? I'm so glad you called."

There was a pause on the other end of the phone, then a woman's voice spoke. "I'm sorry, Caitlin, it's Dana. After the long surgery last night, a few complications developed, so Donovan didn't get much sleep. He's resting right now. I know he was concerned about connecting with you as soon as possible, but I didn't want to wake him. I thought I'd just call and update you so you wouldn't worry."

Caitlin felt disappointed but understood the situation. "That's kind of you, Dana. Will he be able to get here this evening after he's had time to rest?"

Dana paused for a moment before answering. She was making this all up on the fly and hadn't planned it all out yet. "I can only repeat what I heard him tell Jack, the horse's owner. He said he needed to keep a close eye on Daisy for at least the next 24-48 hours, and it would be a good week before the horse could go back home. Did he explain to you last night what was wrong?"

"Yes, the horse had colic. How serious was it?" Caitlin asked in a concerned voice.

That's an easy answer, Dana realized. All she needed to do was tell the truth. "The intestines were twisted, and we almost lost the horse during surgery. Luckily, Daisy is fairly young and strong. However, there can still be some complications after a surgery as serious as this one. That's why Donovan needs to stay close to the clinic."

Caitlin felt somewhat disappointed. "I understand, Dana. Thank you so much for updating me. Can you please ask Donovan to call me when he wakes up? I'd like to speak to him before I leave tomorrow morning."

Dana hesitated, wondering how she could prevent the two of them from getting any cozier than they already seemed to be. Last night Caitlin seemed to be the only thing Donovan had been interested in talking about during the surgery. She hadn't spent all of her time dedicated to Donovan since Marie's death to have him fall for some American now. "I'm glad to help in some way. I'll pass on your message."

Before she could say thank you, Dana disconnected their call. Meghan gave Caitlin a puzzled look. "That was Dana, Donovan's Technician. He's resting after performing a difficult surgery last night. She'll have him call me when he's awake."

Meghan thought that sounded rather odd. "Why did she call you?"

Caitlin explained further, "She said she didn't want me to worry. Some complications set in early this morning, so she let me know Donovan wouldn't be able to make it back into Dublin before I leave. She said she'd have him call me when he wakes up."

Loud noises emanating from the children interrupted their conversation. They were begging to ride the bus to the museum. Meghan agreed it would be a fun experience for everyone.

Caitlin just shook her head at Meghan. "Will we have time to do all that and get back in time to go to church with your folks this evening?" Meghan assured Caitlin the museum was close, and they had plenty of time.

The entire afternoon ended up being one fun adventure after another—a welcomed distraction. The highlight for Caitlin was getting to know Grace and Liam better. They were witty, funny, and utterly delightful children. Caitlin even felt a little jealous of Meghan having two beautiful children already and another one on the way. Her thoughts drifted off as she imagined herself walking hand in hand with Donovan, a toddler in tow. Anything was possible. Maybe her luck would change if she just took a chance on romance.

Back at the clinic, the object of Caitlin's affections felt bombarded by emotions upon waking. Donovan tried to get his bearings after his overextended nap. "Dana, have you seen my cell phone anywhere? I can't seem to find it." He had meant to call Caitlin much earlier.

"No, I haven't seen it. Maybe you left it on your desk. Do you want me to go and check?" Dana offered.

"Yes, would you? By the way, what time is it?"

"Almost 6 o'clock, I ordered some food to be delivered within the next half hour. I knew you'd be hungry."

Donovan realized Caitlin and his parents would be on their way to church any minute now. "Thanks for anticipating my needs, but can I ask why you let me sleep so long? I should have been keeping a closer eye on Daisy."

Dana didn't hesitate with her answer. She had planned out everything she was going to tell Donovan to the nth degree. "Aidan and I have been taking turns. We knew you were exhausted. We wanted to give you time to rest up in case there were any additional problems later tonight you needed to handle."

Irritated by having someone else make decisions for him and still cranky from being overtired, he snapped at Dana. "Fine! Now could you see if my phone is on my desk? And, please, bring it to me if you find it. I'll be with Daisy." He stomped off, thoughts of Caitlin bombarding him from every direction. Every minute that passed was one minute closer to her leaving the country, and it was tearing him apart. For some reason, he wanted to get down on his knees and plead for her to stay just a bit longer until they could figure out what they were going to do about whatever was going on between them.

Dana disrupted his train of thought with a rehearsed sugar-coated sweetness, "I'll go look for your phone. It has to be around here somewhere."

As they parted ways, Dana patted her lab coat pocket to make sure his phone was still where she'd left it. Then she walked to his office and waited for a few minutes. The longer she could delay Donovan from connecting with Caitlin, the better her future chances were of becoming Mrs. Donovan O'Malley. In less than 24 hours, Caitlin would be on the opposite side of the Atlantic Ocean, and she could begin to relax again.

While Dana continued to deceive Donovan, the O'Malley clan entertained Caitlin. She enjoyed attending the evening mass with them at St. Anthony's and getting to meet Brian, Meghan's husband. After being apart for almost a week, joy radiated from the couple, a sign of true love. Caitlin hoped she'd look the same way at her husband after nearly ten years of marriage.

After mass, Sean and Bridgett invited Caitlin to join them for a late supper. Everyone congratulated Brian on the news of the baby. He didn't seem upset when he learned his wife had shared their happy news with her family while he'd been away. Brian just placed his hand lovingly on her belly and smiled.

They also listened to Caitlin explain how she and Donovan had discovered Noreen's husband was one of her relatives. They likened it to somewhat of a miracle. They had many reasons to celebrate.

As the night went on and Caitlin hadn't heard back from Donovan, she started to feel like an ocean of silence lay between them. And she was drowning in it. When Caitlin tried to call him, his phone immediately went to voicemail. She had an early flight and knew she needed to get back to her room to pack her things before it got too late.

She didn't realize Daisy had continued to suffer from discomfort and some pain following her surgery, keeping Donovan occupied. By the time he got her settled down for the night, he realized he still hadn't found his phone. Dana and Aidan had gone home for the night, but Dana had promised to be back early in the morning to take his place. He still planned to try to reach Dublin before Caitlin got on the plane. She had a morning flight, and Donovan was sure she was trying to get some sleep before leaving. He just wished he knew what time her flight was departing.

In the end, he decided to call the Inn and leave a message at the front desk for her. "Hello, this is O'Malley's Inn. Would you like to make a reservation?"

"No, this is Donovan O'Malley."

"How can I help you, Dr. O'Malley?"

"I'd like to leave a message for Caitlin Sullivan. I don't want to disturb her since it's late. Could someone slip a message under her door, so she sees it when she gets up in the morning?"

"Yes, sir." Donovan proceeded to give him the clinic's number so Caitlin could call him there and let him know her flight departure time. Then he sat back in the reclining chair to try to get some sleep while still being available if Daisy got restless in the night. His team was on standby if he needed them.

The next morning, Caitlin painstakingly made the final preparations for her trip to the airport. She had no appetite, and her heart seemed to ache at the thought of leaving without seeing Donovan one last time. As Caitlin placed her suitcase near her room door, she noticed a piece of paper on the floor. She retrieved it and slowly read Donovan's message, which immediately sent her into a panic. By the sound of it, Caitlin only had a few minutes in which to call him before Sean would be there to carry her luggage to the car.

She perched herself on the edge of the bed, and with the note positioned in her lap, she entered the clinic's number into her phone. After three rings, someone answered. "O'Malley Veterinary Clinic, Dana speaking."

"Hi, Dana, it's Caitlin. Is Donovan there? He left me a message to call him, and I'm just getting ready to leave for the airport," she spoke breathlessly.

Dana looked around to make sure she was alone before answering, "I'm sorry, he just left a few minutes ago to head home to take a shower and get some rest. He spent the entire night here with Daisy. I just arrived a few minutes ago to take the next shift. I'm sorry you missed him."

"No problem, I'll try calling his cell phone."

"I'm sorry, Caitlin, he misplaced his phone yesterday and still hasn't found it," she lied.

"Oh." She heard a knock at her door. "I have to go now. Please tell Donovan I'm sorry I missed being able to talk to him before I left."

"I certainly will," Dana promised.

"One more thing," added Caitlin, "please tell him how thankful I am for his help in Killarney."

"Of course, it's just the kind of person he is. I don't know what any of us would do without him, especially me," she added with purpose. "Have a safe trip home."

Just as Dana hung up the phone, Donovan stepped into the office area. "Who was on the phone? I hope it isn't another emergency. I need some rest."

"No emergency, it was Caitlin. She was trying to get in contact with you just before she got on the plane. I thought you'd already left for home. She told me to tell you she's sorry she missed you and thank you for all of your help over the past week.".

"Did you get her cell number so I could call her back?"

"I'm sorry, I didn't think of it because she seemed in a hurry to board her plane and hung up," Dana lied once more. "Oh, that reminds me, I found your phone a few minutes ago."

About time, he thought to himself. "Where did you find it?"

"In the wastebasket by your desk. It must have accidentally fallen in there." Dana pulled the phone out of her pocket and sandwiched it in between her hand and his. Rubbing her thumb over his, she smiled innocently at him, "I promised to pass on her message to you, and it put her at ease."

Nothing more he could do about it now, he admitted to himself. "Thanks, Dana. I'm heading home to get some rest now. Thanks again for all your help this weekend. I'll see you tomorrow morning."

She placed her hands on his shoulders and looked into his eyes before saying, "We make a great team, Donovan. I'm always here for you whenever you need me," she subtly reminded him.

"I know, Dana, and I appreciate it. Until tomorrow." Donovan trudged out to his car, exhausted from the poor sleeping conditions at the clinic. He'd spent most of his time resting on an uncomfortable cot in one of the exam rooms or the old recliner chair in the equine patient care area. He looked forward to going home, eating breakfast, and then taking a long relaxing shower before jumping into bed to catch up on his sleep.

He pulled up in front of his home, feeling dog-tired and depressed at the idea of Caitlin flying back to Minnesota. He'd been to Minneapolis once when he'd spoken at an American Kennel Club Convention several years ago. He didn't know when he'd ever been back in the area. Who was he kidding anyway? As much as he liked Caitlin, the chances of continuing anything more than a friendship at such a distance would be difficult. Sure, they got along and enjoyed each other's company, but was he ready for a deeper relationship? Maybe he shouldn't put off dating any longer. If Caitlin could make his heart sing, perhaps it was a sign he was ready to move on finally.

Two hours later, just after Caitlin had powered her phone down for the flight home, Donovan finally got around to sending her a text message: *Found my phone. Sorry I missed seeing you off. I hope you enjoyed your time in Ireland. Have a pleasant flight home.*

It wasn't much, but with time and miles now increasing their distance apart, it was all he could muster.

# Chapter 17

Almost a week had passed since Caitlin's return home. Chaos closely followed. Multiple projects were due for completion at the museum, but none of the busyness seemed to eliminate the distractions causing her restless feelings. At present, there were three men in her life interfering with her day-to-day routine.

Caitlin's boss was overjoyed by her return to work because he required her assistance in meeting upcoming deadlines. Not a problem, but Jonathan had persisted in asking her out to dinner throughout the week. He didn't seem to want to take no for an answer, and she lacked any interest in accepting his offer. Everything he seemed to do lately irritated her. Jonathan was a reminder that no man would ever measure up to the one she'd left behind in Ireland. She knew what she wanted in a life partner, and every man in the future would have to compete with her memory of Donovan O'Malley. Yes, Donovan was the second man weaving his way in and out of her thoughts throughout the day.

But Caitlin realized a large part of her angst had to do with putting off her phone call to Jeremy. Yes, he was the third man messing with her ability to concentrate. She needed to make it clear to her former boyfriend once and for all, getting back together was totally out of the question. Caitlin wouldn't be meeting Abbey at the Bridal Salon for another hour, so she decided there was no better time like the present. She didn't want to be distracted when she needed to focus on Abbey's final wedding dress decision.

Jeremy answered her call on the second ring. "Hello, Caitlin? Is it really you?"

"Yes, Jeremy. I'm sorry I didn't return your call sooner, but once I got back from Ireland, I found myself immersed in my work." Honestly, she'd been avoiding making the call, but he didn't need to know.

"No problem. I'm glad to hear your voice. I didn't know if you'd ever talk to me again after our last conversation."

Caitlin knew she needed to be completely honest today, no matter how hard Jeremy would take it. She anticipated he'd try to twist the facts around regarding their breakup in an attempt to get her to fall headfirst into his chasm of self-pity. But she knew she needed to stand firm and squelch any thought he had of getting back together. "Well, you upset me when we last spoke. I'd rather have this conversation face to face, but this phone call will have to do."

Jeremy didn't know where to begin. He wanted to say all the right things and not scare Caitlin off. He took a deep breath in, figuring anywhere was better than nowhere. "Caitlin, I want to start by apologizing for my behavior last fall. I let a pretty face lead me astray. You'd been so busy at work, and honestly, I felt neglected."

She couldn't believe he was indirectly blaming her, the nerve of the man! "A pretty face? Really? What a lame excuse for cheating on me, cracking the foundation of our relationship. A lot has happened in the last six months, and Jeremy, I've moved past whatever happened between the two of us."

"Wait. How can you move on in such a short time?" he demanded, his tone building in urgency. "We were together for nearly two years. I still love you, Caitlin. I always have. If you hadn't given up on us so quickly, we could have worked things out when you were still here in Boston. I'm sure we'd still be together. My relationship with Sarah was nothing compared to ours."

Caitlin was offended. What planet was he from, she wondered? Her response came sternly and confidently. She didn't have time for this nonsense. "Jeremy, did you continue to see Sarah after we broke up?"

His response came quickly. Jeremy had thought about what he would say ahead of time if this question came up. His goal was to convince Caitlin she was partly to blame for what had transpired, making it easier for her to forgive him. Jeremy had been a fool to stray and deeply regretted it. "Yes, I figured once you broke things off with me, it didn't matter anymore. I continued to see Sarah for a few more months. But she wasn't you. Her beauty was superficial, and we had little in common. In hindsight, I regret the time I wasted on her."

Jeremy wondered if Caitlin believed him, he could only hope. Jeremy missed her and truly regretted his poor decisions. He would be the first to admit his actions had been relatively immature. And, in hindsight, he'd come to realize how much he genuinely loved Caitlin. He didn't want to lose her.

Caitlin could only shake her head at what she considered shallow remarks. He didn't seem to be taking responsibility for his actions. "I guess we learn from our mistakes, don't we, Jeremy? I've moved on, and you should, too. There is no more us."

"But Caitlin, I've learned from my mistakes. I believe moving on can still mean us being together. Sarah means nothing to me. I want you back in my life. It hasn't been the same since you left," he almost seemed to whine.

Jeremy wreaked of insincerity. Caitlin thought he was putting on an act, and she expected more from a 32-year-old man. "I forgive you, but I don't trust you. I'm not about to start a long-distance relationship with you or anybody else." An image of Donovan entered her mind. Well, maybe there was one exception.

"But Caitlin, I love you. We can work something out. I'd be willing to relocate and find a job near you," he continued, his words fading into the distance while Caitlin's mind wandered off in search of the new direction she wanted to take in life.

Avoiding long-distance relationships, moving to a new city to work, and being closer to someone you loved—she understood Jeremy's desires. But only Donovan proved to be the object of her affections. Caitlin didn't wish to continue any relationship with someone who didn't hold a candle to him. She didn't want Jeremy to move closer to her—instead—she wanted to return to Dublin.

"I'm sorry, Jeremy, I have absolutely no interest in getting back together with you. I may even be moving soon."

"But Caitlin, what are you saying? Where would you go?" He wasn't happy. Things weren't going the way he'd planned.

Caitlin was honest not only with Jeremy but with herself. "Everything's up in the air right now, and I'd rather not say. I'm sorry, I must go now. I'm meeting Abbey at the bridal shop in less than an hour. Jeremy, as much I loved you at one point in my life, my feelings have changed. I don't have time to waste on rehashing a relationship that you weren't committed to in the first place. I wish you the best in life, but it won't be a life with me. Goodbye!"

She ended the call immediately, not wanting to hear any more arguments about her final decision. It was over between them. Now she had to ask herself, did she dare risk everything and take the job in Dublin—to fill a void in her life—and turn friendship into romance?

When Caitlin entered the bridal shop, Abbey and her two other bridesmaids were waiting for her. Susan and Rachel had already donned their two dress choices. Susan wore a cranberry, V-neck halter gown, with an open slit on the left side. A sash accentuated her narrow waistline, and the gathered skirt billowed from her hips to touch the ground.

"Susan, you look lovely. This dress is very flattering on you."

"Thanks, Caitlin. I like the one Rachel is wearing as well." Caitlin and Abbey both turned to look at the sleeveless, burgundy chiffon dress Rachel wore. She walked an imaginary catwalk modeling the knee-length gown.

"I like them both, but Rachel's dress would feel cooler on a hot summer's day," Abbey commented.

Rachel twirled around in her dress, and the skirt flared out. "I agree, and I'd love to dance around in this dress. So, are we in agreement? The dress I'm wearing would be the better choice?"

They unanimously agreed. One crucial decision made and one more to go. Which wedding dress should Abbey choose?

The bridal consultant helped take final measurements to determine their dress sizes, announcing a tentative delivery date. Rachel and Susan apologized. They couldn't stay any longer due to previous commitments.

When Abbey's friends had departed, her consultant left to gather Abbey's final three wedding dress choices. It allowed the sisters a few minutes for a private conversation.

"Well, Abbey, how are you holding up? I'm sorry I've been too busy to talk since my return from Ireland," Caitlin apologized.

"It's okay. I know you've been playing catch up at work. How does it feel to be back home? Are you missing Ireland or a specific Irishman?" she teased.

Caitlin sighed, "I have mixed feelings, especially after talking to Jeremy on the phone just before I got here."

Abbey was stunned. "What? Why did you talk to Jeremy? Are the two of you thinking about getting back together?"

"Of course not! I forgave him but explained I really had moved on, and our relationship is completely over. There's no going back. I realized it before I even left Ireland." Caitlin admitted to her sister.

Even though they were interrupted by the consultant bringing in the wedding dresses, they continued to talk as Abbey tried on the first. Caitlin began to explain about her interview at the National Library and the possibility of a year working in Dublin.

Abbey couldn't believe how perfect the whole thing sounded. "I'm so excited for you, Caitlin. You should definitely take this job and see where things go."

"The job may sound wonderful, but I don't have it yet. I'm going to wait and see what happens. If the National Library offers me the job, I may decide to take it. Then again, I may not. In the meantime, I'm just going to take things one day at a time and see where life leads me."

"It's probably all you can do now. I'm praying whatever lies ahead will lead you directly to your happily ever after."

"Me too, Sis. Me too."

Their conversation paused as Abbey stopped to model the first dress she'd tried on. "I love this dress, but the neckline seems to be a little too plunging. I'd be afraid I'd fall out of it in the middle of a conga line."

Caitlin grimaced at the thought, pulling up on the shoulders of the dress. "They might be able to adjust the neckline. But why don't you try on the next dress before requesting any crazy alterations."

The second dress had a tulle tank V-neck gown with a layered skirt. Abbey liked the comfort of the fit and how the skirt floated when she began to follow through on a few waltz steps.

"Ohh, wow! I prefer this over the first dress. Help me out of it, and I'll try on the last one." She felt relieved the final dress selection was going easier than she thought it would.

Once changed, Meghan turned to look at herself in the full-length mirror. The last, an off the shoulder mermaid dress made of beaded lace, looked lovely and fit Abbey's body like a glove. The only negative, she found it harder to move in.

"Well, Caitlin, I think I've made my choice."

"The second dress?" she hoped.

"Yes, I truly love everything about it."

Just then, Abbey's odd sense of problem-solving kicked in. "Hey Caitlin, it seems to me your life's choices are similar to mine."

Caitlin prepared herself, she knew Abbey was about to stretch an analogy.

"Like me, you currently have three choices staring you in the face. One choice, Jeremy, who you've already walked away from once. Can he even be trusted if given a second chance?"

Caitlin shook her head emphatically. "Absolutely not! Next!"

"Your second choice is Jonathan. I know you've gone out a few times and have a love for history in common, but if you ask me, he's rather stuffy and would cramp your style. I believe your boss would bore you to tears over time."

"Oh, Abbey, you're hilarious! What's my third choice? The one you'd pick for me. Donovan?"

"Why Caitlin, whenever you mention Donovan or anything about your time traveling with him, you light up like the Chrysler Building. I haven't heard you say one negative thing about him. Of course, he's your third choice—the perfect choice," she said with conviction.

"You make it sound so easy, Abbey," she sighed.

Caitlin had to admit she had stronger feelings for Donovan than she would like to admit. "I enjoyed every single minute I spent with him. He's rather charming, to say the least, and comes from a wonderful family. They made me feel right at home. Especially Duncan, his dog."

"So, like the dress I'm officially wearing at my wedding, you've made your choice. Donovan is the perfect fit for you. And what are you going to do about it, dear sister?"

"Take the job in Dublin if they offer it to me?"

"You've got it, Sis! It's a no brainer if you ask me." Their discussion ended there as they hustled to finish up their business and head to lunch to toast the hard decisions they'd made.

With only a short walk to one of their favorite restaurants, it wasn't long before they were celebrating the road ahead in both their futures.

# Chapter 18

A month after returning home from Ireland, Caitlin had fallen into a state of melancholy. She couldn't shake the feeling of sadness brought on by the separation from her newly found Irish family and friends. Is this how her great-grandfather had felt after leaving his family back in 1927? Caitlin contemplated what it would feel like never to set foot in Ireland again. Ridiculous! She knew she was acting a little overdramatic, slightly irrational. She planned on returning, but she couldn't deny her feelings, as strange as they seemed. They were real. She'd lost her heart to Ireland and its people, especially Donovan. She had logically arrived at this conclusion.

There were many times Caitlin considered texting or calling Donovan over the past month. Just out of curiosity to see if they still had some kind of connection. What did she fear most? That time and distance apart had already put a dent in whatever feelings had been simmering between them. Besides, it worked both ways. If he had any feelings for her, he would have attempted to connect in some way.

With only a week until Abbey's wedding, the anticipation had been building, blissfully distracting her. Today she was keeping her dad company while Abbey worked the afternoon shift. With a little twist of the arm, her sister had also convinced her to stay overnight.

Michael Sullivan wiped his mouth with his napkin and sighed contentedly, feeling full after a relaxing dinner with his eldest daughter. "The meal was delicious, Caitie! It's been a long time since I've had such a tasty Shepherd's Pie. Did you use your mom's recipe?"

"Yes, but I made a few adjustments," she explained.

"No matter, I still enjoyed it. I'll be honest. You surprised me tonight. I expected takeout food with you in charge. Your mom loved to cook, but you were always buried in a book when you were growing up—while Abbey was her glorified *sous* chef. What suddenly inspired you to cook a fancy meal tonight?" Their eyes met across the table, and Michael could see the confused emotions settled within his daughter's misty green eyes. She indeed was an Irish beauty.

Caitlin let out a big sigh before making her confession. "Oh, Dad, to tell you the truth, this has been going on for about a month. Since I returned from Ireland, I've had a desire to recreate some of my favorite meals from the trip. Shepherd's pie happens to be one of my favorite dishes and my most recent comfort food. I'm feeling a little stressed out this week."

Michael looked across the table at his daughter, studying the expression on her face. Since her return from Ireland, something seemed different about her. It was almost as if she'd left a part of herself behind, leaving an almost haunted look on her face. "What's going on with you, Caitie? You've been acting rather absentmindedly since you returned from your trip."

"It's hard to explain, Dad. Something about Ireland affected me to my inner core. The longing to return has been overwhelming, almost as if a spell has been cast upon me." A tear escaped at that moment, slowly making its way down her right cheek. She quickly wiped it away before her dad could notice it.

"I can only imagine the multitude of emotions you encountered on your trip. I promise we'll go and visit as soon as my doctor okays me for travel. We can immediately start making plans on where to go, what to see, and whom to see. Isn't planning half the fun of taking a trip?" Her dad reached his hand across the table for hers. As she placed it in his he gave it a little squeeze. If he didn't know better, he would suspect a man had something to do with her recent change in behavior, but she'd only been gone a week. It wasn't possible to fall for someone in such a short time, at least not from his perspective.

"Yes, Dad. I look forward to making those decisions with you." She released his hand and stood. "Now, I'm going to put away the leftovers and clean up the kitchen. Why don't you relax and watch some TV?"

"Sure, thanks again, Caitie. I don't know what I ever did to deserve such wonderful daughters. I'd be lost without you and Abbey." He got up and kissed her tenderly on the cheek.

Caitlin immediately started to feel guilty. She'd been keeping an enormous secret from her dad and younger sister. Earlier in the week, she'd received a phone call from the National Library with a job offer. Making the right decision weighed heavily on her mind. She wondered if it was the right time to take a job in Ireland with Abbey getting married—even a temporary one. With her mother's passing and now Abbey moving into her own home, her dad would be alone again. She felt torn over the thought of leaving the country to chase after her dreams when it would mean leaving her dad by himself in the process.

Caitlin contemplated the idea of accepting the offer while she hastened to clean-up. Afterward, she joined her dad in the living room. They had a few pleasant hours together in front of the TV—briefly catching up on life during the commercials. Caitlin learned her dad's doctor had cleared him to go back to work part-time the week after Abbey's wedding. This was good news. Her dad had great friends at his workplace, and they stopped by now and then, but more daily contact with them would be the final dose of medicine he needed to make a full recovery.

Susan, his in-home caregiver, had also helped speed along his healing. Lately, Michael didn't need her as often as in the beginning stages of his recovery, but they continued to enjoy spending time together. She'd been a great help in overseeing her dad's rehab, and now, even when Caitlin or Abbey were present, Susan seemed to show up when it was time for their dad's scheduled walks. She usually brought along her collie dog named Chauncy, and their dad would get dog therapy and exercise simultaneously. Afterward, they'd sit around and visit over a cup of coffee and some homemade treat Susan had baked. Caitlin suspected they'd developed feelings for each other, but Abbey had just made light of the idea. If Susan were still around to keep her dad company, maybe she could accept the new job. She was so tempted.

At 9 o'clock, Michael yawned deeply and announced, "Caitie, it's time for me to go upstairs and get ready for bed." Caitlin noticed this was earlier than usual for her dad. In the past, he had a habit of shortchanging himself on sleep. Of course, she didn't realize her dad was heading upstairs to make his nightly phone call to Susan, a pleasant habit he'd gotten into since his injury.

"Goodnight, Dad. I'll see you in the morning. I promised Abbey I'd wait up for her."

"Sounds good, but don't keep her up too late. She needs to get her beauty sleep with the wedding just a week away," her dad teased.

Caitlin chuckled, "Of course, Dad." As tired as Caitlin felt, she planned on keeping her promise. Hopefully, she could stay awake until Abbey got home around midnight. Good thing she'd brought along a book of Irish folklore she'd checked out from the local library.

After attempting to concentrate for a quarter of an hour, reading proved to be a fruitless endeavor. No matter how hard she tried, she couldn't focus. Her mind kept drifting off. Abbey had been flying higher than a kite this week as her wedding date drew nearer and all the last-minute details were a big part of Caitlin's distraction. That and missing Donovan. She didn't want to ruin things for Abbey, so she tried to put on a happy face whenever they were together. It had become a difficult task. She kept thinking about what Meghan had told her over the phone after receiving the Library's job offer.

They'd conversed earlier in the day as Caitlin tried to decide whether to accept the job offer or not. As interested as she was in taking it, she questioned her real motivation. Caitlin still had a notion Donovan might be in a serious relationship with Dana after Meghan alluded to the fact that they'd gone out a few times since she'd left Dublin.

Meghan tried to convince her friend she knew her brother well. "Donovan has no feelings for Dana other than friendship. They'd been working together for years, and nothing developed in the past. I certainly don't see any sign of any emotional connection now."

"But Meghan…"

"Don't worry, Caitlin. It's you he cares about," Meghan emphasized. Whenever she mentioned Caitlin's name in Donovan's presence, a forlorn look took residence on his face, and he became more distant. She knew he was suffering from their separation.

Caitlin promised she'd let Meghan know the minute she made her final decision. She still felt a little apprehensive about accepting the job. There were too many unknowns. Could her dad handle her living so far away? Would living in Dublin bring her closer to Donovan, or would she suffer emotionally if her feelings were only one-sided? What should she do? She had a lot to consider. In a sense, she had to admit to herself—she was a big coward when it came to pursuing love this time around.

The phone rang unexpectedly. It was Caitlin's sister. "Hi, Abbey, what's up? Are you going to be delayed at the hospital?"

"No, Caitlin, but I wanted to tell you to look up tour information about The High Kings. You know, the group you've been talking about and whose music you play nonstop," she rattled on sarcastically.

Talk of The High Kings perked her up. "Oh? Are they on tour in the U.S.?"

Abbey continued excitedly, "Yeah! I heard something on the radio about their band performing in Minneapolis. I didn't catch all of the details. Maybe they'll be close enough for us to hear them in concert."

"Well, even if they are in the area, there might not be any tickets available. Besides, it might be when we're busy with your wedding. Next Friday we have the groom's dinner, and we have family flying into town for the wedding…"

Abbey interrupted, "Humor me, Caitlin, just check. I'll be home in about half an hour, and then you can fill me in on what you've found out. It'll be fun to see them if it works out."

"Yes, I'd like that. I'll check," Caitlin promised.

"Thanks, see you soon."

When Abbey arrived home half an hour later, she immediately spied Caitlin pacing back and forth in the living room. Startled, Caitlin jumped, then paused before sitting down on the couch in front of her open laptop. An image of The High Kings stared back at her. Caitlin's red nose and puffy eyes hinted she'd been crying.

"What's wrong, Caitlin?" Abbey raced over to sit down next to her sister. "You look as if someone has died."

"No, just feeling a little sentimental, I guess."

"What did you find out about the concert?" Abbey questioned, taking a seat next to her sister.

"The High Kings perform at Cedar Cultural Center in Minneapolis on Thursday night next week. Two days before your wedding."

"Great! That'll work for me," Abbey announced. "I bet Dad and Tim would love to go with us to the concert. It would be a great final family outing before the wedding! Are there tickets still available?"

"Yes," Caitlin answered hesitantly.

"Do they have four seats together?"

Caitlin pointed to the screen, "It's general seating."

"Great! We'll leave early enough so we can get halfway decent seats and sit together. If all else fails, I can sit with Tim, and you can sit with Dad. We can bring Dad's rolling walker for him to sit on in case we have to wait too long in line before the concert starts."

Abbey seemed to have thought through everything rather quickly, almost as if she had done some preplanning. Caitlin disregarded the possibility. She then acknowledged to herself that going to the concert would be therapeutic.

By the time she'd mulled over the idea, Abbey had already bought the tickets on-line. "Done!" she exclaimed. "I secured four tickets for Thursday evening. The door opens at 7 o'clock, so we have time to eat supper here first and then ride into the city together. What do you think?"

"Sounds good. The band usually does a meet and greet after the concert. I want to introduce you to the guys and get a chance to say hello. Dad will love the Irish folk music. But, as much as I'll enjoy going to the concert, it won't change things. The music will make me miss Donovan even more, and he'll still be an ocean away."

"Oh Caitlin, I've said it before, and I'll say it again: there are times when we have to just surrender to the possibilities and let go of the unknown. I don't think God would have sent you on your adventure in the first place without a purpose. You even said you felt Ireland was pulling on your heartstrings, not just Donovan." She paused for a moment then continued, "What would it hurt to accept the job at the National Library for one year if they offered it to you? Just see what happens. If it's meant to be, it will all work out."

Maybe she needed to take a chance and just walk through the door God had opened and see what He had in store for her. Finding the steamer trunk in the attic had opened the first door. She had walked through it into a wonderful adventure. Getting to know Donovan and his family had indeed been a blessing. His family had opened the next door, a door to her heart. They helped her find family members who could've been lost to them forever. Now the real test remained in a temporary move to Ireland—should she walk through this newly opened door, or should she shut it and possibly regret it for the rest of her life?

"Abbey, you're a smart little sister. I know how much you and Tim love each other. You want the same for me, a love for a lifetime. The kind Mom and Dad had. I have a confession to make."

"What's that?"

Taking a deep breath, she shared the secret she'd been holding back. "Abbey, I got a call from the National Library last week with the job offer for Meghan's position. I'm seriously thinking about accepting, but I don't have to let them know my final answer until the week after your wedding."

"Yes! Your answer should be yes! You have to go!" Abbey shouted.

"Shh! You'll wake Dad," scolded Caitlin. "I'll take your suggestion into consideration."

Abbey pulled her sister into a great big bear hug. "Enough excitement for one night. We'd better get some sleep now. I think Dad has plans for us to go to mass together in the morning."

"Yes, time for bed. Luckily, I'm exhausted. The mattress on my old bed has seen better days!" Caitlin complained, hoping she could get some restful sleep instead of tossing and turning like she'd been doing since her return from Ireland.

# Chapter 19

The week slowly dragged by for Caitlin in anticipation of The High Kings' upcoming concert. She felt excited yet apprehensive about seeing them again. Caitlin predicted it would only make her miss Donovan more than she already did. It had proved to be a big distraction at work, especially since she had to make a final life-altering decision about whether or not to accept the job at the National Library in Dublin.

Fortunately, Caitlin had permission to leave work a few hours early on Thursday to avoid traffic delays. Tonight the concert, tomorrow the groom's dinner, and then the wedding. The next two days would be busy. Excited for Tim and Abbey, she tried to move past her personal feelings. Caitlin was determined to take her sister's advice to relax and have fun.

A high-spirited conversation took place during their meal of take-out pizza. Everyone seemed excited about the upcoming events of the week, especially Michael Sullivan. He looked forward to spending time together with his siblings after being apart for almost two years.

"Uncle Will and Aunt Patti will be arriving late Friday evening. They'll meet us at the church on Saturday," Michael explained.

"What about Aunt Mary? I've been trying to get a hold of her all week, but I haven't had any luck. I left her numerous messages, but she never got back to me," Caitlin shared. She looked forward to seeing her aunt again and divulging explicit details about her trip to Ireland.

The puzzled look on her dad's face was priceless. "I'm surprised. We've been talking just about every day this week. Aunt Mary said she'd be here tomorrow in time for the groom's dinner, she's staying at the same hotel as Uncle Will and his family, and she's bringing a guest with her."

How odd, thought Caitlin. "I wonder who it could be?"

Her dad shrugged, "She wouldn't say who. It's supposed to be a big surprise."

Abbey giggled as a possibility entered mind.

"What's so funny, Abbey?" Caitlin asked, confused by her reaction.

"Maybe Aunt Mary has met someone special, and she wants us to meet him."

"At her age?" Their dad could not fathom the idea.

"Dad, you never know when you're going to meet the love of your life," Abbey stated. That silenced him. He was quite aware of the fact. "Aunt Mary is an intelligent, witty, and rather attractive middle-aged woman. I would think many men would be interested in someone like her."

Caitlin agreed with her sister. "I think the reason she's never been in a serious relationship has to do with her being married to her job for the last 30 years. Maybe her priorities have changed."

Their dad shook his head, "I disagree. I just think she's never met the right man. If she had, she wouldn't have been able to resist getting married. I know how I felt when I met your mother. All rational thoughts escaped me, and my universe suddenly revolved around her. She became my reason for living."

Caitlin understood what he meant. She'd felt the same way ever since meeting Donovan. He was never far from her thoughts. If her aunt had met someone, it had to have been after her visit in April. Otherwise, she believed her aunt would have said something to her.

Tim, who'd been quiet most of the meal, finally spoke up. "It's getting late. We'd better clear the table and head off to the concert. I'll drive tonight if no one minds." Caitlin and her dad both agreed. It would be more relaxing if they didn't have to drive. Abbey and Tim had other underlying reasons.

The lively conversation they started at dinner continued on the ride to the Cedar Cultural Center. Family time was rare these days, so every moment was precious, and the conversation usually escalated into some sort of riotous outbreak. Abbey and Tim had been planning their wedding with Caitlin's help for almost a year now. Tonight's excitement centered around the disbelief that the time had finally arrived for them to walk down the aisle.

"Tim, it's too bad we have to postpone our honeymoon."

"I know, Abbey, but we'll have more time to spend together if we wait until later," Tim promised.

Michael overheard Abbey and Tim talking about a delayed honeymoon from the back seat. "What did you say, Tim? You aren't going on a honeymoon right after the wedding?"

"It's all right, Dad. Tim's graduate classes begin the Monday following our wedding. Not the best timing, but he only has a few credits left to complete his master's degree. Then he'll be qualified to apply for a job as a high school principal," Abbey proudly announced.

"Exactly. We've decided to take our honeymoon trip abroad during my spring break in late March. Neither of us has traveled overseas, and we're looking forward to a new adventure together." With no further discussion, only silence filled the air. A father could wish things for his daughters, but they were adults and would make their own decisions in the end.

The light traffic sped up their arrival time as they drove onto the University of Minnesota campus to enter the 19th Avenue Parking Ramp. From there, it was just a three-block walk to their venue. A line for the concert had already formed about half a block long. They quickly joined it and began waiting for the doors to open. It was a lovely summer evening with clear skies making the wait rather pleasurable.

It didn't take Caitlin long to become lost in thought. She looked up at the marquee to see *THE HIGH KINGS* listed at the top. She couldn't believe they were here. Knowing they toured in America gave her hope of seeing them in future concerts. All the band members were such fun-loving, energetic guys. They elicited laughter from their audiences due to their delightful sense of humor. She was counting on them tonight to lift her spirits. She sorely needed it.

When the line began to move, they slowly walked along until they were inside. Once they had found their seats, Caitlin said, "I'm going to get a bottle of water before the concert starts. Does anyone else want something?"

"I'll go with you. I'm going to get a beer for your dad and me," Tim offered.

"Okay."

As soon as they were out of sight, Abbey got up and disappeared. Even her dad didn't know where she'd gone when Tim and Caitlin returned.

"Where's Abbey?" asked Caitlin.

"I don't know. I guess she just got up to stretch her legs. Oh, here she comes now," her dad pointed out. Abbey had emerged from behind a door to the right of the stage.

Caitlin found this a little strange. When she tried to question her sister regarding where she'd been, Abbey just ignored her and squeezed past Caitlin to get to her seat on the opposite side of Tim. Shortly afterward, the band members started to come onto the stage to start the show, making it impossible for her to get to the bottom of things. All else escaped her mind. The High Kings were about to perform.

They started the show by introducing themselves and naturally transitioned into singing a song Caitlin had come to absolutely love since her first encounter with the band, "The Rocky Road to Dublin". Caitlin let herself relax for the first time in weeks, content seeing her family clapping along to the song. Amazed at this multitalented group of musicians, she took a moment to appreciate their newest member Paul's fine flute playing.

After an hour of performing, the audience had such a good time The High Kings chose not to take a break and play straight through.

Near the end of the concert, Darren began introducing one of Caitlin's favorite songs, "Next we're going to sing a classic folk song, Red is the Rose." His smile seemed to sparkle from behind the microphone as he spoke, "With this song, we bring a special message from Ireland to a mutual friend who is seated in the audience tonight. Caitlin Sullivan, where are you lass?"

Caitlin was speechless. She looked around at her family. Did Caitlin hear correctly? How would the band know she was in the audience? What was going on? Then she remembered Abbey had suspiciously disappeared earlier. What had she been doing?

"Well, Caitlin. We don't have all day. We know you're out there," Brian spoke up. All the audience members seemed to be looking around for some movement from the crowd. She didn't know what to do.

"Caitlin, they're talking to you. Wave your hand or stand up or something," Abbey insisted.

When Caitlin hesitantly raised her right hand, it seemed as if all eyes were staring directly at her. She could feel a blush begin to travel across her face. How embarrassing.

"Ah, there you are, lass. Stand up so we can see you better." Caitlin slowly rose from her seat, then Darren continued, "Our dear friend Donovan O'Malley has asked us to sing a song in your honor tonight. He said you would understand the meaning behind its lyrics," Darren informed.

Completely caught off guard, Caitlin suddenly felt as if the only way to survive her embarrassment was to hide her face in her hands and sink deeply into her chair. What is going on, she wondered?

Darren gestured for her to be seated and then gave the rest of the guys a nod of the head to start. She slowly settled back to listen as Finbarr began to sing the first verse acapella.

*Come over the hills, my bonnie Irish lass.*

*Come over the hills to your darling.*

*You choose the road, love, and I'll make the vow.*

*And I'll be your true love forever.*

Now, what message did Donovan mean to send by these words? Did he want her to go back to Dublin to be with him? Was he proposing marriage? Is that what "make the vow" meant? She wondered as the band began singing the refrain. She shook her head slowly. Maybe she was reading way too much into this. Could this be what he wanted her to think?

*Red is the rose that in yonder garden grows.*

*Fair is the lily of the valley.*

*Clear is the water that flows from the Boyne.*

*But my love is fairer than any.*

Then Darren began to sing the second verse, and by the time they reached the second refrain, recognition set in, and tears were rolling down Caitlin's face.

*'Twas down by Killarney's green woods that we strayed*

*When the moon and the stars they were shining*

*The moon shone its rays on her locks of golden hair.*

*And she swore she'd be my love forever.*

When Brian began the third verse, she felt a gentle touch on her right shoulder. Through tear-filled eyes, she looked up to see Donovan standing next to her. She thought she was dreaming, but he held out his hand for her to take, pulling her into his waiting arms. They just stood embracing as Brian finished the verse, and the guys began another chorus.

*It's not for the parting that my sister pains.*

*It's not for the grief of my mother.*

*'Tis all for the loss of my bonny Irish lass*

*That my heart is breaking forever.*

As the band continued to repeat the chorus, Donovan led Caitlin to the back of the room for a more private reunion. They looked at one another for a moment before Donovan leaned in to kiss her. Caitlin was too stunned to be embarrassed. She closed her eyes and just melted as Donovan's lips touched hers, and she felt him slowly take her in his arms and deepen the kiss.

The audience's thunderous applause at the end of the song was almost deafening. Donovan released Caitlin and turned toward the band, nodding at them, and mouthing the words "thank you" to his friends. He then proceeded to take Caitlin's hand and pull her toward the door Abbey had come through earlier.

"What are you doing here?" Caitlin asked breathlessly.

"Just come with me, and I'll tell you." They stepped through the door and into the hallway, away from the crowd where they could hear each other. Donovan stopped and turned toward Caitlin. "I couldn't wait for you to return to Ireland. I had to see you again and explain why I never made it back into Dublin to see you off."

She tried to focus on what he was saying as the band broke into song with the audience joining in on "Friends for Life", one of their signature songs. "Dana explained everything to me on the phone, and I understood you had an emergency you needed to handle. She also said you'd misplaced your phone. I know why you couldn't make it back to drive me to the airport, but I was disappointed. I had a wonderful time with you in Killarney, and I admit I didn't want it to end."

A frown appeared on his face when he began to explain what had transpired during her last full day in Dublin. As forgiving as she seemed, he felt he needed to explain. "First, my phone disappearing seemed a little strange. Later I figured out Dana was behind the whole missing phone business and had been harboring feelings for me since Marie's death."

"Is that why you've been dating her lately?"

"Now, where did you get such an idea?"

"When I finally got up the courage to text you last week, you didn't respond, and Meghan mentioned you'd been out with Dana."

Leave it to his sister to omit the essential details to make Caitlin jealous. "We had worked overtime and were both hungry, so I treated her to a late supper, nothing more."

"Hmph!"

Donovan chuckled, "Caitlin, the only woman I'm interested in growing closer to is you. It wasn't until you left Ireland that I realized you'd taken a piece of my heart with you." He wasn't going to beat around the bush. He needed to convince Caitlin then and there that she was the only one who had a place in his heart. He hadn't come this far for there to be any more misunderstandings. As he lowered his mouth, all the reasons why rushing things was a bad idea flashed through his head in rapid succession, but none compared to the urgent hunger inside him to claim this woman for his own.

When his mouth brushed against hers once, then twice, Caitlin gave a small intake of breath. He started to ease away but didn't make it far before she wrapped her arms around him, sending all thoughts of taking things slow out of his mind.

Caitlin couldn't believe Donovan was standing right there in front of her. It was like she was experiencing the loveliest dream from which she hoped never to awaken. She didn't care what had happened in the past. He was here with her now.

"I've missed you, Cait," he whispered in her ear, sending shivers up and down her spine.

"I've missed you, too," she returned.

Suddenly applause broke out again from the other side of the door, and the band members started filing into the hallway.

"Break it up already," teased Brian.

"So, have you two worked things out now? Are you friends again?" asked Darren.

"Friends for life," affirmed Caitlin, trying to lighten things up. The band was overjoyed to have been a part of their friend's reunion.

"Are you including all of us?" Finbarr interjected.

"Definitely!" Caitlin promised.

"Well, we have to head back out to our awaiting fans and sign a few autographs," Darren explained. "It's a pleasure seeing you again, Caitlin. I wish we had more time to visit."

"I feel the same way. It's been wonderful listening to your music again. It won't be the last time for me. I promise!" The guys generously acknowledged her praises before reentering to greet their fans with Darren leading the way.

Donovan held the door open for Caitlin as they followed the band back into the main concert hall. Some of the audience was slowly exiting, giggling, and chatting as they went, while others moved towards the merchandise area. Caitlin watched the band cut across the stage before noticing her family patiently waiting for her to return to their seats.

Caitlin took Donovan's hand this time, dragging him toward the emphatic wave of her sister. Caitlin saw Abbey tap their father on the shoulder and point in her direction. A huge smile spread across his face. By the time Caitlin and Donovan had reached her family, they'd moved into the aisle to welcome them.

Caitlin began her introductions. "Abbey, Tim, Dad, this is Donovan O'Malley, Meghan's brother."

Her father stepped forward first. Donovan held out his hand to a firm handshake. "I'm Caitlin's dad, Michael. It's a pleasure to meet you finally. I've heard a lot about you and your family. Thank you for being such a good host to my daughter while she was in Ireland."

"It was my pleasure, Sir. Trust me. I don't know how I'll ever repay your family for sending Caitlin our way. We had the adventure of a lifetime," he admitted as he pulled Caitlin to his side and casually wrapped his arm around her. Immediately after setting eyes on Donovan, Michael realized why his daughter had been so distracted since she'd returned home from Ireland.

Abbey spoke next, "Hi, Donovan. We've already met, but I'd like you to meet my fiancé, Tim Baxter."

Relieved their plans had succeeded, Tim enthusiastically greeted the Irishman. "Hello Donovan, I'm glad you were able to make it. Abbey and I are relieved this little surprise worked out. We'd like to officially invite you to join us tomorrow evening for our Groom's Dinner and then our wedding on Saturday."

"Yes, please, you could be Caitlin's plus one," added Abbey.

A strange expression appeared on Donovan's face, "Plus one?"

"It means you'd be her date. She doesn't have one yet," Abbey explained.

"Well, I should hope not!" he exclaimed. He hadn't come all this way for only a few minutes of her time. Abbey had promised him some quality togetherness before he had to fly back home. He wasn't taking any chances of Caitlin distancing herself from him again. Even his sister had promised she had an idea to get Caitlin back to Ireland as quickly as possible; only she wouldn't say how.

"What?" Caitlin couldn't believe what Abbey had just said. Everything was happening so fast. She stood there in awe listening to the rest of their interaction, finally realizing the two had done some extensive planning regarding this little reunion.

"It would be my pleasure. I don't fly back to Dublin until Sunday. I'd love to join in on your celebration and spend more time with Cait," he said as he pulled her closer to him, rather possessively.

Confusion showed on Caitlin's face, but Donovan felt assured by their previous interactions that she was more than happy to have him there, just currently embarrassed by all the attention directed toward her.

"Is it okay with you, Caitlin?"

She paused slightly before answering, "Of course, I'm still adjusting to the fact that you're here." Nothing could be more accurate. The shock had begun to wear off, and a sense of peace enfolded her like a mother's embrace.

"Honestly, I'm a little surprised by your warm reception, especially after I missed seeing you off at the airport in April. I didn't know if you'd be happy to see me again."

A smile immediately spread across her face. "Of course, I'm happy to see you. I just can't believe you're here," she repeated.

The reaction she had experienced to his kisses alone had clarified her strong feelings toward him. When she had pressed up against him, she had lost all sense of reason. She'd kissed him with a hunger that seemed to match his own. Honestly, she felt a little embarrassed by her own reaction.

Caitlin and her family continued to visit with Donovan until most of the audience members had cleared the area. Then he did the honors and introduced each of the band members to Caitlin's family.

"Are you in town long?" Caitlin asked.

Brian was the first to respond. "No, we're on the road again tomorrow."

"Too bad, I would have invited you to Abbey's wedding and tried to convince you to play a few songs for their dance. You would make the perfect wedding band!"

"Well, maybe for the next family wedding," added Darren, along with a wink aimed at Donovan.

"I plan on bringing my dad to Ireland for a visit. Maybe we'll get to see you in concert on my return trip."

"We'd love to see you again," Brian concurred.

"Thanks, everyone, for helping with this unbelievable surprise. I don't think I'll ever forget it. I promise you'll see me again in the not-too-distant future," Caitlin promised the band.

"We're counting on it, Caitlin." Darren patted Donovan on the shoulder as he nodded with a smile. Then the band turned their attention back to the last few fans waiting for autographs.

Donovan thanked Abbey and Tim for helping with his grand surprise. "What a delight to finally meet you. I look forward to getting to know your family better over the next few days. Thank you so much for allowing me to crash your wedding to spend more time with this fair lass."

"It'll be a pleasure to have you join our celebration," Abbey assured him.

"Now, if you don't mind, I'll give Cait a ride home in my rental. Is that all right with you, Cait?" he asked, his eyes pleading for her to answer in the affirmative.

"Sure," she agreed, feeling a need for some closure after such a big shock in seeing Donovan again.

Abbey placed her hand on her dad's shoulder just as he was about to speak. She didn't want to take a chance on him interrupting any extra time her sister and Donovan might have together. Then Donovan began to escort Caitlin toward his car in total silence, unsure how to start to say what he felt still needed to be said. Being the gentleman, he went to open the car door for her, but she held out her hand for the keys instead of getting in.

His confused look forced her to explain, "We're in my territory now. I'll drive so you can focus on explaining to me exactly why you're here."

Once they were both in the car and Caitlin had readjusted the seat and mirrors, she started the engine. As she pulled out of the parking spot, Donovan began hesitantly. "So, you were surprised to see me?"

"Definitely. What on earth are you doing here without contacting me first?"

"Abbey and Meghan talked. By the sounds of it, they determined your mood had changed for the worse since you returned from Ireland. Abbey wanted to get my take on what happened between the two of us because she was highly suspicious that I was the cause of those changes."

"And what did you tell her?"

"I told her we enjoyed our time together, but it ended unfortunately in an abrupt manner. It was only a coincidence The High Kings were in this area on their American Tour, so they agreed to help us out with our little scheme to surprise you. Were we successful? Were you pleasantly surprised?"

Not taking her eyes off the road, she reflected briefly before answering. "Honestly, my head is spinning, and my heart rate is still a little faster than normal. We've barely communicated with one another since I got home, so yes, I'm surprised. Since I'm confirmed this isn't a dream, I'm wondering why you traveled all this way to see me?"

Caitlin wasn't making this easy for him. "Plain and simple, I missed you and felt terrible about how we parted." If truth be told, he'd been totally out of sorts for a good week after she'd left. He kept reminiscing about the time they'd spent together. He felt he needed to be honest with her if they were ever going to strengthen what he perceived to be the start of a good friendship with the potential of turning into a lasting relationship.

"I haven't been the same since you left and for some reason have been very distracted since you flew out of my life," Donovan began in all sincerity, "I like you, Caitlin Sullivan. It's plain and simple. I know a long-distance relationship sounds crazy, but I'm here to put my heart on the line and tell you I want to take a chance on us being more than just friends."

She wondered if his sister had told him about her job offer. "We wouldn't see much of each other except once or twice a year. Unless you're planning to move to the States."

"I know, Cait. I was thinking we'd start by just connecting more often. I know I was a little assertive when I kissed you, but the minute my lips touched yours, I knew I hadn't just imagined our strong connection."

Caitlin, thrown off by Donovan spilling his emotions out on the floor, almost missed her turn off the highway into Maplewood. She wasn't ready to make a final decision about the job in Dublin just yet, but she knew whatever transpired over the next two days would help her make her final choice.

"I'll admit we seem to get along easily. We've had some fun times together. Let's just see how things go while you're here."

"Deal!" Donovan agreed immediately, reaching out to squeeze her hand. A smile lit up his face. He felt hopeful about spending quality time together at Abbey and Tim's wedding festivities. The question was, if their relationship evolved into something more permanent, would she be willing to take the leap and move to Ireland? He couldn't leave his family business to live with her in America, of that he was sure. But what he was surer of was his determination to move mountains in order to convince her to make a home with him in Ireland.

Once they arrived at Caitlin's place, they agreed to call it a night and get some much-needed rest before a busy day ahead. Donovan wrapped his arms around Caitlin in a tight hug before leaving for his hotel, promising to pick her up the next evening for the groom's dinner. He had a busy schedule the next day, seeing some clients he wanted to squeeze in while he was here. Afterward, he could devote the rest of his time to the woman who had somehow captured his heart.

# Chapter 20

The wedding rehearsal the next day went smoothly. Tim and Abbey had scheduled a few hours in between to relax before gathering friends and family for the Groom's Dinner at a local Italian restaurant. Tim's parents were staying at a nearby hotel, and he had promised to pick them up before swinging by to get her. Abbey assured Tim she'd be watching for him from the house, so he didn't need to walk to the door to pick her up. She kept checking her hair and make-up in the hallway mirror in between glances out the window. Abbey wanted to look perfect tonight for Tim on their last evening together before becoming husband and wife. She peeked outside once more just as his car pulled up in front of the sidewalk.

Abbey shouted to her sister from the bottom of the stairs, "Caitlin, Tim, and his parents are waiting out in his car. I'm leaving now. We'll see you at the restaurant."

"Okay, we shouldn't be far behind you," Caitlin shouted back before making her way to her dad's bedroom in hopes of keeping him on schedule. She gently wrapped on the door. "Are you ready, Dad? Donovan should be here shortly."

"Come in here," he ordered. "I need some help with my tie. No matter what I do, it doesn't seem to be right," he complained from the other side of the door.

She entered slowly, fighting to prevent herself from laughing at the picture her dad made. He stood in front of the floor-length mirror, with the tie wrapped around his fingers, frustration written on his face.

He saw her reflection behind him in the mirror, "Now don't look at me like that, Caitie. You know your mother always helped me with my ties. I don't think I've worn one since her funeral, and if I recall correctly you were the one who tied it," he muttered.

She could hold back her laughter no longer, "I seem to remember. I hate to say this, but you need to start learning how to do this independently. There are plenty of online videos you could watch to help you. Tonight is Abbey's last night staying with you, and I won't always live such a short distance away."

"What do you mean by that? Where are you going? Does this have something to do with the Irish fellow coming to pick us up?" her dad confronted her. "Is he the reason you haven't been yourself since you returned from Ireland?"

Realizing she'd accidentally opened up a can of worms; Caitlin waved her hands in the air to stop him from continuing to ramble on. "Calm down, Dad. I've told you about Donovan before. He's Meghan's brother, and I've become friends with her entire family, including Donovan. "

"Friends don't usually kiss like the two of you. I had my eye on you last night at the concert, young lady. You're not fooling me. Something is going on between the two of you."

Michael was no fool. He'd seen the way the two had looked at each other. Who did she think she was kidding? He wasn't born yesterday. Fortunately for Caitlin, his thoughts were interrupted by the doorbell.

Caitlin could just see the wheels turning inside her dad's head. One last check of his tie and she steered him into the hallway and down the stairs to the front entryway to get their coats. The doorbell rang again, Donovan to the rescue.

Donovan discreetly greeted Caitlin with a quick kiss on the cheek before turning to shake hands with her dad. Smart move on his part, Caitlin noticed. It seemed to help settle her father down a bit. He was already marrying one daughter off this week, she didn't think he was ready to see the second enter a serious relationship so soon after.

"It'll be nice to meet more of your family tonight, Mr. Sullivan. Your daughter has shared wonderful stories about all of you."

"I can just imagine." He turned and stared earnestly at his daughter. He wanted her to know he had his eye on her, and he knew what was going on. They couldn't fool him. "Donovan, you can call me Michael. Hopefully, by the end of the night, we'll be friends."

Caitlin began to relax, and lovingly smiled at her dad. She didn't know how much change her dad could handle at one time. Despite all her befuddled thoughts, she kept thinking about the job waiting in Dublin and what a move to Ireland could mean for her.

Her dad seemed to ask Donovan a million and one questions in the short time it took them to reach the restaurant. Once they'd arrived, one of the wait staff led them to a private dining area. Caitlin could see that the entire wedding party had come. She observed Abbey chatting with Caitlin while Tim stood on the opposite side of the room having a serious conversation with his brother Roger.

The other groomsmen were engaged in an animated conversation with Tim's parents. Dave, Susan's husband, seemed to be in the process of telling some tale of adventure about Tim. Greg, Tim's co-worker, kept adding details to the already embellished story causing Tim's parents to break-down laughing. By the look of things, everyone had arrived except Aunt Mary and her mystery guest. Caitlin suspected she was up to something.

"Let's all take our places so the servers can do their job. My sister should be here shortly," the father of the bride announced, joy radiating from his face as intense as the summer sunshine.

Everyone quickly found their place at the large, beautifully decorated table. Only two seats remained empty just to Caitlin's left. The servers efficiently delivered water glasses and had finished taking everyone's drink orders just as Aunt Mary swooped into the room.

"I'm sorry we're late. We had a hard time finding a parking spot," she announced loudly to the group. It was apparent by Aunt Mary's rambling that she was excited about her big surprise. She moved aside so everyone could see her guest for tonight's dinner and tomorrow's wedding. Caitlin and those family members that knew the guest just stared at him in awe. It was none other than Jeremy.

"It can't be," sighed Caitlin, followed by Abbey's loud gasp. Donovan glanced around the table, confused by all the sour expressions on the Sullivan family's faces. He could see this guest of Aunt Mary's was an unwanted surprise, especially to Abbey and Caitlin.

"For those of you who don't know my guest, this is Jeremy Fisher, Caitlin's boyfriend from Boston. I decided to surprise her by bringing him along."

*Ah, so this is Jeremy,* Donovan thought, as he connected the face to the name.

"Former boyfriend, he's my former boyfriend," Caitlin stressed loud enough for the entire party to hear. She was fairly sure she was going to pass out; she felt a bit light-headed.

Aunt Mary joyfully added, "But hopefully not for long. Here you sit next to Caitlin, Jeremy, and I'll sit next to my brother. Michael, maybe you could introduce us to your other guests here tonight. I don't know everyone."

Ever the gracious host, Michael recognized the uncomfortable situation his sister had forced upon them, and he was determined to make the best out of a bad situation. He slowly started by introducing Tim's parents, followed by the groomsmen, the bridesmaids, and Donovan.

"Mary, I'd like to introduce you to Caitlin's good friend from Ireland, Donovan O'Malley. He helped Caitlin track down our second cousin and his family in Killarney."

"Oh, I see," she managed to breathe out, recognizing the big mistake she'd made. If Donovan O'Malley had come from Ireland to see Caitlin, something must be brewing between them. She realized she was in big trouble by the unspoken message Caitlin's eyes were sending her way. Jeremy seemed to be oblivious to the whole uneasy situation.

A general discomfort grew around the table. Caitlin, feeling blindsided by Jeremy's unexpected arrival, skipped over any small talk, and immediately excused herself to the bathroom. She was angry. Less than a month ago, she'd clearly told him their relationship was over. Yet, he still decided to show up out of the blue, thinking something would magically change. Typical Jeremy, always out to serve himself and take advantage of her aunt in the process. He was somewhat clueless when it came to social graces.

Having witnessed the whole awkward exchange, Abbey followed her sister out of the room to make sure she was okay.

Caitlin's abrupt absence left Donovan and Jeremy with just the empty seat between them for company. Jeremy, ever the alpha male, quickly sized up his competition and went on the attack, "So, Donovan, what brings you here?"

Donovan's answer was short and sweet, "I'm here on business and to spend some time with Caitlin."

"You've traveled a long way for a visit," Jeremy prodded.

"Yes."

"Specifically to see someone you've only briefly met," came Jeremy's left jab.

Donovan noticed his attempt at stirring things up. He could tell Jeremy intended to get back together with Caitlin, so he decided it was best to stake out his territory. "Our time may have been brief but significant. Memorable enough to want to see each other again and continue to develop our relationship. We've decided to see where this weekend leads. I have a good feeling about it," he continued.

Jeremy didn't like what he was hearing, especially the mention of them having spent time together in Ireland. Nope, he did not like the sound of it.

Aunt Mary overheard the last part of the conversation and leaned over Jeremy. "That's nice, Donovan. Friends of Caitlin's are friends of the family. It's a pleasure to meet you even if Caitlin didn't tell me anything about you when we talked earlier," she said, insinuating it was Caitlin's fault this whole uncomfortable mix-up had occurred.

Donovan couldn't help smiling when he tried to lighten things up by replying, "Well, Aunt Mary, Caitlin did tell me about you, and it was all flattering. By the way, she looked lovely in the outfit you bought her." The smile on his face slowly spread to Mary's, and she heaved a sigh of relief. His willingness to forgive might be her only saving grace when extending an apology to her niece.

Talking to Abbey had calmed Caitlin down a bit. By the time they returned to the party, things had begun to settle down. That's when everyone's appetite kicked in. With the party distracted by the food, Caitlin leaned toward Jeremy and, in a quiet voice, began to speak her piece. "Why are you here, Jeremy?" she seemed to growl under her breath at him.

"Caitlin, come on, give me a chance. You said you preferred to have a conversation in person, so Aunt Mary arranged to make it happen. How can you be mad at me for taking her up on the offer?" he challenged.

In her head, Caitlin started to count to ten. This man could make her blood boil, and she found it hard to believe she had ever loved him. "Jeremy, it was just a figure of speech. I said all I had to say to you over the phone the last time we spoke."

"What does this Donovan fellow mean to you? Is he why you won't give me another chance?"

"Donovan and I are just friends, Jeremy, nothing more. But that doesn't have anything to do with us." She took a deep cleansing breath before continuing, "I'm going to be respectful of the fact Aunt Mary brought you here from Boston, so let's make a deal. You can escort Aunt Mary to Tim and Abbey's wedding as planned, but you won't intrude on my space without my permission, and you will not harass Donovan in any way."

He studied her face carefully before commenting further, "So, you are sweet on him, aren't you?"

"My feelings for Donovan are none of your business. Now let's eat our meal and try to be sociable for the rest of the evening. I want to avoid the spotlight casting its light on us instead of Abbey and Tim," she firmly resolved.

Donovan had attempted to listen in on their conversation, and he wondered just how far Jeremy would go to get Caitlin back. He knew he hadn't come this far to abandon his plan of strengthening their budding friendship. He hoped it would become much more.

Later in the evening, after dropping off Caitlin and her dad, Donovan was tempted to give his sister a call. She was always so good at offering him words of wisdom, but he soon realized it was early morning in Dublin. She would never forgive him for interrupting her beauty sleep. He'd have to delay talking to her until morning and focus on getting a good night's rest. Tomorrow was going to be another emotionally packed day. He had a lot riding on his ability to persuade Caitlin of his feelings for her.

# Chapter 21

The big day had finally arrived, and a buzz of excitement filled the air as Caitlin gathered with her sister and the other bridesmaids at the beauty salon for the ritual wedding preparations. Donovan was scheduled to meet Caitlin at the church for the wedding in the early afternoon. Until then, he used his time to accomplish a few things. First, he made a brief phone call to his sister. Meghan seemed to be in good spirits.

"Why if it isn't the devil himself calling me from America," she teased. "What's up?"

"I need some advice, dear sister. I met my competition for Caitlin's affections. His name is Jeremy Fisher, and he's from Boston."

"What does this Jeremy have to do with Caitlin?"

"He's Caitlin's former boyfriend. He arrived yesterday with her aunt. By the panicked look on Caitlin's face, I could tell his appearance had been a complete surprise to her. She doesn't know this, but one evening when we were together in Ireland, I noticed a text from him on her phone proposing marriage. Now he's here, and he doesn't seem to be backing down no matter what Caitlin says to him."

"Caitlin never mentioned him to me in all the conversations we've had. He can't mean that much to her. Did you get a chance to talk with her after meeting up with this Jeremy fellow?"

"No, we were with her family all evening. Hopefully, after the wedding today, we'll get some quality time alone. There will be dinner and a dance afterward. I'll be Caitlin's escort," Donovan proudly announced.

Meghan interrupted, "Now see here, he's not much competition for you if she's planning to spend her time with you. Now that should mean something."

"Thanks, Sis. I hope so." he sighed.

"Well, I've had enough practice over the years trying to head you in the right direction. Between you and Sheamus, I don't know who's the bigger fool. Now don't give me any more of your blarney. If I'm not mistaken, you've already won Caitlin's heart."

"Thanks for the vote of confidence, Sis."

"Donovan, good luck!"

"Thanks!"

Now to act. Before heading to the church, Donovan needed to find a wedding gift for the happy couple and a little something special for Caitlin to show her how he felt. A short drive from his hotel, he found a quaint shop called "Irish on the Grand" on the outskirts of St. Paul, only a 15-minute drive from the church. Within half an hour, he'd found the perfect piece of jewelry for her and a lovely Irish Wedding Blessing picture frame for Tim and Abbey.

Fortunately, when Donovan explained his situation regarding the wedding gift, the shop clerk found a decorative gift bag to place the wedding gift in as well as a small card for him to sign. With time to spare and the loud rumbling sounds emanating from his stomach, he found a quaint restaurant in the neighborhood where he grabbed a quick bite to eat, something to tide him over until the wedding dinner. With his hunger fed by a cheeseburger and fries and his thirst quenched by a large glass of iced tea, he was off to the wedding.

Donovan's thoughts spun round and round in his head on the short drive to the church. Along the way, he tried to rehearse the words he would use to convince Caitlin of his strong feelings for her. She had promised to ride with him to the Community Center, where the reception and dance would take place. During their time alone, he planned to pull any weeds of doubt from her mind regarding pursuing a long-distance relationship.

He noticed the bridesmaids posing with the bride for a photo as he pulled into the church parking lot. Once parked, he walked in their direction, where he found Caitlin and her sister standing near a large maple tree. Together they painted a beautiful picture, and he couldn't resist taking out his cellphone to snap a photo before they could notice him. Caitlin somehow felt his presence and slowly pivoted until her eyes caught his.

*Donovan could be the groom today, the way he's dressed,* she thought to herself. He had arrived wearing a slim fitting black business suit, white shirt, and black tie. He looked rather debonair. She noticed he'd groomed his beard since she'd seen him the night before. The twinkle in his blue eyes and a nod of his head let her know he, in turn, appreciated how she looked in her formal attire. He walked toward her until they stood face to face.

"You're looking rather handsome this afternoon, Dr. O'Malley."

"Why, thank you, Miss Sullivan. You look rather stunning yourself. What's going on here? Where are all the men?"

"Abbey doesn't want Tim to see her before the ceremony. She's more traditional than me when it comes to weddings."

"Yes, I recall you complaining about that fact when we were in Ireland. You said you wouldn't be hiding away on your wedding day but front and center to greet your guests as they entered the church."

Caitlin was shocked that Donovan remembered her comments and wished she could take back her earlier rant, regardless of how she truly felt. "We're trying to get a few photos taken where the bride and groom aren't together. Then after the wedding, they'll quickly take the rest of the photos before heading to the reception. The wedding will be starting soon. Why don't you go into the church and let one of the ushers know you're supposed to be seated with the bride's family."

"I'll do just that." He confidently stepped in closer and decided if he planned on planting a metaphorical garden of love in Caitlin's life, he would start with a kiss on her sun kissed cheek. As he walked toward the church, he couldn't resist looking back to smile at Caitlin. Her gaze had attentively followed in the direction he'd taken until a tall, rather serious looking man joined her. He moved within a foot of Caitlin, and placing a hand on her shoulder, began to have what looked like a rather intense conversation. Donovan wondered who the man could be. Did he have more competition for Caitlin's affections other than Jeremy? He didn't like the idea. He realized he would just have to wait and see. Her charm and intelligence were bound and determined to attract any man within a hundred yards. He could feel a seed of doubt enter their lovely garden. How would he be able to compete with these men who lived in closer proximity to her?

Donovan tried to leave his insecurities behind once he entered the church. He observed the ushers quickly seating the guests. He didn't have long to wait before finding himself seated next to Caitlin's Uncle Will and his wife, Patti. Aunt Mary briefly introduced them. She seemed to be on her best behavior after yesterday's fiasco. Not Jeremy, who sat to her right, smiling in an irritatingly smug way at him.

Donovan's focus of attention changed the minute the processional music started to play. He turned to glance down the aisle toward the entrance of the church. Tim looked relaxed as he waited patiently at the foot of the altar. The bridesmaids slowly began walking down the aisle escorted by the groomsmen to the piano and flute accompaniment. Donovan watched for the first sign of Caitlin. She appeared, coupled with the best man, Tim's brother Roger. She held a beautiful bouquet of red sweetheart roses and baby's breath. Entranced by the vision, he didn't take his eyes off her until the music suddenly changed, and Abbey appeared to float down the aisle on her father's arm, wearing a beautiful ivory wedding gown. Donovan hadn't been at a wedding since his sister's almost eight years ago. Happy memories rippled across his mind.

Upon reaching the foot of the altar, Michael Sullivan hugged and kissed Abbey before shaking Tim's hand. Then the bride linked her arm in the groom's and pivoted to stand in front of the priest. Donovan watched intently as the wedding began. Now and then, he would sneak a peek at Caitlin to watch her varied expressions during the ceremony. He knew she would make a beautiful bride someday.

The celebration of the wedding within the Catholic mass proved to be simple yet memorable. The guests broke out into applause as the happy couple exchanged their first kiss as husband

and wife before making their way back down the aisle. Donovan felt a sudden swell of sadness flow over him, throwing him off balance. His thoughts drifted into the past, recalling his lost love—Marie— until he caught sight of Caitlin slowly following behind her sister. A glance in his direction and her smile seemed to light up the room. Just what he needed to lift his spirits.

With the wedding ceremony finished, the bridal party formed a traditional receiving line to greet their guests. After the photographer took a few more formal photos, they drove the short distance by car to the reception. Donovan had been patiently waiting all day to have some time alone with Caitlin. Their drive to the reception would be his first opportunity.

Always the gentleman, he opened the car door and helped her in. Once they were on their way, she asked, "What did you think of the wedding?"

"Truly lovely, and your sister looked radiant. Tim looked every bit the happy groom."

"A match made in Heaven."

"From the little I've seen of the two together, I can see their joy. I look forward to getting to know them better over time," he hinted.

"Sadly, it probably won't happen today. I'm sorry you won't be able to sit with us at the wedding party's table. My dad promised to keep you company and entertain you until I'm free to join you."

"It's going to be rather painful not spending every moment with you, yet I'm sure I'll survive with the help of your family," Donovan exaggerated. "I would like some private time for the opportunity to discuss something important with you before the evening ends. My flight leaves rather early tomorrow morning."

"Oh! Here it is!" Caitlin gasped. "Take the next turn to the right. We're almost at the Community Center. Do you see the large building over there?"

"Yes, I do."

Donovan made his turn in time, and when the car had come to a full stop, Caitlin reached over to take Donovan's hand. She leaned in toward him and made a vow. "Donovan, when the meal is over, we'll have all the time in the world to talk. I hope you'll save a dance for me, too."

"That's a promise I'm going to make sure you keep. As far as a dance goes, one would never be enough." He leaned in even closer to capture a kiss from her eagerly awaiting lips when suddenly they were startled by a rap on Caitlin's window. Annoyed, she turned and rolled it down, and Jeremy's head popped into view.

"Your Aunt Mary wants to talk to you before she sits down to eat. Can you meet her in the lady's room?"

"I suppose so. Why don't you go in and find your table? I'll bring Aunt Mary to you when we've finished talking."

"Sure thing, but why don't I walk you in?" he offered.

"Jeremy," she warned.

"Yes?"

"I already have an escort," she reminded him. "Go on ahead. I'll see you later."

Donovan started to consider Jeremy a real nuisance. He seemed to be self-centered and lacked manners. He tucked Caitlin's arm in his for the short walk to the building where they parted ways. Caitlin walked directly to the lady's room to check on her aunt.

Caitlin spotted her aunt standing in front of a floor-length mirror. She looked pretty, polished, and just a little bit playful in the vintage inspired A-line silhouette, which flattered her trim figure. The velvet rose shade with embroidered floral embellishments, and a satin ribbon added an elegant flourish. She made a pretty picture in pink.

Following a short discussion, Caitlin discovered her aunt felt a need to be officially forgiven for her impulsive choice to drag Jeremy with her from Boston to the wedding without discussing it with her niece.

Relieved, she gave it freely. "Aunt Mary, you know I could never stay mad at you for any reason. I forgive you, but I'm counting on you to keep Jeremy occupied. I don't want him to interfere with my time with Donovan, short as it is. Can you do this for me?"

"Of course, my dear," she promised.

Love is a fragile flower opening to the warmth of spring, Caitlin realized. A sudden heavy outburst of rain could do damage, and while her aunt might have brought light rain to the party, Jeremy could easily be the downpour that could beat it to the ground. She knew things didn't always go as planned. When in life does anything ever go smoothly when it comes to love?

Caitlin guided her aunt to the family table. Donovan had already found a seat next to her father, directly across the round table from Jeremy. She smiled and nodded at him before moving to the large rectangular table nearby reserved for the wedding party.

The meal began with a tasty strawberry spinach salad, followed by a grilled balsamic chicken breast with fresh tomatoes, garlic, red onion, basil, and shredded Parmesan cheese sprinkled on it. The side dishes of scalloped potatoes and grilled asparagus were all delicious but had difficulty settling in Caitlin's stomach. For some reason, she felt very apprehensive about Donovan and Jeremy sitting in such close proximity to each other, with her being outside of the hearing range of their table. If only she knew what Jeremy had up his sleeve, she could relax a bit, but she didn't trust him or his promises.

A movement to her left redirected her attention toward the best man as he stood confidently, gearing up for his toast to the bride and groom. It would be her turn next. She needed to breathe deeply and calm herself for the task.

Roger looked relaxed as he began his short speech. "Tim, Abbey, this day has finally arrived, and I can already tell that marriage between the two of you is going to be one big happy adventure. Never in your entire relationship have I seen you question your love for one another. You are devoted individuals who make a difference in the world through your chosen professions. May you bring the same devotion to your marriage. Here's to a long and happy life together. Cheers!"

"Cheers!" echoed the crowd, as glasses clinked around the room.

Caitlin took a quick sip from her champagne glass before standing up to take her turn. She slowly gazed around the room before her focus landed on Donovan, quickly diverting back to the bride and groom. "Abbey, from one sister to another, I'd first like to tell you how amazing you look today. I am so proud of the woman you've become and happy you've found the man of your dreams."

*Thank you*, Abbey, mouthed back to her.

"I'm so grateful you and Tim included me in the planning of this blessed event. I look forward to watching your love grow in your new relationship as husband and wife." Directing her gaze towards Tim, she added, "Tim, I couldn't have chosen a better match for my sister. You've always been there for her and the rest of our family during the good and bad times. The support you offer gives her the strength she needs to keep going on a daily basis. I look forward to meeting your children in the future and adding the name 'aunt' to my credentials."

Turning out toward the guests, she lifted her glass and concluded, a celebratory note in her voice, "Best wishes to our newly married couple Tim and Abbey Baxter and may you all be as blessed as they are today in finding the love and support you need in your lives." Her focus landed on Donovan as she ended with a triumphant, "Cheers!"

As everyone responded, she noticed her dad had become teary-eyed. Blowing him a kiss brought a smile to his face. The gesture did not go unnoticed by Donovan. Her words had touched him, as well. Listening to her speech only confirmed for him that Caitlin was the one who could make a difference in his life, helping to heal his bruised heart and support him through the good times and bad. Life could deliver some hard blows. Donovan's burdens would lessen with the right support behind him, and his blessings become more abundant.

Following the toast, the bride and groom shared the traditional piece of cake. To their guests' delight, Abbey couldn't resist making a mess of Tim's face after he'd fed her so delicately. To retaliate, he kissed her, transferring some of the frosting. Caitlin happily captured the moment on camera.

The Community Center had a large dance floor, and about 15 minutes after the cake cutting, the D.J. started to play the first song. The groom had chosen "Everything" by Michael Bublé. Tim and Abbey took the dance floor together, followed shortly by the rest of the wedding party. Once the dance ended, Caitlin made her way over to Donovan's table. She immediately felt guilty. He sat alone, having been abandoned by the rest of her family members. They'd either stepped onto the dance floor or moved to another table to visit.

"Thank you for waiting so patiently for me, Donovan. I thought my dad would at least keep you company until I arrived."

"Your dad stepped onto the dance floor only a minute ago with a woman named... Susan?"

Donovan pointed toward the dance floor, and sure enough, Caitlin spotted her dad dancing with Susan Brown, to the song

Abbey had chosen as their second song, "Make Me Feel My Love" by Adele. The expression on their faces was a real give away. It showed how their relationship had somehow changed from friendship to something more when Caitlin hadn't been paying attention. How interesting, she thought, maybe leaving for Ireland wouldn't be such a shock to her dad's system.

Donovan had been waiting for this moment all day when he could finally have some time alone with Caitlin, and she already seemed distracted by others around them. He felt somewhat nervous as he began to speak, "Now that you're here, I don't care where anyone else went. I just hope the wait was worthwhile, and you're mine for the rest of the evening."

"You may have to share me with a few people, but I want to spend as much time with you as possible," she promised.

Donovan reached into his pocket. "The evening will fly by way too quickly tonight, and I'm intent on leaving a small parting gift to ensure you don't forget me."

Caitlin panicked at first when he used the word parting, but when she watched him pull out a jewelry box, her heart fluttered. He extended his hand toward her, and she hesitantly took it from him. As she eased open the box, inside, she found a beautiful sterling silver bracelet with a 14-karat gold plated heart. The bracelet's sterling silver hoops interlocked around one another, meeting on opposite sides where two trinity knots lay. The centered art showed two delicate hands holding the gold heart, adorned with a shimmering crown.

"Why Donovan, it's beautiful. Wherever did you find it?"

"At a little Irish shop not far from my hotel," he answered. He looked directly into Caitlin's stunning eyes and found himself lost in the green hues of a forest in summertime.

She shyly batted them at him, knowing the bracelet represented a gift from the heart. "Only you would be able to find an Irish shop in the middle of Minnesota," she smiled. "I've seen rings with these same symbols before. What's the meaning behind them?"

"This bracelet holds two different Celtic symbols used throughout history." He pointed to the two trinity knots surrounding the Claddagh. "These knots celebrate the unity and complete perfection of the Christian trinity. The centered heart represents the importance of love, loyalty, and friendship in life."

Donovan could see Caitlin appreciated the symbolism behind his gift and the message he wanted to share, suggesting his desire for them to be a couple. "It's beautiful. Would you help me put it on?"

"I'd be honored." He carefully lifted the bracelet from the box and unhooked the clasp, placing it around her wrist before refastening it. The DJ began to play another slow song, at the perfect time. "Dance with me, Caitlin."

"I'd love to." Donovan took her hands and gently pulled her up off the chair. They walked with hands entwined to the dance floor, where he gently took her in his arms. Caitlin felt almost mesmerized by the music as they floated across the floor together in a simple waltz. It was apparent he had dance experience as he confidently maneuvered her around with ease.

They returned time and again to the dance floor as a variety of music played throughout the evening. In between dances, they sat and talked with each other and some of the other guests. Caitlin made sure she introduced Donovan to as many people as possible because she wanted them to know he was special to her. She noted his words and deeds, and they were embedded in her mind. She would remember them long after he had returned home.

At one point, her boss stopped by to ask her to dance. "Donovan, I'd like to introduce you to the curator at the museum where I work, Jonathan Richardson."

He stood up to greet him. "Nice to meet you, Jonathan. I'm Donovan O'Malley."

Jonathan seemed to look him up and down before stating, "So, you must be the man Caitlin met in Ireland."

Donovan didn't know how to respond to his comment other than with a confident nod.

Jonathan noticed his failure to communicate successfully, "What I meant to say was, are you the man who assisted her in finding her family in Killarney?"

"Yes, I am."

"Well, I appreciate all the time you spent helping her. Where Caitlin is concerned, failure is not an option. We rely on her at the museum, and I admit I feared she would ask to lengthen her time in Ireland if she couldn't find the answers to her questions. I would have had to deny any request for an extended time abroad," he added. "She's a rather determined woman, and I feared the way she might react to my response."

"Fortunately, you avoided such an unpleasant situation."

Before he could say anything more, Jonathan turned to Caitlin and asked, "May I have the next dance?" After she nodded, he took Caitlin's hand and walked her onto the dance floor.

Donovan noticed the ease in which Jonathan held Caitlin in his arms as they began to dance. They were comfortable with each other. As Jonathan swung Caitlin around to the quick beat of the music, their laughter flew across the floor and slapped Donovan in the face. What would happen when he returned to Ireland? How many other men would she have waiting in the wings attempting to steal her heart the minute he left?

As the song neared the end, Donovan got up to reclaim his dance partner just a moment too late. Jeremy swooped in out of nowhere and was allowed to lead Caitlin further away from Donovan's reach. He had to strain to keep an eye on them.

Partway through the song, Donovan noticed Jeremy guide his dance partner toward a door leading into a garden area visible through a large glass door. He quickly crossed the floor to follow them, stopping just inside the door. Donovan tried to discreetly watch the pair, attempting to keep out of view. He didn't know why he was so paranoid, but ever since overhearing them at the restaurant the night before, he still suspected Jeremy wouldn't easily give up on Caitlin. There were no hard and fast rules about love when it came to the competitive pursuit between two potential suitors. He feared the upcoming distance he would be putting between himself and Caitlin might destroy the close friendship they'd begun to develop and any further hope of something more. His life was in Ireland, and he didn't foresee any change in the future.

At first, Caitlin wore a strained look as she and Jeremy conversed. After a few minutes, her face broke out into a brilliant smile, breaking the tension between them. Then without warning, Jeremy abruptly pulled Caitlin into his arms. Donovan could only see Jeremy's face, but he noticed Caitlin had reached around and returned his embrace, now patting him gently on the back.

When Jeremy spotted Donovan, he stepped back slightly and took Caitlin's face in his hands, turning their warm embrace into a kiss. A passionate looking one from where Donovan stood. Caitlin tried to pull away, but Jeremy held her face tightly between his hands to prevent her escape. From Donovan's point of view, he'd seen enough and briskly walked away. Jeremy hadn't given up on rekindling their romance.

Jeremy knew his chances weren't good, but for some reason, he didn't want to play the nice guy and give up Caitlin to this Irishman from across the sea. She'd been his girl first, and he wouldn't abandon his mission quite yet.

When Caitlin had finally gained her freedom, she snapped. "How dare you kiss me! I made it clear earlier I wanted nothing more to do with you."

"I'm sorry, I got carried away by my feelings," Jeremy apologized. "I still love you, Caitlin. I can't change how I feel."

"Oh, Jeremy, you're impossible. I think you'd better leave now. I'll make sure my aunt gets back to the hotel later. Now I need to return to my date," she emphasized.

"Fine!" Jeremy stalked off, huffing, and puffing childishly.

Caitlin made her way back inside. She didn't find Donovan at first, but when she did, he made some excuse about it getting late and how he still needed to pack for his trip home.

"I have an early flight tomorrow, Cait. Can you get a ride home with your dad? I don't want you to miss any of the festivities tonight, and it's already getting late. I need to get back to my hotel."

"I understand, Donovan. Thanks for a lovely time over the past few days. I promise I'll be seeing you again in the future. Can I walk you to the car?"

Confused by what he'd seen, Donovan wanted to make a quick escape. He needed time to digest everything he had witnessed and sort out his own emotions. "No, it isn't necessary. Enjoy your family and friends and what's left of the celebrating tonight. We can keep in touch until we see each other down the road." He hugged her briefly then hustled off into the night without saying goodbye to anyone else.

Caitlin became confused at the sudden change in Donovan's demeanor. Then it dawned on her; he must have seen her in the garden with Jeremy. Maybe the whole fiasco had been a part of Jeremy's ultimate plan to hinder her blossoming relationship with Donovan. He had lied to her when he promised to play by her rules. It was the straw that broke the camel's back. There would be no going back for her. The path ahead seemed clear. No one could be more perfect for her than Donovan, and she wouldn't give up. She realized she had a big decision ahead of her, and there was only one thing she could do now, surrender to her biggest fear.

# Chapter 22

A light sprinkling of August rain fell as Donovan finished bandaging a cut on his last patient for the day, a sweet Border Collie from the nearby animal shelter. Throughout the week, a multitude of animals had flooded into the clinic needing his medical expertise. Exhaustion had him looking forward to heading home for the weekend to relax.

He envisioned Duncan laying by his feet as he reclined in front of a burning fireplace, but a red-haired woman soon replaced the image. It was his genuine desire—Caitlin tightly wrapped in his arms. It had been two long months since he'd last seen her, with only periodic text messages shared between them. They seemed to have difficulty finding the time to connect due to their busy work schedules and the time zone difference. Caitlin promised they'd see one another again, but it seemed like a distant fairy tale to him.

Distracted by a movement to his left, he turned to see Dana picking up unused bandaging materials and putting them away in the nearby drawer. "Donovan, would you like to join me this evening for dinner? I'm going to heat some of my mom's corned beef and cabbage soup. It's been a busy week for both of us, and we could just relax and enjoy a good meal together."

Although he'd forgiven Dana for her deceitful maneuvers to distance him from Caitlin earlier on, her continual attempt to embed herself in his personal life had strained their relationship in the workplace. If things didn't change soon, he felt he'd have to let her go, despite her excellent work skills.

Before Donovan could respond, Aidan popped into the examining room. "Donovan, there's a call for you from your sister. It sounds urgent."

"Sorry, Dana, we'll finish this discussion when I return."

"Of course."

He rushed to the phone, thinking something had happened to one of his family members, maybe his grandad. "Hello? Meghan?"

Meghan's tone of voice sounded nothing like an emergency. "Good evening, Donovan."

"Is something wrong? Aidan made it sound like this was an urgent call."

"Well, it's only an emergency because I forgot to call you and tell you about our plans."

He paused, then with a sigh, asked, "What plans, Meghan? What's going on?"

She took a few deep breaths to calm herself. She didn't want to seem too anxious. "Well, it won't be long before the newest Rafferty appears on the scene. Brian and I convinced the rest of the family to get together tonight before our time is otherwise occupied. It wouldn't be the same without you, big brother."

"Well, I don't know. It's been a long week. I'm exhausted and planned on heading home for some well-deserved rest."

"Please," she begged, "there's room for you at the Inn. You could stay overnight. We have a special dinner guest coming that I'd like you to meet."

Donovan went on high alert. "Meghan, what are you up to now?"

"Nothing. I just want our whole family to meet the woman the Library hired as my replacement," she assured him. "It's her first day in Dublin, and I didn't want her to spend it alone. Meeting one more friendly face would help her feel more at home. She'll need all the friends she can get."

He stopped to think it over, "In other words, she isn't from the area?" he continued.

"No, but she has family living not too far from here. She'll be starting at the Library on Monday. I'll work with her for a few days before I begin my leave of absence. I can't wait to get off my feet as the doctor ordered. You'd think I was an elephant by the look of my ankles at the end of the day."

Donovan would do just about anything for his sister, within reason. He decided he might as well humor the pregnant woman. "All right, I wouldn't want to disappoint an expectant mother. I'll join you this evening, but you have to make one promise."

"What's that, Donovan? Anything. I really want you here."

"Seriously, Meghan. You must promise to stop your matchmaking. No matter how young and pretty she might be."

"Donovan, did I say she was young and pretty? For all you know, she could be old enough to be your mother."

"Is she?"

"No, but don't worry. There'll be no matchmaking tonight by me or anyone else in the family. Now, are you coming or not?"

He realized he preferred to spend the evening alone, but his two choices tonight seemed to be Dana or his family. Rest assured, if he didn't go into Dublin, Dana would make him feel obligated to join her. "Okay, sis, I'll come. I'm going to head home to change my clothes and grab my overnight bag. I'll be there in just a little over an hour from now."

He couldn't help but chuckle at his sister's antics. If he were honest with himself, tonight's family time would breathe new life into his soul. They were the best medicine for his lonely heart, and the atmosphere of the pub would have a healing power of its own. As much as he had tried to forget Caitlin, memories of her haunted him daily. He had tried to suppress his feelings for her, but she had a way of invading his thoughts.

Dana, who'd been impatiently waiting by his office door, walked further into the room as Donovan ended his conversation. "So, you're going into Dublin tonight?" She sounded extremely disappointed, and he knew she would be.

"Yes, while I appreciate your offer of a hot meal, my sister has a bit of celebrating to do, and she wants to include the entire family. I plan on staying overnight. We've been so busy around here I haven't had much time to spend with my family lately."

"Fine, I'll see you then on Monday unless you need me for anything."

"Thanks for all your hard work today, Dana. I hope you realize I appreciate everything you do around here as part of an important team of professionals."

Dana could take the subtle hint, he appreciated her as a coworker, but his feelings didn't go any deeper than friendship. Maybe it was time for her to move on. He seemed too distracted lately to give her the time of day.

"I know... thank you. Have a wonderful evening, Donovan."


Back in Dublin, the excitement continued to build. The Rafferty family had dressed up for the evening, including its youngest members. "Now remember children, when you start getting tired, Great Grandad said you could lay down upstairs until it's time to go home. But first, you'll get to meet the person who's going to do my job while I stay home with you and the new baby."

"Is it someone we know?" asked Liam, smiling from ear to ear.

"Maybe."

"I can't wait until the baby comes," Grace chimed in.

"Me, too. We'll spend lots of time doing fun things together," Meghan promised.

Liam couldn't resist asking, "Does it mean we'll be able to get a puppy? If you're home, there would be someone to take care of him when we're at school."

Brian intervened, "Someday, you'll be ready to have a puppy, but not right now. First, we must adjust to having a new baby around the house. Then we can think about adding yet another mouth to feed."

The children giggled at his comment. Liam put his hands on his hips and looked directly at his dad. In a solemn voice, he said, "Puppies don't eat much, Dad."

"Yes, but they do eat, son."

"Enough, everyone, it's time to get going." Meghan reminded them, "We don't want to be the last ones to arrive for the family celebration!"

They weren't last to arrive; Donovan trailed after them by a quarter of an hour. Once the last member of the family had joined them at the pub, they quickly fell into a lively discussion. Even

Sheamus and Maggie had joined them. Maggie happened to be the only non-family member dining with them tonight, except for Meghan's guest.

"Hey Maggie, what are you doing here? Did Sheamus finally give you some time off to enjoy yourself? Can this place even function without you at the helm?" Donovan teased.

Sheamus realized his older brother was attempting to ruffle his feathers. "Why Donovan, didn't you hear? Maggie and I have been dating for almost a month. But you know she's been like a family member much longer. Everyone seems happy I've finally accepted the fact there's no getting rid of her. Being the oldest, though, I think you should have to take the plunge first, so you better get a move on before Maggie does the choosing for you."

Everyone chuckled just before Bridgett scolded, "Behave yourselves, boys. Tonight is about having a relaxing evening and enjoying each other's company, not your sibling rivalries."

Her sons just laughed at the remark. Donovan leaned over and hooked his arm around his brother's neck, drawing him in closer and whispering in his ear, "It's about time you started taking Maggie more seriously. She's been pining after you for over a year now." Sheamus pushed himself away from his brother, a goofy smile beaming on his face as he took his seat next to Maggie.

Donovan surveyed the seating arrangements and noticed there were only two empty seats left. That meant the guest of honor would be sitting next to him. He looked over at Meghan, then the chair.

Meghan responded to the unspoken question. "Relax, Donovan, I made a promise."

Aengus caught Donovan's attention by the mischievous grin on his face. "How've you been, son? We haven't seen you for several weeks now. What have you been doing with yourself?"

He frowned at his grandfather. "Working," he grumbled.

Aengus redirected his attention to Meghan in order to register a complaint, "When's this mystery guest you invited going to arrive? I'd like to eat before my bedtime!"

"Oh, Dad, we'll be eating soon enough. Besides, you're going to stay for some of the music tonight, aren't you?" Sean asked.

"Our guest should be here soon. She's staying at the Inn until she can find her own place. I promised we'd help her search for an apartment next week," explained Meghan.

Donovan didn't like the sound of that. "Who's the 'we' in that offer? I assume you mean you and Brian."

"Not really. I know everyone in our family wants my replacement to have an easy transition to her new job, which includes helping her find a comfortable place to live. Don't you want to help make her feel at home here in Dublin?"

"Of course, we do," her mother tried to reassure her. "We'll all pitch in and help in whatever way we can."

A cell phone vibrated, and everyone looked toward Meghan. "I'd better check this."

The entire table sat quietly, waiting as she read her message. "She's on her way down from her room now. Let's all put on our best smiles and refrain from asking too many personal questions at one time." They all promised.

As they waited for their guest, Donovan chatted with his niece and nephew, who sat directly across the table from him. At one point in their lively banter, Liam and Grace dropped their mouths wide open. Donovan wondered who on earth had entered the room. It was like a domino effect watching one face after the other change expressions. Aengus got a strange look on his face while his parents were smiling like Cheshire cats. He turned slightly to his left to see who had grabbed their attention in such a manner. Who could put such a variety of expressions on their faces?

Just inside the pub's entrance stood Caitlin, wearing a long-sleeved free-flowing turquoise colored dress that hung several inches above her knees. She looked like a woodland fairy with her red hair braided to one side and wavy tendrils hanging on either side of her face. Donovan went into an almost trancelike state as she walked toward the back of the room where they were seated.

Donovan didn't know what to think. Then it dawned on him, Caitlin was Meghan's job replacement. By the time he'd let the idea sink in, the entire table had rushed over and surrounded Caitlin. The children jumped up and down to get her attention while his mother wrapped her in a warm embrace. He could feel the rapid increase in his heart rate before his feelings shifted more toward anger. How could she have come all this way and never hinted even once of her job prospect? Was she playing some kind of game with his feelings?

When the noisy greetings had subsided, his family seemed to part like the Red Sea, expecting him to act the part of Moses and head for the promised land. Donovan's family watched anxiously to see what would transpire. Caitlin waited in anticipation, shaking like a leaf. Donovan had returned to a transfixed state. Finally, he spoke gruffly, his face stern yet otherwise void of any positive emotion, "Hello, Cait."

Meghan, frustrated by Donovan's relatively unmoving greeting, stepped forward. "Caitlin, we're glad to have you join us tonight. You know everyone here. Why don't we all sit down, and Sheamus will have his staff bring out our meals."

Caitlin felt disconcerted. A monkey would have given her a more emotional reunion than Donovan. Had she been wrong to keep the news from him? They'd only sporadically communicated since their reunion in June, and she had wanted her decision to be focused on wanting the job versus her feelings for Donovan. She hoped her decision didn't backfire on her. She was determined to take one day at a time and enjoy all the opportunities that crossed her path.

When she moved closer to the table, panic over Donovan's reaction set in when she realized her chair stood next to his. He pulled it out for her. Things appeared to move in slow motion as she anticipated the next words to flow from Donovan's thin sultry lips. She stood momentarily transfixed on them before slipping into her seat.

Her nerves felt like the strings of a guitar pulled so tightly they were about to break. The result? "Surprise!" she yelled out. "I'm so happy to be here. I hope no one is disappointed that I'm the one who will be temporarily filling Meghan's position at the Library."

"Best surprise ever!" Aengus admitted before turning to his son and daughter-in-law. "I suspect you knew about this the entire time, didn't you?"

"Of course, and we had the devil of a time not spilling the beans where you're concerned. It's the hardest secret we've ever had to keep." Bridgett confessed.

She elbowed Sean to get him to agree with her. "Sure enough!"

Donovan swiveled in his seat to face Caitlin, and she could see the look on his face had begun to soften. He looked like he wanted to say something. The rest of the table eyed the couple as they patiently waited for Donovan to speak. The words, "I can't believe you're here," came out in a calm voice. "I hope you had an uneventful flight."

Immediately, Caitlin realized Donovan had been caught off guard by her appearance rather than angry with her. And to break the ice, she responded cheerfully, "Fortunately, there were no medical emergencies onboard, Dr. O'Malley. What would we have done without you?" She placed her hand on his knee, causing a chain reaction.

A smile slowly spread across his face. "You would have managed." Relieved that the tension had broken between the two of them, the rest of the table fell into a lively conversation—Donovan and Caitlin's attention unbroken.

Caitlin sincerely apologized by saying, "I hope you'll forgive me for keeping this news from you. I don't want you to feel uncomfortable about my taking this job. It seemed like a wonderful career opportunity. One that would allow me some additional time in Ireland."

Donovan took her hands in his without looking away. "Why would it make me uncomfortable? I'm the one who almost threatened you with the idea we could never be more than friends because I would never consider leaving my country to move elsewhere. And now, here you are. Wait! Jeremy won't be visiting while you're here, will he?"

"Oh, Donovan! Don't underestimate my feelings for you. Your visit helped me make my final decision to accept this job. You need to have a little more confidence in your own charm."

He leaned in a little closer. "So, you'll be here for about a year?"

"It all depends."

"Depends on what?"

"Well, several things."

"Can you be more specific?"

"The National Library assured me if my work is satisfactory and Meghan chooses to lengthen her leave; they would extend my contract indefinitely."

"That's a big if. Is there anything or anyone else that might be able to convince you to stay in Ireland longer than a year?"

"As long as my heart calls me to stay here, I will stay."

"That sounds promising," he proclaimed as his grip on her hands tightened.

"I hope you'll be interested in convincing me to lengthen my stay…" she murmured as he lowered his mouth firmly onto hers, determined to leave no doubt in her mind as to what he wanted. Caitlin kissed him back as her heart raced to the finish line.

By this time, the table's attention had come back to the reuniting couple, just in time to hear him say, "How about indefinitely?" Donovan posed.

A broad smile spread across Caitlin's face. Donovan had just confirmed her decision to take this job had been a good one. The rest of the family couldn't believe what they'd just witnessed. They sincerely hoped this story would have a happy ending.

Still in their own little world and unaware the entire table had turned their attention back to the two of them, Donovan leaned forward once more. Caitlin did the same, meeting in a simple promising kiss inconveniently interrupted by the wait staff bringing in their meals and drinks. To Donovan's family, it looked like their two hearts had finally surrendered to love.

# Chapter 23

Accepting the National Library job had been the best decision Caitlin had made in her entire life. Seven incredible months had passed, and everything seemed to be falling into place. She took pleasure in assisting visitors daily as they sifted through documents, then followed the clues to fill in the missing links on their family tree. Several had connected with relatives in Ireland just as she had. She'd even made headway in tracking down some of William Murphy's nieces and nephews. The number of family members she'd met in Ireland continued to grow, making her time there very fruitful.

The most gratifying reward she'd received by taking the Library job was her strengthened relationship with Donovan. There had been no guarantee that closer proximity would lead to anything more than friendship, but the risk had paid off. She'd never been happier.

Meghan and her family enjoyed the arrangement, too. Her 5-month-old daughter Erin, along with Liam and Grace, were reaping the benefit of their stay-at-home mom. They were happy, thriving, and growing. Brian's earlier promotion had limited his travel away from home to one day a month. If things continued along this path, Meghan would have the option of going back to work or continuing her leave of absence for an additional year. They still had time to make the best decision for their family. The Library had promised Caitlin Meghan's job if she extended her leave. They'd been pleased with the work she'd been doing.

For a Friday, time seemed to move as slow as molasses as Caitlin anticipated Abbey and her brother-in-law, Tim's arrival. They were starting their belated honeymoon in Dublin. Tim's winter break from school had started, and they had nine days to enjoy the Irish countryside. Caitlin felt honored they'd be dedicating their first weekend to hanging out with her and Donovan. Bridgett had been kind enough to reserve rooms for them all to stay at the Inn on the same floor.

Caitlin hastened the short distance home by bus to grab her things for the weekend in anticipation of Donovan picking her up on his way into town. She couldn't believe they'd have the entire weekend together: dinner tonight, sightseeing in Dublin on Saturday, and then a visit to O'Malley Farm on Sunday. Tim anxiously awaited some competitive clay pigeon shooting, guys versus the gals. He didn't realize his wife and Caitlin both had trophies stored in boxes back at their dad's house from their teen years as members of the local trapshooting club.

The Inn was already buzzing with activity because Abbey and Tim had brought along a special surprise. Abbey's dad and Susan Brown had joined them on the first leg of their journey. They had officially started dating a month after the wedding. On top of that, Aunt Mary had flown in separately from Boston. Bridgett had helped them get settled in their rooms on the top floor of the Inn. Currently, they were dressing for the big reunion, which would take place in O'Malley's Pub in less than an hour. They looked forward to meeting the rest of Donovan's family.

"Won't Caitlin be surprised when she sees all of us?" Michael asked as he struggled to put on his shamrock green tie while Mary and Susan waited patiently in his room at the Inn. Susan finally got up and proceeded to help him with it. A tear came to his eye, realizing he had someone to help him now and in the future, taking away the burden from his daughters who had tried to fill the void their mother had left upon her death.

"Yes, Michael. She'll be utterly amazed, but it'll be just the beginning of several amazing revelations tonight." Mary announced.

"Are you referring to my bringing Susan?"

"She's one of the surprises," Mary hinted.

"What else are you referring to?"

"You'll just have to wait and see. Trust me; you'll be amazed," Mary assured her brother.

Michael didn't like being kept in the dark. It made him nervous. No matter what he said to convince his sister, she refused to share any other information. He couldn't imagine what other surprises there could be. He was bewildered.

"Relax, Michael, just enjoy tonight and all the surprises it will entail," Susan advised as she made final adjustments to his suit coat before placing a heart-felt kiss on his cheek.

Abbey and Tim had only a short time to unwind in their room after their long flight. Abbey felt thrilled about seeing her sister after being separated by such a long distance. She showered first to freshen up, blow drying her hair while Tim took his turn. She wanted to look her best tonight to match the importance of the evening's big event. Caitlin didn't like surprises, but Abbey hoped this would not be one of those times.

Sean and Bridgett supervised Grace and Liam while their baby sister took a nap on the floor below. Donovan had stopped by earlier to drop off Duncan and a puppy named Rosie. He told the children he would be delivering Rosie to her new family in Dublin on Saturday. As they waited to go down with the rest of the family to the pub, they played with the puppy.

Grace pulled on her grandmother's dress, "Is Caitlin eating with us tonight?"

"Yes, your Uncle Donovan went to get her."

"Can I sit by her?" she pleaded.

Her grandma tried to explain the situation to her. "I don't know, dear. Caitlin's sister will be with her, and they haven't seen each other since August. You may need to let them sit together. Your Uncle Donovan will probably want to sit on her other side."

This didn't make Grace happy, and she stomped her foot to show she wasn't pleased with this arrangement. She liked Caitlin and wanted to spend as much time as possible with her. Caitlin read and sang to her. They played games together, too. Sometimes she would help the children when they visited the farm to ride the ponies.

"You'll have a lot of time with Caitlin in the future, just not tonight, Grace."

"Okay!" Then she immediately changed the subject. "Can Rosie sleep with Liam and me tonight?" Bridgett laughed. It was surely going to be an entertaining evening, and it had just gotten started.

"We'll see, Grace. I don't know what your uncle has planned for Duncan and Rosie tonight. They may be having a sleepover in his room." A frown appeared on her face. Maybe tonight wasn't going to be as much fun as Grace envisioned it should be, but Bridgett knew better. If everything went the way Donovan had planned, they were all going to have a marvelous evening.

After dropping off the dogs, Donovan stopped in the room at the Inn where he'd be staying for the weekend. It was on the second floor just next door to Caitlin's and down the hall from Abbey and Tim's room. He had stopped to freshen up after a long day at the clinic before leaving to pick up Caitlin. He momentarily stopped at Abbey and Tim's room to check in with them before heading out, wanting to make them feel welcomed and review their plans for the evening one last time.

Abbey heard a loud knock at the door as she inserted a pearl teardrop earring into her right ear. She quickly got up to open the door. Donovan stood looking rather dreamy in a pair of brown dress pants and a cream-colored Irish knit sweater. His neatly trimmed beard and tousled dark black hair added a rather laid-back look to the picture he painted.

Donovan stepped toward Abbey, encompassing her in a warm, welcoming hug before greeting Tim in the same manner. "It's so good to see you both. And don't you look just lovely tonight, Abbey," Donovan complimented her as he admired her in her long-sleeved, emerald green dress adorned by a strand of pearls and matching earrings.

"I'm heading to pick up Cait. We'll meet you in the lobby around 6 o'clock. Thanks again for helping with another big surprise. I'm indebted to you both."

"We were happy to help, and I can't wait to see how my sister reacts to the many surprises you have in store for her tonight!" Abbey acknowledged.

Tim nodded in agreement. "Now, Donovan, you'd better hustle if you're going to get Caitlin back here in time to get the real party started." Tim placed his hand on Donovan's back and walked him out the door.

Fifteen minutes later, Caitlin ushered Donovan into her relatively small living room as he attempted to hide a package behind his back. She couldn't help noticing how handsome he looked. "Is that a new sweater?"

"No, it's the one I bought from the gift shop at Muckross House almost a year ago."

She'd never seen it on him, so she didn't recognize it. "You look very dashing in it. Did you know Irish sweaters remind me of my grandfather? When Grandpa Pat passed away, I hung onto the one he wore all the time, which was knit in the O'Sullivan clan pattern. I feel like I'm wrapped up in one of his big hugs every time I wear it."

Caitlin, confused by how Donovan seemed to keep his distance from her, finally realized he'd been trying to hide something. "Hey, what do you have there?"

Donovan held out the gift bag he'd been trying to hide. "A present for you."

"Why on earth are you giving me a present?" she asked.

Donovan just smiled. "Don't ask questions, just look inside," he demanded.

Caitlin sat down on the sofa. Upon removing the tissue paper hiding the gift from view, she couldn't believe her eyes. Inside lay a beautiful cream-colored cable knit cardigan with a pattern matching the one on Donovan's sweater. And the secret he withheld from her at the time? Her sweater bore the O'Malley clan's design.

"We're a matching pair now. Is there some message behind this?"

"Yes, but I'll share it with you later this evening. For now, all you need to know is I thought it was time you had an Irish sweater that fits you. I've noticed you wearing your grandfather's sweater, and it gave me an idea. I want you to wear this sweater, so you'll think of me wrapping my arms around you instead of your grandfather. I want to be the person there for you whenever you're happy, sad, and every kind of emotion in between."

Donovan helped her put it on, then stepped back to get a better picture of her ensemble. He ran his eyes over her dark green pants and thin turtleneck sweater, making a note of the fact she, like her sister, had included green in their outfits in honor of her grandfather, whose birthday would have been earlier in the week on St. Patrick's Day.

"You look lovely."

Caitlin stepped forward, wrapping her arms around his neck to pull him close, running her fingers through his silky hair. He smelled so good, like some kind of masculine soap and a laundry detergent that smelled like a mountain meadow. She breathed in deeply. She couldn't believe she'd almost passed on the job in Dublin. If Donovan hadn't visited her in her hometown, she might never have taken the risk.

"Thank you, Donovan. I love the sweater, and more importantly, I love you!" she proclaimed, a kiss the exclamation at the end of her sentence. "Now, let's get going. I have my bag packed and can't wait to see my sister and Tim."

"Of course! Let's go!"

Caitlin kept glancing over at the man of her dreams on the short drive to the Inn. She hoped they'd enjoy their time with Tim and Abbey tonight and, better yet, continue to make memories together with family and friends for years to come.

When they arrived, Abbey and Tim were sitting comfortably in the lobby, waiting. Abbey spotted her sister the minute she walked through the door. She raced across the lobby and greeted Caitlin by lifting her off the floor in a big bear hug. They began giggling and complimenting each other on their outfits while the men just stood and smiled.

"Well, Tim, do you think we can get the ladies to follow us next door to get something to eat?" The anticipation of revealing not one but several surprises had begun to cause Donovan to sweat profusely. If they didn't get moving soon, his newfound nervousness would start to show.

Tim concurred by rubbing his belly. "I hope so, Donovan. I'm ready for a good hearty Irish meal and a Guinness."

The ladies glanced at them and nodded. Caitlin announced, "We're more than ready. Lead the way, gentlemen."

Donovan's stomach was tied in knots as he anticipated revealing his big surprise. He hoped Caitlin would overlook his jumpiness. He'd been planning this night for the last month.

"Greetings, Donovan, Caitlin, and friends," Maggie welcomed. "You must be my party of four." She winked at Donovan, making him even more nervous. He didn't want her to make Caitlin suspicious.

"Yes, Maggie. May I introduce Caitlin's sister, Abbey, and her husband, Tim? They're here in Ireland for their honeymoon."

"Ah, how exciting. Have you ever been to Ireland before?"

Abbey's brief response, "No, never."

"Well, I'm sure you're going to have a grand time. Come this way."

Abbey and Tim followed directly behind Maggie, with Donovan and Caitlin bringing up the rear. Surprisingly, the pub seemed quiet to Caitlin. Usually, you couldn't hear yourself think on a Friday night.

They passed a few couples, but no one she recognized. When they got further toward the back of the pub Abbey and Tim separated and a group of people huddled together yelled, "Surprise!"

Stunned, Caitlin froze in her place. "What's going on?"

Donovan wrapped his arm around the lass he'd grown to love over such a short period and began, "Cait, you're not the only one who can pull a rabbit out of a hat. When Abbey and Tim decided to come this way for their honeymoon, I started planning a bigger reunion for the woman who crossed an ocean to spend more time with me. They've brought a few people along with them."

Caitlin scanned over the crowd of people in front of her. She immediately spied her dad standing next to Aunt Mary. As swift as a flash of lightning, she flew across the room to him. They embraced, tears flowing down their eyes simultaneously. "Oh, Dad, I've missed you so much!" she managed to say before noticing Susan Brown standing just behind him. Without letting go of her dad, she reached out to take Susan's hand in a firm welcoming grip and spouted out, "Oh, Susan! It's so good to see you. I can't wait to hear the story about how you came to be here."

Susan smiled shyly, then looked directly into her eyes and softly said, "Someone has to look after your dad now. The two of you girls will be too busy taking care of your men. Your dad figured he'd never make it to Ireland if he waited for you to take him, so I've promised to be his new travel buddy."

"Oh, Susan, you are the perfect match for my dad," Caitlin assured her.

Before they could say anything further, her dad released her from his crushing grip. Aunt Mary stepped in for a hug of her own. "My dear, it's so good to see you! I couldn't let you have a family reunion without me, and your Uncle Will and Aunt Patti are going to join us before the weekend is over. We're all going to travel together to Killarney on Monday with our new family members leading the way."

It took Caitlin a moment to realize William and Noreen Murphy, as well as their son John and his wife, had also joined in on the big surprise. After warmly greeting them, she surveyed the members of the O'Malley clan who had gathered with them as well. What a wonderful surprise. Both of their families were together in one place.

"Oh, my, I can't believe you're all here!" she cried out just as Donovan reclaimed his place by her side. He took her left hand, and before she could say anything else, he went down on his right knee in front of the crowd of loved ones gathered before them. They seemed to hold their breath as Caitlin stood, looking stunned.

"Cait," Donovan began, "From the moment I met you on the plane coming home from Boston, you played with the strings of my heart. I could see you were a beautiful woman immediately, and not only on the outside but from within. I knew you had a heart of gold."

He briefly scanned the crowd. "My family saw it when they met you as well and began to make hints here and there...Some were none too subtle, right, Grandad?"

"I tell it like I see it, my boy!" Everyone roared at his comment.

"Yes, you're a wise man, but I was blinded by a lost love. How did I know God would bless me in my life not once but twice? I thought it would be folly to begin to woo the lass. She lived an ocean away, and a long-distance relationship in my mind just wouldn't work because I knew I couldn't commit to leaving my homeland to be with her."

"You weren't the only one who had a fear of a long-distance relationship," admitted Caitlin.

"Cait, I panicked at one point in fear of my competition for your affections. With me clear on the other side of the Atlantic Ocean I had no way of protecting you from the hungry wolves circling about you."

"My dear, no man in America could take your place in my heart. You had nothing to fear."

"Maybe, but how was I to know you'd be willing to listen to your heart and surrender to the unknown. You proved your willingness to take a risk by coming back to Dublin just to give me a better chance. You started a new job, uprooting yourself from family and home. You took a chance on me—on love."

"It was well worth the risk," she whispered.

"Today, I want to prove your risk has been worth the taking." He pulled a single solitaire diamond ring from his pocket and continued by saying, "Will you, Caitlin Sullivan, do me the honor of becoming my wife?"

A tear escaped, flowing down her cheek as she nodded, "Yes, Donovan O'Malley, it would be an honor to marry you."

He slipped the ring onto her left hand. Then stood up and pulled her into his arms, sealing the promise with a kiss. A joyous outburst broke out. Sheamus and Maggie had slipped into the room to join in the celebration.

After a second heartfelt kiss Donovan got everyone's attention once more. "Caitlin, as you can see, we're celebrating for more than one reason tonight. Being together with our loved ones is a big part of that. I have one more surprise, but it isn't for you, my love."

"Grace and Liam come here. Your mom and dad have something to tell you." The children rushed over to Donovan. Meghan stepped forward, holding her daughter Erin. From behind her, Brian appeared carrying something squirming around in his arms.

Liam and Grace looked up, "Rosie!"

Brian knelt in front of his children and said, "Your mom and I have finally agreed with your Uncle Donovan. We believe you are ready to have your own dog. If you promise to help take good care of Rosie, he's willing to give her to you."

Donovan added, "But you must promise to love her and take care of her."

"We promise!" The children vowed, rushing toward Rosie. Then Duncan barked for joy, wagging his tail exuberantly. It wouldn't be a true celebration without the entire family present.

# Book Discussion Questions

1. Which character did you relate to the most? Why?

2. If you were making a movie of this book, who would you cast?

3. Caitlin's journey is fueled by her desire to discover missing leaves (people) on her family tree. Have you ever experienced the same kind of desire to learn more about your own family history? And, to connect with living relatives you've never met? Explain.

4. Ireland has a rich history, did this story bring up any topic you would like to learn more about or a desire to travel to Ireland?

5. Have you ever felt tied to the customs and culture of your own heritage? What are some of the traditions you actively engage in?

6. Each character in this story experienced loss in some way. Despite their journeys looking different, they found a way to move forward in life. Can you relate to one of the challenges they faced? What strategies helped you cope?

7. What did you think about the challenges Donovan and Caitlin faced on their journey from friendship to a more lasting relationship? Where would you imagine them being five years from now?

8. In what ways do you think Donovan's profession as a veterinarian influences the way he interacts with the other characters in the story?

9. There is a strong theme of family throughout this book. In what ways do you think Donovan and Caitlin's families have helped shape their lives?

10. If you got the chance to ask the author of this book one question, what would it be?

## ABOUT THE AUTHOR

Rebecca Mattson is the author of the romance *Surrender to the Unknown*, her first published novel. You may ask, Why did she wait so long to publish something when her first story was completed in high school? Life got in the way. But deep in her heart, with love for reading and writing, she dreamed of one day having her stories grace the pages of a book to be placed in the hands of family, friends, and anyone else who cared to join her on an adventure she created.

After 37 years of teaching, retirement allows her the time to pursue two things she really enjoys: reading and writing. Motivators for creating this story were: her actual search for members on her family tree, her love of history and background in historical research (public history certification), and her father Lavern, a Scandinavian by descent (Norwegian and Swedish) born on St. Patrick's Day because everyone is Irish on St. Paddy's Day!

Made in the USA
Monee, IL
02 April 2021